MY
HEALER
BEWITCHED AND BEWILDERED

ALANEA ALDER

PUBLISHER'S NOTE

This is a work of fiction. Any names, characters, places and incidents are the product of the author's imagination or are used fictitiously, and any resemblance to actual persons, living or dead, business establishments, events or locales is entirely coincidental.

The scanning, uploading, and distribution of this book via the Internet or via any other means without the permission of the publisher is illegal and punishable by law.

Please purchase only authorized electronic editions, and do not participate in or encourage piracy of copyrighted materials. Your support of the author's rights is appreciated.

www.sacredforestpublishing.com

P.O. Box 280

Moyock, NC, 27958

Digital ISBN-13: 978-1-941315-04-0

Print ISBN-13: 978-1-941315-05-7

Sacred Forest Publishing

Cover Design and Interior format by The Killion Group

http://thekilliongroupinc.com

DEDICATION

~Omnia Vincit Amor- Love Conquers All~

PROLOGUE

Colton growled low; even in his sleep, he couldn't bear to see the fear in his mate's eyes. Unease grew in the pit of his stomach as he watched her pace back and forth in her family room. He watched in terror as the front door was kicked in and ferals rushed inside.

"Run! Call for help! Come to Lycaonia!" he yelled.

It didn't matter how loud he shouted, she couldn't hear him. He watched helplessly as one of the ferals stalked closer to his mate, a raised knife in hand, and then... nothing.

Colton's eyes opened, and he stared into the darkness. Groaning, he rolled over onto his back. He went over every aspect of the dream, trying to figure out where his mate was. The previous dreams had only involved his mate looking worried or anxious. Never before had she been in any physical danger.

He could only pray that she was safe; it was all in Fate's hands now.

CHAPTER ONE

Rheia Bradley paced back and forth in front of the large picture window in her family room. Last night's dream had spooked her so badly that she'd asked Radek Carson, one of her oldest friends, to swing by the house. He had taken over as Sheriff when her father retired, he always knew how to cheer her up and ease her fears.

She breathed out a sigh of relief when she saw headlights flood her driveway. She walked over to the door and waited, knowing if she simply swung it open without checking to see who it was, Radek would never let her hear the end of it. A minute later, there was a knock, and she checked the peephole. Sure enough, the bastard had covered it with his thumb.

"Stop wasting time, Radek," she yelled through the door.

"Just checking," was his muffled reply. She opened the door and grinned; Radek hadn't come alone. Beside him were the other members of the paranormal squad that patrolled their small town of Jefferson. Outside the confines of the four paranormal pillar cities, Vanguard squads blended into human first-responder teams. To avoid the issue of appearing ageless, the Vanguard members rotated from city to city, occasionally returning to active duty status as a Unit Warrior in one of the four pillar cities.

She opened the door wide; Radek walked in smiling and ruffled her hair. Ever since childhood, she always likened him to his animal. The bear-shifter was huge and barrel-chested. When not in his sheriff's uniform, he stayed in jeans and his favorite, worn biker jacket. She always joked with him that if the townspeople saw him riding around on his bike, there would be less crime. She crinkled her nose when he leaned down to kiss her cheek; his scruffy beard was scratchy. Laughing, he kept walking to make room for the others. Behind him, the fire marshal, Marco Rodriguez, a jaguar shifter, winked and she blushed. He chuckled and kept walking through to the family room. Marco could make even the old women at the bingo hall feel beautiful. He epitomized Latin good looks and always flirted with her outrageously. To this day, despite the number of years he'd been doing it, he could make her cheeks burn. Levi Sorrel stepped over the threshold and gave her a hug. He was one of the town's police detectives and excelled at complex puzzles. Smiling, the witch handed her a small sachet of lavender and chamomile. Growing up, he had taught her about different herbs and their uses; she knew that these two herbs in particular helped to soothe frantic nerves. She squeezed his hand in thanks. Dax Vi'Eaereson followed behind Levi, his huge body filling the doorframe. Dax worked with Marco in the fire department. She'd heard more than one woman around town threaten to set their house on fire to get the two men to save her. Where Marco was dark eyes and lean muscles, Dax was tall, as were all fae, with long golden hair. Built like a linebacker, he had amber colored eyes. Without saying a word, Dax leaned down and kissed her forehead before moving inside. The last of their squad, Athan Durant, a vampire and her girlhood crush, walked in, closing the door behind him. He was the squad's only paramedic. His vampire senses and attunement to blood helped him treat many human injuries and diseases. Athan had borne her girlish infatuation with the grace of a gentleman, neither breaking her heart nor encouraging her. His royal blue eyes smiled at her warmly before he pulled her into a hug. She let herself sag for just a moment, soaking in his strength and support.

"We are here now, honey. Come into the family room so I can visit with my niece, and you can tell us what has you so frightened. Then we can kill it and head home." He pulled back and kissed the tip of her nose. Smiling, she let him take her hand and lead her into the room.

Radek had already scooped up her daughter, Penny, and she was firmly ensconced on his lap. They were playing with Penny's favorite hidden object book. It was almost a year to the day since Penny had come into her life. Radek and his team had arrived at the scene of a brutal double homicide and, to their shock, found the tiny girl wedged between the wall and the bed. The blankets not only masked her scent, but also kept her out of sight. Radek bundled her up and gave her to Athan, so he could bring the child to her. Athan, upon arriving at her house, thrust the girl into her arms and said, "She cannot go into the system; she is one of us."

Radek had Levi manipulate the computer systems so that Penny was officially hers, but they all soon discovered that forging adoption papers had been the easy part. Penny was nearly catatonic for the first six months that she'd lived with Rheia. She had tried to balance the needs of a traumatized child with her career as a doctor at the local hospital. When it became evident that Penny needed more care than she was providing, she took a leave of absence. She used the inheritance she'd received upon the death of her parents to raise her daughter. It saddened her that her parents never got to meet Penny, but she believed that, in a way, the money they'd left her was their way of helping their granddaughter.

"Penny, darlin', why don't you go up to your room and arrange your baby dolls so your uncles can see how well you've learned how to clean?" Rheia suggested. Penny was only four; she didn't want her to hear about the nightmare. Penny looked up at her from Radek's lap and stared at her. Without changing expression, the little girl hopped down and walked toward the stairs.

Shaking her head, Rheia reached out and pulled her in for a tight hug. "I know I treat you like a little girl, but guess what, squirt? You are. Let me protect you for as long as I can, yeah?"

When Penny looked up, her eyes softened, and her small arms tightened around Rheia's waist. This was as close as she came to a smile. It wasn't much, but it was a dramatic improvement over how non-responsive she'd been when she first moved in.

Penny let go and headed up the stairs. When Rheia turned to face the room, the men were trying not to grin. "I know, I know! She acts as precocious and surly as I did when I was a child." She walked in and took the seat next to Radek, surprising her adoptive brothers. She only turned to Radek or Dax when she was feeling scared or threatened. Both men were so imposing that she always felt comforted by their presence. Levi was her go-to movie-watching buddy. He knew how she took her coffee and what sweets to bring her for a visit. Marco's specialty was revenge served cold. He was a master at the cat and mouse game. The longer his prey suffered psychologically, the better. His sunny disposition hid a vicious nature. True to his animal, he was either purring or lashing out. Athan, however, did not believe in a long, drawn out revenge scheme. He would smile, nod, then go out and happily murder anyone who hurt her. The bond they shared ran deep, and she knew there wasn't much the older vampire wouldn't do for her.

Radek wrapped a beefy arm around her shoulders and pulled her close. "Okay, Pumpkin Dumpling, tell big brother Radek what has you so upset."

She took a long shuddering breath. "It's probably nothing; it's just that I can't seem to shake this nightmare. The bone-numbing terror is as fresh to me now as it was in my dream. I can't stop shaking." She held up her trembling hand.

"What happened in the dream?" Levi asked, concern on his face.

"I'm here in the family room, pacing. It's as if I know something bad is going to happen. Suddenly the front door is kicked in and these savage looking men run in. One of the men approaches me, smiling; I can tell he's insane. Just as he raises a knife, I hear a man's voice shout and then..." she trailed off.

Radek started to rub up and down on her arm. "I'll tell you what, pumpkin; we'll check all the windows and the doors before we leave. I also have a kick bar in my trunk that you can use on the front door to prevent anyone from kicking it in. Next week, we'll install an alarm system that will not only immediately alert the police, but will also send a page out to us. Does that make you feel better?"

She took a deep breath and nodded. "I think so." She looked around the room and the men were smiling at her. She knew they would do everything to make her feel safe in her childhood home. She'd been their adopted little sister for over twenty years now. She got the feeling that even when she was old and grey, they would still treat her like a child.

She stood and walked over to stand between the family room and the kitchen. "Let me put a frozen lasagna in the oven, although I don't know if I'll be able to stand the smell. In my nightmare, the attackers smelled like rotten cheese, I woke up gagging." Swallowing hard at the memory, she turned toward the kitchen when, suddenly, Athan's hand grabbed her upper arm. When she looked up, his eyes appeared a bit wild.

"What did you say about how they smelled?" His tone was serious. She looked around at the other men; they all looked worried.

"They smelled like death and old cheese. It was disgusting. Why?"

Athan pulled her into his arms. She turned her head to see the men were already moving. Levi's hands were glowing as he spoke low. From the Latin she'd learned in med school, he was asking for protection. In all the years they had spent together, he'd never once cast a spell in front of her. Dax left the room and went out the front door.

Radek stepped in front of her. "Rheia, this is very important. Is there anything else you can remember from your dream? Anything at all, no matter how small?"

She shook her head then paused. "Just the man's voice. He sounded so desperate when he yelled. He said, 'Run! Call for help! Come to Lycaonia!'."

Marco's olive-toned skin drained of color. Cursing under his breath, Radek pulled his phone from his pocket. Rheia heard the front door open and close. Dax returned with a large duffel bag, which he set on the coffee table. When he unzipped it, she saw it carried an arsenal.

"You can't have that around Penny! Is that..."— she looked closer"Is that a grenade launcher?" She practically screeched.

Marco turned to Athan. "I'll leave her to you." He walked over to where Dax was already loading weapons. He picked up a shotgun and took up a position in front of the picture window.

She looked up at Athan. "What's going on?" She had been scared of her nightmare, but now, she was terrified.

He ran a hand over her hair. "Even though you have known about paranormals most of your life, we have tried to keep the scarier details about our world from you. You know about the four pillar cities and roughly how mates work, but what we have not told you is that our people have been waging a long-time war against something we call ferals. They are paranormals who have lost their souls. That horrible smell you described from your dream is the decay of a person's body, rotting from the inside out."

She stared at him. "You're telling me that those things are out there, right now? That what I dreamt is real?"

He nodded. "The man you heard in your dream said the word 'Lycaonia'. That is the name of the shifter paranormal city. It is about eight hours south of here. A couple of months ago, my contact in Lycaonia called me. A spell was cast to bring all the unit warriors their mates. Shortly after that, according to my contact, the Unit Commander, Aiden McKenzie, began dreaming of his mate. There is a pretty good chance that the voice you heard in your dream belongs to your mate," he explained.

Rheia was stunned. All her life, she secretly dreamed of finding a paranormal of her own for a mate. Her last boyfriend had fallen woefully short of the standards she had set, using her brothers as examples of manhood. In addition to being self-absorbed, he'd left the night she brought Penny home and never returned, saying he didn't want a child in his life.

"Maybe he will be a vampire," Athan said softly. When she looked up, his eyes were twinkling.

"I hope to all the Gods she does have a mate. I, for one, am not willing to lose her to old age," Dax said, walking up to hand Athan a gun.

"Aiden, I have a situation here," she heard Radek say, holding his phone in one hand, his gun in the other.

Marco walked over to her. "I'm heading upstairs to pack for Penny. Did you want me to pack for you as well?" he asked.

"Pack?" Her head was swimming.

"Honey, you can't stay here. You have to go to Lycaonia," he explained gently.

"But my house! My things!" she protested.

"We can pack up all your things and send them to you," Dax offered.

"What about my house? This is temporary, right? I can come home later when you kill these things, right?" she asked desperately.

Marco shook his head, sadness in his eyes. "Pumpkin, if your mate is in Lycaonia, that's where you belong."

"This was my parents' house. I grew up here! Why is this happening now? Penny's been here almost a year?"

Marco growled low. "That sonofabitch Bruce Johnson at the *Herald* just released an exposé about the recent murders and linked them back to Penny's parents. He let the cat out of the bag that a little girl may have witnessed the murder and survived. He also mentioned that a local humanitarian and surgeon adopted the poor orphan. He must've hacked the records because that was not for public consumption."

"Let us get you and Penny to safety, then we can figure things out," Athan said, squeezing her hand.

She turned to Marco. "Our suitcases are in my closet. Pack as many of her things as you can, she'll need familiar things around her. I'll be up in a second to pack my clothes." He jogged up the stairs and out of sight.

"Commander, this is Radek Carson ... no Radek. I'm the Vanguard squad leader in Jefferson. Yes, sir. We have an issue and I need to send someone to Lycaonia for protection. Yes, sir. It's ten p.m. now, she should be arriving around six a.m. Can you have someone watching out for her? Yes, sir, yes, sir. I'm going to give her directions. Your idea to have unit warriors outside the four cities is starting to pay off, isn't it? Protecting paranormals has always been our goal, but if we can save even one mate, then this entire program will have proved itself invaluable... yes, sir. I'll check in later with more details. Goodbye, sir." Radek ended the call and turned to her. "Aiden McKenzie will have someone waiting for you, to escort you into the city. You need to go pack, Pumpkin Dumpling." He pointed to the stairs.

Feeling numb, she turned and walked up the stairs. She went to Penny's room first. Marco was making her dollies walk then jump into the suitcase. Penny watched intently, a serious look on her face. The little girl didn't have much. She had refused all of her toys from her parents' home except a small, handmade cloth doll. Rheia believed that Penny's mother had made it for her. Penny had rejected everything else, including her old clothes.

Even later, Penny hadn't expressed much interest when they went shopping, so the amount to pack for her daughter was painfully small. Not wanting to disturb the two, she turned and made her way to the master bedroom. It took her two years after her parents' fatal car accident to move into the master bedroom. Marco had left the large and medium size suitcases open for her on her bed. Looking around the room with a critical eye, she decided to pack her clothes and toiletries in the large suitcase and pack her sentimental items in the medium suitcase.

She emptied her small closet and nightstand into the large suitcase and frowned. She had a lot of space left over. Coincidentally, she hated clothes shopping as much as Penny did. She lived in her scrubs mostly, rotating between the same seven pairs. The rest of her wardrobe was comprised of some T-shirts, a couple pair of jeans, sweaters, a couple nightgowns, and undergarments. Her clothes selection was as pitiful as her daughter's. She transferred the clothes and toiletries to the medium suitcase and zipped it shut. In the larger suitcase, she packed the small set of fairy tale books her father had read to her as a child, all of her mother's jewelry, her own favorite books, a small shoebox of keepsakes, three photo albums, and the accordion file that held all of her legal papers. Looking down at the nearly full suitcase, she realized there was only one more thing she had to have with her. She turned and raced downstairs to the kitchen. Lovingly, she wrapped her mother's china tea service, which included a teapot, a creamer, a sugar bowl, and four cups with saucers in her kitchen towels and headed back upstairs with them in a laundry basket.

When she'd first moved to this house, she hadn't been that much older than Penny was now. She could clearly remember her mother sitting her down at the table and making her a pot of sweet chamomile tea. All the ugliness of her past slipped away as she sat holding that delicate teacup. She carefully packed the small tea service in the suitcase using her kitchen and bathroom towels to keep it safe. She zipped up the suitcase and stood back.

"You ready, hun?" Marco asked. Penny peeked out from around his side, holding his hand.

Rheia nodded. "Yes. Surprisingly I was able to get most of my personal things into two suitcases. Everything else is just household items, but the things that matter will be going with us." She walked over and scooped Penny up, and the small girl laid her head on her shoulder.

"We're going to a very nice place, Penny. It's called Lycaonia. It's a city where all the people are like your uncles," she said, walking down the stairs. Behind her, Marco easily managed the three suitcases.

Penny looked up and pointed at her chest with her thumb. Rheia nodded. "Yes, darling, people just like you. Won't that be nice?"

Penny scrunched up her face for a second, thinking about it, then nodded.

"Okay, here are the directions. Things are pretty normal until you turn off the highway. No matter how lost you think you are, stay on the dirt road. There will be someone waiting for you," Radek explained, handing her a piece of paper before plucking Penny from her arms. He kissed the toddler's face all over. Penny squirmed, trying to avoid his whiskers. Radek pulled back and smiled at her. Penny, without changing expression, tweaked his nose. He gave a long booming laugh.

"You're not coming with us?" Rheia asked, feeling uneasy. She tucked the directions in her pants pocket.

"Car's loaded, Boss." Marco said, returning from the garage. He handed the keys to Rheia.

Radek shook his head. "You'll be safe in Lycaonia. I'm going to stay with the guys and try to find this threat and eliminate it. There have been too many..." he hesitated. "Incidents lately. I want to find these guys and take care of it."

In Rheia's mind, she translated: *There have been too many murders lately, and we want to find those responsible and kill them all.*

Rheia took a deep breath. "What if..." She didn't want to sound childish. She was a grown woman, a doctor even. She shouldn't be relying on these men to tell her that everything would be okay.

"What, honey?" Athan asked. The men gathered around to say their goodbyes.

"What if I don't like him? What if he isn't like any of you? What if he doesn't want me?" she said, voicing her greatest fear.

"Oh, honey, you're breaking my heart," Levi muttered and pulled her head close to kiss the top of it.

"You love us, Pumpkin Dumpling, but your mate will complete you in ways that we never will. You're our kid sister. But you'll be his mate, his partner, his equal. He'll see sides of you that weand correct me if I'm wrong gentlemennever want to see. You're our kid sister, for crying out loud!" Radek said, the tips of his ears turning red.

"Ah, you mean sex." Rheia grinned.

Levi gasped and covered Penny's ears. Rheia rolled her eyes. "It's a natural part of life, Levi."

"Not for you," Marco grumbled.

"If he hurts you, just call us. We have no problem explaining very thoroughly how he should treat our baby sister," Athan said, his blue eyes turning dark.

Rheia turned to Penny. "I wonder what they'll be like when you find your mate?" For a second, Rheia thought she saw the hint of a smile on Penny's face.

"That will never happen! Our Penny baby isn't allowed to mate. Ever," Marco growled.

Penny rolled her eyes. Rheia's heart swelled with pride. Penny might not be her daughter by blood, but this tiny kiddo was turning out just like her.

"Okay, enough crazy talk. You head to Lycaonia, find your mate, tell him if he hurts you, we'll skin him alive, and Penny stays a baby girl forever. Got that?" Radek demanded.

"Yes, sir!" Rheia laughed, taking Penny from his arms.

She was just about to head toward the garage when she heard a loud bang and the sound of splintering wood.

"Run!" Radek yelled. The men turned and ran toward the family room, blocking the danger so she and Penny could escape.

Heart in her throat, Rheia clutched Penny tightly and ran into the garage. She opened the driver's side door and got in. Penny scrambled over to the passenger seat and hit the button to lock the doors.

"Good girl! Now, get the seatbelt on and hold on tight. We don't have time to get you in your car seat," she said and started the car. She hit the garage door button. Slower than she could ever remember it moving in the past, the door rose. Before the door was completely up, the same feral from her nightmare appeared behind her car, grinning at her in the rearview mirror.

"I don't think so!" she muttered and threw the car in reverse. Pressing her foot down on the accelerator, she had a second to appreciate the surprised look on his face before he disappeared under her car. Both she and Penny bounced up and down as they ran him over.

The car screeched to a halt at the bottom of the driveway before she executed a K-point turn that would have made her father proud. She slammed her foot down on the gas pedal and sped away.

After a few minutes, a small, warm hand took hers. She looked over and saw Penny was watching her closely. There was neither fear nor panic on her face. Her brave angel was trying to comfort her.

"Oh, baby, we'll be okay, and your uncles will be okay, too. We'll get settled in Lycaonia, and they'll come to visit, and this will seem like a really bad dream. You'll see." Penny nodded and pulled her hand up and kissed it sweetly.

"I love you, too, baby girl. I know one thing; my mate has a hell of a lot to live up to," Rheia said, trying not to think of what could be happening to the men they'd left behind.

Looking serious, Penny nodded again. She let go of her hand and popped her left thumb into her mouth.

"Get some sleep, baby. I'll drive for a bit and put some distance between us and the house. Then we'll stop for a snack somewhere, and I'll put you in your car seat, okay?"

Penny nodded again.

Radek, Athan, Dax, Marco, Levi... you'd better be okay.

CHAPTER TWO

Colton leaned against the SUV and sighed. He looked down the long, dark dirt road that circled the outskirts of Lycaonia. There was still no sign of their unexpected visitor. When Aiden had knocked on his door the night before and asked him to take this early morning lookout, he'd jumped at the chance. He'd do anything to avoid another sleepless night. Looking out at the pre-dawn sky, he had to admit, even if only to himself, that the odds this was his mate on her way to him were slim. However, waiting out here in the frigid temperatures was preferable to watching his mate die in his dreams.

In the distance, he could see a faint glow. As it moved closer, he realized that it was a car coming toward him. He pushed away from his SUV and walked until he was in the middle of the road. The sun was just coming up, providing enough light for him not to worry about being run over. Slowly, the car rolled to a stop a good distance away. Seconds later, the driver's side door opened, and a small figure got out.

"Hello there!" he called. "My name is Colton Albright. I'm your escort into Lycaonia."

"How do I know that?" a female voice yelled.

Huh?

"Do you have any ID?" she asked.

He scowled. "Do you mean the official Lycaonia ID that states I'm a wolf-shifter from a secret paranormal city? No, I left that in my other pair of pants."

"You don't have to be snarky about it," she admonished.

He squinted, trying to see if she was kidding. He could see the outline of her body, but not much else. "You're going to have to trust me. I'm going to get in my car and drive to the Alpha estate where you'll meet with the Unit Commander. He's in charge of placing you in a safe house. I suggest you pay attention; the turn-off is well hidden." Without waiting for a reply, he turned and got into the car. Grumbling, he fastened his seatbelt. "Pain-in-the-ass woman."

When he began to pull away, he noticed that she stayed right on his ass. He thought about tapping his brakes but didn't feel like explaining to Aiden why the SUV needed repair work, not when Aiden's own car was still being rebuilt after his mate torched it. Smiling at that particular memory, he cranked up his iPod. His compilation of songs from *Supernatural* blared inside the SUV. As soon as they got to the estate, he would drop the crazy woman in Aiden's lap and go watch reruns until he passed out. He was always surprised at how much they got right.

When they arrived at the estate, he couldn't help himself, he slammed on the brakes, bringing the SUV to a screeching halt. Sure enough, the car behind him hit the back of his car. Since they weren't going very fast by then, there wasn't a lot of damage.

Shouldn't have been following so closely.

Smirking, he grabbed his iPod and got out of the car. He was making his way to the front door when he heard an angry woman's voice behind him.

"What in the hell was that?" she demanded.

Turning, he watched as the woman fought with the seatbelt still wrapped around her arm. In a fit of anger, she threw it to one side and slammed the car door. She marched toward him, and as she got closer, Colton felt his stomach drop. He knew her. She had the same heart-shaped face framed by sun-kissed, light brown hair as the woman in his dreams. Her eyes were a perfect mixture of blue and grey. He had only ever seen those eyes anxious, sympathetic or afraid, but never pissed. She was just as beautiful in life as she had been in his dreams.

She stomped up the porch stairs and began poking him in the chest.

"What kind of immature stunt was that? I have had one of the worst nights of my life and you pull this shit? You're lucky my brothers aren't here; they would..."

He watched as she stopped and realized what she'd said. Tears filled her eyes at the mention of her family, though her expression remained defiant. With a shaking hand, he reached out and cupped her face.

"Thank the Gods," he whispered. He couldn't keep the tremor out of his voice.

She looked puzzled at first and then her eyes widened.

"You're the voice from my dream, aren't you? They said that the voice might belong to my mate," she whispered and stood stock-still.

He nodded before he pulled her close and simply held her against him.

She pushed against his chest with both hands and stepped back. "You weren't an asshole in my dreams," she said bluntly.

He grinned. She was spunky. "And you weren't a prickly bitch in my dreams, either."

Her mouth dropped, and she just stared at him. Seconds went by before she began to smile. "I can't believe you said that. Aren't you going to try to woo me or sweep me off my feet?"

He shrugged. "Something tells me you're not the type of woman who wants to be swept off her feet. In fact, I'm willing to put money on the fact that you're the type of woman who likes to be in charge."

She winced. "Actually, yeah." She squinted up at him. "And you're okay with that? Most men like meek women."

He gave her his most wolfish grin. He was pleased when he saw her eyes widen at his expression. "I don't have to be in charge, but that doesn't mean I'm not dominant." He leaned in and buried his nose where her neck and shoulder met. He inhaled deeply, shuddering at her scent. He bit down lightly and heard her gasp. Almost instantly, he could smell her arousal. "Just because I'm not always in charge, doesn't mean I'm not an Alpha," he whispered, letting his lips dance on her skin.

"Colton let the poor woman get some air," Aiden boomed behind him.

Colton stepped back and turned to face his childhood friend standing in the open doorway. The look on his face must have been impressive because

Aiden swallowed visibly. The rest of his unit stood next to Aiden in the foyer, smiling at him.

"She's your mate, isn't she?" Aiden asked.

Colton nodded. "Yes, she is." He turned to the woman. "This is Aiden McKenize, the Unit Commander. Aiden this is..." He stopped. "What is your name, anyway?"

Aiden burst out laughing and Colton flushed slightly. Growling, he frowned at his friend. "We hadn't gotten that far yet."

Aiden smirked at him, arms crossed over his chest. "And just how far did you get?" he teased.

Colton thought about it for a moment. "We've pissed each other off, exchanged insults and she's damaged my car."

"So, pretty much on par for the Alpha Unit," Sascha's voice said from their left. Colton looked over, and the men from the other units stood grinning up at him from beyond the porch. "Har har, guys. At least she didn't set my car on fire."

"Hey!" Aiden protested.

"His car was set on fire? Is it safe here?" his mate asked.

Colton felt his smile threaten to split his face. "Yeah. Meryn, his mate, blew his car up for being a dick; he totally deserved it. As for being safe, look around, sweetheart. These men represent the best the paranormal world has to offer. There's no safer place." He wrapped an arm around her shoulders. "Come on, honey, let's head inside. You can tell me your name and why you're on the run."

"Wait! I have to..." She turned back toward the car.

Laughing, he pulled her back. "We can get your bags later."

She pulled free and shook her head. "You don't understand." She jogged back to her car and opened the back door behind the passenger seat.

Frowning, Colton and most of the men gathered around the car. When his mate lifted a small bundle out of the car, his brain couldn't make sense of it. It looked like a tiny body pillow wearing a coat. His mate set the bundle down and reached down to grasp a small hand. Hand? Blinking, Colton gawked down.

"Colton, my name is Rheia Bradley, and this is my daughter, Penelope Carmichael. She likes to be called Penny."

Colton stared until multicolored dots appeared before his eyes. A solid whack to his back brought him to the present, and he inhaled sharply, choking on his own spit.

"Breathe, you damn fool!" Sascha chided.

Gasping for air, he bent over and put his hands on his knees. "I think I'm dying!" he wheezed.

He looked up and saw his mate roll her eyes. "You're not dying, but I think you are having a panic attack. Just breathe, Penny won't bite, I promise."

Colton took deep breaths while staring at the ground. When he saw two small purple shoes appear, he looked up. Bright green eyes surrounded by dark lashes peered up at him. Rich brown ringlets spilled from outside the coat's hood. She had tiny, pink, bow-shaped lips and wore a serious expression. She raised her hand and placed it on his cheek. She was warm, very warm, too warm to be a human. This tiny child was a shifter, and she was now his daughter!

His legs gave out, and he fell to his knees in front of Penny as he looked into her eyes. The universe screeched to a halt around him and shifted. He knew eventually he would fall in love with his mate, but the love he would have for Rheia would be different than what he already felt for this child. He had fallen instantly in love with his daughter, and Gods help the ones that were after her, because there was nothing he wouldn't do to keep her safe.

Five minutes ago, he had been a bachelor; now he had a mate and baby girl. His world was changed forever. He smiled at her and she tilted her head. Slowly, giving her time to pull away, he reached for her and scooped her up when she didn't protest. Standing, he turned and faced the men.

"I'm a father!" he announced, forgetting that the men around him had been there the whole time.

Cheers went up from the men as they crowded around to meet Rheia and Penny.

"This is my mate, Rheia and my daughter, Penny. Aren't they beautiful?" he asked, beaming.

"Being a father is nothing to play at," Rheia chided, her hands on her hips, frowning at him again.

"I'm not playing. You're my mate and she's your daughter, that makes her my daughter," he rebutted.

She blinked. "Just like that? Poof! Just like that, you're willing to sacrifice everything and become a parent?" she demanded.

Colton frowned, confused. "Of course. Isn't that how it works with humans?"

"Not exactly," she confessed.

"Well, that's how it is with me. She's already mine, aren't you, princess?" Colton asked Penny.

Yawning, the girl nodded, popped her thumb in her mouth and laid her head down on his shoulder.

Colton melted. "Let's head inside. My baby girl has to be getting cold. Darian, Keelan, can you bring in their suitcases?" he asked.

"Sure thing," Darian said. He and Keelan opened up the driver's side door and popped the trunk.

"Now wait a minute. You can't just expect me to let you walk off with my daughter. Hey! Get back here!" Rheia called as he walked toward the house.

"Is your mommy always so grumpy?" Colton asked. Penny shook her head.

"Just with me?" This time she nodded.

"Perfect," he sighed.

"Colton!" Rheia ran in front of him and held her arms out. "Give me my daughter," she said in a dangerous voice.

"Sure. I just figured you must be exhausted from driving all night, I was trying to help." He carefully placed Penny in her mother's arms. "If you only accept one thing right away and without question, let it be this: There is nothing I wouldn't do for her. In my heart, she is the same as my own flesh and blood; I would die for her, for both of you." He hated the indecision and pain he saw on her face. Smiling, he reached out and thumped his mate between the eyes. He winked at her stunned expression.

Slowly, her features began to relax. "Just give me time. I lost my home today. I don't know if my brothers are alive. I met you and the whole world turned upside down. She's all I have." Rheia gripped Penny tightly.

"You have me now. Oh, and them." Colton jerked his thumb behind him where nearly thirty men began to look anywhere but at them, trying to appear busy.

"I feel better already," she joked. The men smiled.

"Come on, prickly pear, I'll introduce you to your housemates and then we can go to bed."

Rheia stumbled at his words. He caught her elbow to keep her upright and keep her from dropping Penny.

"I'm not going to bed with you," she protested.

Colton rubbed his chin. "I bet you will. What do you think, Penny?"

Penny held out her hand and gave him a thumbs up.

"Oh, Penny, you don't know what he's saying." Rheia walked past him into the house. Colton closed the door behind them.

"Maybe she does," Colton said and looked around. "I know it's early, but are Meryn and Beth up yet?"

Gavriel nodded and Aiden exhaled. "Meryn will be down in a few minutes. She said that it is too early to be alive, but she wanted to meet Lycaonia's newest citizen, I think she has been getting bored."

The men shuddered.

Ryuu walked in from the dining room and bowed to Rheia. "My lady, my name is Ryuu, I am the squire for this home. If you need anything at all, please don't hesitate to bring it to my attention." He turned to Penny, his face softening considerably. "And who is this treasure?"

Penny hid her face in Rheia's neck; she peeked out, staring at Ryuu with one bright green eye.

Rheia rubbed the girl's back. "My name is Rheia Bradley, and this is my daughter Penny."

Ryuu placed a white-gloved hand over his heart and bowed to the little girl. Penny wiggled her fingers at him. Colton was surprised to see Ryuu in western style dress; he had come to associate the squire with the traditional Japanese style clothing he normally wore. It was a shock to see him looking like a turn of the century Victorian butler.

Behind them, Beth and Meryn walked down the stairs arm and arm. Beth looked immaculate as usual, her blonde hair in a braided up-do. Today, she wore a charcoal grey business suit. Beside her, Meryn couldn't look more like Beth's opposite if she tried. Her short brown hair was sticking up in every direction, in what she called her "wild" look. Colton thought it was perfect for her. As usual, she was in jeans and today's T-shirt had a large blue box on it. Though awake, Meryn looked disgruntled and angry. Yawning, she stomped down each step, whereas Beth glided down gracefully. Beth stopped and eyed Ryuu's attire with a curious expression before turning to Rheia.

"Rheia, we heard your introduction to Ryuu as we were walking down. Welcome to the Alpha estate. My name is Elizabeth Monroe and this is Meryn McKenzie," Beth greeted Colton's mate cordially. "Your daughter is beautiful." Beth's smile was kind as she waved at Penny.

Penny however was staring at Meryn who was swaying slightly beside Beth and blinking drowsily. Meryn looked over, caught Penny staring and began to stare back. With their eyes locked, neither one of them looked away. As the silence grew, everyone began to look around uncomfortably. Finally, Penny extended her arm. She pointed at Meryn's shirt and gave a thumbs up.

Meryn's eyebrows shot up and she smiled. It was rare to see Meryn smiling before coffee. Colton noticed Keelan was edging behind Darian nervously. It was no secret that Meryn, before she had her coffee, scared the poor witch to death.

"Cool kid. Come here, brat." Meryn simply plucked Penny from Rheia's arms and started walking toward the dining room. "I'm hungry and I know my squire has food somewhere. Speaking of which..." She stopped, then turned to look behind her and tilted her head. "Yup, I was right. Ryuu, you do have a great ass." Without saying another word, she went into the dining room. Aiden was sputtering and growling like a bear with a thorn in its paw as he followed her.

"Who is that strange woman who has my child?" Rheia asked, turning to Colton, her eyes a bit wild.

"That's Meryn, she's Aiden's mate," Colton explained.

"The one that set the car on fire?"

Everyone nodded.

Rheia turned and hurried into the dining room.

Colton looked around, fighting to keep a grin off his face. "So. Who's hungry?" He threaded his fingers behind his head and walked into the dining room whistling.

Rheia's hands itched to take Penny away from the odd, short woman, but Penny looked perfectly content sitting on her lap looking at the woman's shirt. Trust her daughter to find another Whovian in the house. She had no one to blame but herself; she had indoctrinated Penny into the fascinating world of *Doctor Who* when she was desperate to find something the child liked. She stumbled across an old DVD one day and Penny was hooked.

Rheia watched Meryn carefully. "So are the two of you shifters?" she asked pointing to Meryn and Beth.

Beth nodded. "I'm a *lepus curpaeums...*"

"Beth's a bunny," Meryn interrupted.

"Meryn, quit baiting Beth," Aiden chided then smiled at her. "I'm a bear shifter."

"Who is growly and stubborn, but my teddy bear," Meryn whispered loudly to Penny.

Rheia looked around the table. The dark haired man sitting next to Beth spoke up next. "Gavriel Ambrosios, vampire. I am also Beth's mate."

"Über vampire. Dark Prince, even." Meryn continued with her commentary. Gavriel shook his head, smiling at her antics.

The man with long golden hair looked around before continuing. "Guess I'll go next. I'm Darian Vi'Alina, fae."

"Super tall. Doesn't say a lot, but very sweet. He's always willing to get the hidden boxes of snacks down from the higher shelves for you," Meryn smiled at Darian who winked back.

All eyes swung to the red headed man who was blushing furiously next to Darian.

"I'm Keelan Ashwood, witch," he said, then looked at Meryn anxiously.

"Keelan is very thoughtful and courteous. He always goes out of his way to make sure I have my coffee in the morning." Meryn beamed at Keelan, who laughed nervously.

Rheia turned to Meryn, "What are you?"

"We haven't figured that out yet," Colton quipped.

Meryn glared daggers at him, but he just laughed. Ignoring him, she turned back to Rheia. "I'm human."

Rheia noticed that Meryn's mate watched Meryn interacting with Penny with a gentle smile on his face. For all his bluff and bluster, he was a softie just like Radek. Rheia gasped and dug for her phone. How could she forget?

"Sweetheart, what is it?" Colton asked, his face filled with concern.

"I need to call home; I need to know if my brothers are okay." She looked down and nearly cursed aloud. Her phone was dead. In all the chaos, she had forgotten to plug it in while she was driving.

Aiden cleared his throat. "Rheia, Radek called me early this morning. He told me to tell you that everyone was fine. He said he also suspected your mate was here in Lycaonia." He shot a droll look at Colton who grinned back at him. "He said to tell her mate that if he ever hurt her, his Vanguard squad would come and personally remove his skin one inch at a time. He sounded very serious." Aiden's mouth twitched.

Colton turned to her, a serious expression on his face. "How many brothers do you have?"

She smiled at him sweetly. Now that she knew her family was safe, it felt like a huge weight had been lifted from her shoulders. "Five."

He exhaled loudly. "Perfect."

"So who's your favorite doctor?" she heard Meryn ask. Penny held up four fingers.

"Fourth Doctor, huh? Mine's a tie between Ten and Eleven. Ten because he was so painfully lonely and Eleven because he wasn't afraid to kick butt," Meryn explained.

"Congratulations on raising a well-rounded daughter. I personally love Classic *Who*, not many younger folk go back and watch the older seasons," Beth said turning from Meryn and Penny.

Rheia smiled. "Thank you, Beth, right?" Beth nodded. Rheia paused. "Let me ask you something. Is this mating thing real? My brothers explained a bit how it works. As a child, it seemed like a fairy tail ending, as an adult it feels like it's moving too fast."

Rheia noticed Colton flinched at her question and ignored it. Love at first sight only happened in cheesy 80's power ballads and Disney movies.

Beth smiled. "It is. I know it must seem strange to you, being human, but I think you already knew the answer to that question before you asked it. For the record, Colton has to be one of the most selfless men I've ever met. I think he'll be a good match for you."

Rheia snorted. "You don't even know me."

Beth raised an eyebrow and leaned back in her chair to look her up and down. "Smell of professional grade antiseptic soap, Gods-awful polyester scrubs, Naturalizer shoes, and the willingness to adopt a child not even of your own species? RN?" she asked.

Rheia shook her head. "Surgeon. I was working overnights in the ER when Penny came into my life. And scrubs are not God awful, they are comfortable, and I never have to worry about what to wear," Rheia refuted.

"My mate is gorgeous and smart." Colton winked at her.

Rheia sighed dramatically. "Too bad, I don't like blonds."

Colton's head whipped around to stare at her, slack jawed. She continued to look at him without cracking a smile. She could tell he didn't know if she was joking or not.

"Seriously?" he asked.

She shrugged indifferently and smiled up at Ryuu as he placed a plate of food in front of her. "You don't have to serve me, just let me know where the food is. I can make Penny's plate," she offered.

"See! It's not just me." Meryn pointed to Rheia.

Rheia looked around. "What?"

Beth answered. "Rheia, Ryuu is the house squire. In human terms, I think the closest thing that you have is a butler, but in the paranormal world, it goes beyond that. Here, we treat squires with reverence. They command a great deal of respect as they are the ones who run the homes of the high ranking families."

"High ranking? Who here is high ranking? Wait, didn't she say that Ryuu was her squire?" she asked pointing to Meryn.

Beth fought a smile and nodded. "Aiden, when he takes over from his father as the Elder for all shifters, will be the highest ranking paranormal in the world. Meryn, as his mate, will also be highly regarded."

They all watched as Meryn turned her waffle into a cartoon face using whipped cream and chocolate.

Rheia leaned back. "That just doesn't seem right to me."

Ryuu handed her a cup of coffee by the saucer. "Would it help you to understand if I told you

Meryn is single handedly restructuring some of the oldest paranormal traditions for the better? She looks at the world with fresh eyes. The changes she has made will save thousands of lives."

Meryn waved a waffle-laden fork around. "I know, I know. I look and sound like an immature teenager. It's not that I don't know the societal norms, I just don't give a flying fu..." She looked down at Penny. "Fig. Most of society are assholes. Why would I care what they think?"

"I agree with you," Rheia said, sipping her coffee. She paused and looked down at the cup. "Holy Mother of God," she said breathlessly. She turned and looked up at the handsome squire.

Meryn and Beth giggled. Beth winked at her. "I know exactly what you're thinking. Impeccable manners, gorgeous, can run a house, cook incredible food and brew the nectar of the Gods, is this man real?"

Rheia let out a sigh of relief. "Thank God, I thought it was just me."

Meryn shook her head. "No, we all have crushes on Ryuu. Plus, he spoils us." Meryn blew kisses to her squire. Around the table, Aiden and Gavriel growled low. Rheia noticed her mate wasn't acting particularly possessive. She didn't know if she liked that he wasn't acting like a caveman, or was upset because he wasn't.

Colton caught her staring and winked. "One. You're my mate, once I claim you, no other man will even compare," he said, oozing confidence. "Two. He feeds me, too. I have a man crush on him, so I can't get mad," he shrugged.

Rheia began to laugh so hard she had to put her cup down. "Oh Lord, I think I'm punch drunk, because he's just not that funny," she said, wiping her eyes. Around the table, the men chuckled.

Colton stood, glaring at the men. "I am so that funny. But you're exhausted, come on, honey. Time for bed."

Rheia stopped laughing and scowled up at him. "I told you, I'm not going to bed with you."

Colton walked over to Meryn and picked Penny up. "And I made a bet with my baby girl that you would. Let's go see who wins. Last one upstairs has to make the bed!" he shouted and sprinted from the room.

Rheia looked around. "Is he serious?"

Aiden nodded. "Yes. He never makes his bed."

Sighing, Rheia walked out of the dining room. She found Colton and Penny waiting for her in the foyer. She raised an eyebrow. "I thought we were racing."

He shrugged. "I remembered you haven't been upstairs yet, and I'd have an unfair advantage." He easily carried Penny on his right side. Her daughter was sitting comfortably on his muscular forearm. He offered her his left elbow and smiled. "Come on, honey."

"I'm not going to sleep with you," she said, placing her hand on his elbow.

"Bet you a dollar," he countered.

"Deal," she accepted. No way in hell was she letting him sleep with her and Penny.

CHAPTER THREE

Rheia walked into the room and was pleasantly surprised. Colton's bedroom was neat and tidy, except for the bed, which looked like the blankets had been thrown on haphazardly. He had decorated using different shades of creams, whites, and dark browns. The furniture looked expensive, but broken in and comfortable. Colton set Penny down on the bed and the girl immediately burrowed beneath the covers like a mole.

"Penny, honey, you have to change." Rheia started toward the bed.

Colton caught her around the waist. "Let her be. We'll be getting up in a few hours anyway; we don't want to be up all night." He leaned in and whispered against her ear. "Or do we?"

Shivering, she pulled away and gave him a sour look. They watched as Penny's head popped out of the covers near the headboard. She was in the center of the king sized bed and looked even smaller because of it. She looked perfectly comfortable.

Rheia turned to Colton. "She's a bed hog; there won't be room for three of us." She crossed her arms over her chest.

"Oh? I think there will be plenty of room." Colton stood back and stripped his shirt over his head. Rheia nearly swallowed her tongue. She shot a nervous glance over to Penny who watched them with her normal, serious expression on her face.

"What are you doing?" she whispered. She ogled each defined muscle, there was a definite six-pack, or was that...

"Eight," Colton said, his eyes laughing.

"Excuse me?" she stuttered.

"Eight-pack." Colton flexed shamelessly.

Rheia felt her heart rate pick up. When her breathing changed, Colton stopped flexing and turned to her, his green eyes burning.

"I'll stop teasing since baby girl is here." Taking a deep breath, he turned toward a closed door. "I'll change in the bathroom, be right out." The sight of his muscled back was no less dangerous than his washboard abs; Rheia was shocked when a slight whimper escaped.

When Colton turned back to face her, one hand on the doorknob, he had the biggest grin on his face. Seconds later, he disappeared into the bathroom and Rheia let out a shaky breath. The first thing she did was get out her phone charger and plug in her phone. She took her shoes off and debated on changing into pajamas for only a second. She quickly dismissed the idea, opting instead to stay prepared for any emergency. She lifted the covers and scooted in next to Penny.

"Don't tell him I actually like blonds," she whispered.

A look of concentration crossed Penny's face before she executed a perfect wink. Rheia laughed and pulled Penny into the circle of her body. Since adopting Penny, she lived for her cuddles. She blinked a few times, her eyelids growing heavy. Where was Colton? She heard the door creak and looked up. She didn't see him anywhere. When a heavy weight jostled her feet at the bottom of the bed, she looked down and nearly screamed. A large wolf sat at the foot of the bed, tongue hanging out like the family dog. Penny sat up and reached for the wolf with both hands. The wolf walked forward and lay down on the other side of Penny. The little girl wrapped her small arms around the wolf's neck and snuggled down with a sigh of contentment.

"Colton?" Rheia whispered.

The wolf raised its huge head and swung it over to her. It nuzzled her neck in the same fashion Colton had, before he licked her from chin to hairline.

"Ewww! Colton, that's gross." Rheia wiped at her face with her sleeve.

The wolf made a chuffling noise and settled in next to Penny.

Damn. Looks like I'm out a dollar.

Rheia turned onto her side and watched the huge wolf with her tiny daughter, the contrast made the scene that much more unbelievable. Yawning, she wrapped her arm around Penny and buried her hand in Colton's fur. He sighed, sounding content. Rheia stopped fighting the need for sleep; she knew that if anyone came after them, they would at least have a huge wolf to contend with. It was enough to allow her to fall asleep without worry.

When Rheia woke up, she experienced a momentary sense of panic. Where was Penny? She looked around to find the bed and room empty.

"Okay Rei, no reason to freak out, she's probably with the strange people you met a couple hours ago." Rheia tried to open her eyes and gave up; it felt like they were glued together with sand and Elmer's. Grumbling to herself, she swung out of bed and fumbled with her shoes. She walked to the door Colton had gone through to change and opened it. The bathroom was clean and the bright white surfaces gleamed back at her mockingly. Everything about this man, down to his bathroom, was bright and cheery.

She washed her face and gazed at her reflection. She looked like an angry bitch. She sighed; she really did hate the process of waking up. She found her suitcase and pulled out a fresh pair of scrubs. She changed quickly and walked out of the bathroom. She put her dirty clothes on top of her suitcase and left the bedroom, heading toward the open staircase. She was amazed at herself for not falling head first down the stairs. Vision and coordination weren't quite online yet. She heard voices and followed them to the dining room. When she entered, everyone got quiet and looked up. Colton sat with Penny on his lap. He was peeling tangerines and handing the pieces to her one at a time. The men all stood as she entered.

"Weren't you all here when we left?" she asked still blinking tiredly.

Meryn nodded. "Yup, but that was nearly six hours ago, it's lunch time already."

Rheia grunted and stumbled toward the only empty chair, which, of course, was next to Colton. The men sat when she did.

"Good morning, sunshine!" Colton practically sang out.

She swung her head in his direction and glared at him from half closed eyes. "Why are you being so loud?"

"Oh Gods, not again," she heard Keelan whimper.

Colton visibly gulped. Penny held up an empty coffee cup and shook it in front of Colton's face.

He grabbed the cup. "Ryuu!" he yelled.

Rheia rested her head on her arms. "You do realize that I am medically trained to remove pieces of your body in such a way that you won't die?" she asked.

Ryuu entered the dining room walking quickly, carrying a tray with three steaming cups. He placed one down in front of Meryn, then Beth, before setting one down in front of her.

"Considering your profession, I made yours extremely strong. Please let me know if it's to your liking," he said and stepped back.

She raised the cup and took a sip. Her eyes opened wide, and she looked down at the contents. She took another sip and sighed. It was hot, dark, and bitter. She could almost feel the caffeine kicking in. She sat back, never releasing the cup. She looked to Ryuu. "What is it? It tastes like coffee, but it's very strong, almost too strong, but amazing."

Ryuu smiled and bowed at the compliment. "I

have been studying the different types of beverages that can be made using coffee and espresso. What you're drinking is called a Black Eye. A cup of strong coffee with two shots of espresso. I used a dark roast for the coffee, but used a milder roast for the espresso shots. It was my hope that the two would balance each other," he explained.

"It's wonderful. Could I have this every day?" she asked hopefully.

"Of course, it would be my pleasure."

"All hail the Coffee God," Colton whispered. Beside him, Keelan drew a symbol in the air and muttered. "So mote it be."

Meryn held up her cup. "Ryuu, you cheated me! I'm missing an ounce of coffee."

Ryuu's eyebrows shot up. "I don't even want to know how you knew I changed your coffee levels, but that doesn't change the fact that we are restricting your caffeine intake. This will be your new blend."

Rheia frowned. "Why are you restricting her coffee?"

Aiden beamed at her. "She's pregnant; we're going to have a baby," he said proudly.

Rheia smiled back. "Congratulations." She turned to Meryn. "They're right; studies show that women who take in more than two hundred milligrams of caffeine per day double their risk of miscarriage."

Aiden turned to Ryuu. "What is she down to?" he demanded.

"She's now getting just under two hundred a day, but we've only been measuring coffee. I'll have to restrict other forms as well such as teas and chocolate."

Meryn turned to Aiden. "Don't make me get stabby! I need caffeine! I need chocolate!" Aiden paled.

Ryuu gently tapped her on the nose. "What you *need* is to go to your appointment with Adam later. His last report said you're still anemic, so you'll be getting more spinach and kale at dinner."

Meryn glared at Ryuu. "I love you, Ryuu, don't make me hurt you."

Ryuu smiled. "Trust me, *denka*. You won't even know you're eating something healthy."

"Meryn? Baby? What do you mean stabby?" Aiden asked, turning Meryn to face him.

Meryn shrugged. "You took my gun, so I 'found' a knife."

Aiden frowned. "Where is it?"

Meryn shook her head. "Not telling."

"Meryn!"

"No! We have all kinds of fucking crazy shit happening around here, I want to be able to defend myself. Just because I accidentally shot you, isn't a good enough excuse to take my only

source of defense!" Meryn shouted back.

Rheia looked over to make sure Penny wasn't getting upset at all the yelling, but she should have known better. Penny and Colton both wore identical looks of fascination as they slowly ate their tangerines and watched the drama that was unfolding at the table.

"*Accident?* Accident? How can you call that an accident when you said, 'Don't piss me off or I'll shoot you'? Then you shot me!" Aiden demanded.

Meryn's lower lip stuck out in a defiant manner. "I was kidding! I really wasn't going to shoot you.

But while we're on the subject, I don't know why you're making such a big deal, you healed in, like, a day." She sniffed dramatically. "I think you like upsetting me."

Aiden's mood changed dramatically. He reached for his mate's hand and brought it to his lips. "I'm not trying to upset you, baby, I'm just worried about you that's all. I don't ever want you in a position where you would have to stab someone... me especially."

"I'd feel better if I kept my knife. Please?" she asked.

Aiden sighed. "If it makes you feel better, then okay."

Rheia had to turn her head. Aiden was a bigger marshmallow than Radek. Maybe it was a trait for all bear-shifters to be softies when it came to the women in their lives. She pushed down a wave of homesickness that threatened to overwhelm her.

Colton leaned in so he and Penny were close. "Are you okay?" he asked.

Rheia regarded them as they glanced at her. She looked at Penny then Colton. "You both have the same color eyes," she said.

Colton turned Penny in his lap so he could see her face. They stared at each other. He turned back to Rheia. "She does! She has my eyes. Just like her..." Frowning, he turned to Penny. "What do you want to call me? You know that I am your mother's mate, which makes me your father. But you're old enough to decide what you'd like to call me."

Penny nodded.

"How about Daddy?" She shook her head.

"Dad?" She shook her head again.

"Father?" Again, she shook her head sending her ringlets flying about her face.

Rheia noticed the dejected look on Colton's face. A big part of her wasn't emotionally ready to share her daughter, but another rapidly growing part was already falling for Colton's roguish ways. It seemed to her that he should always be smiling.

She turned to Penny. "How about Papa?"

Penny paused. She thought about it then nodded.

Immediately, Colton's face brightened. "I'm your Papa!" He tickled her and Penny's face broke out into the first smile Rheia had ever seen.

"Oh!" She covered her mouth with both hands and watched as Penny smiled and thrashed around in Colton's arms; she had never looked happier.

Colton noticed her distress and stopped. "What?"

Rheia shook her head and pulled Penny into her lap for a cuddle. "This is the first time I've ever seen her smile." When Rheia pulled Penny back, she was almost afraid to look, afraid the smile would be gone. But it wasn't, it was still there, Penny was beaming up at her.

"You're so beautiful when you smile, dumpling," she said, kissing her daughter's forehead.

Penny leaned in and kissed her cheek before wiggling to get down. Once on her feet, she ran from the dining room. Rheia went to get up, but a hand on her shoulder stopped her.

Ryuu bowed. "I'll watch over her so you can eat your lunch." He placed a towel on the buffet table and followed the little girl.

"Sounds like good advice to me," Colton said, placing three small finger sandwiches on her plate.

"What are your plans for the rest of the day, Rheia?" Beth asked.

Rheia shrugged. "I don't know. Less than twenty-four hours ago, I was in my own home and my biggest concern was helping Penny speak again. Now, I'm far from home, I don't have my brothers or a job. But Penny's never looked happier. It's like she's a different child."

"Can you tell us what happened to her?" Colton asked, wrapping an arm around her chair.

Rheia drew in a ragged breath. "There's not much to tell. About a year ago, Radek was sent to check on a house because a concerned neighbor reported the couple that lived there hadn't been seen in a few days. When he got there, he could tell the door had been kicked in, but then shut again so that no one could see from the road. He said he found Penny's father in the hallway. Radek could tell he had been trying to defend the door to the master bedroom; the poor man had been ripped to pieces. He said as horrible as the hallway was, the scene in the master bedroom was a hundred times worse, blood and chunks of flesh were everywhere. He was about to turn and leave the room for fresh air when he heard a tiny noise. He found Penny wedged, pinned really, between the bed and the wall. She was three at the time. He said the blankets had been thrown over her, and if he hadn't heard the sound, he never would have known she was there. The smell of the blood completely masked her scent."

"When he lifted her out, she was covered in urine and feces. She had been so terrified she hadn't moved from the spot in days. Her legs had cramped, she nearly suffocated under the layers of blankets, and had been surrounded by blood and the stench of death from what was left of her own mother." Rheia had to take a deep breath.

"Dear Gods," Beth whispered. Gavriel pulled her close, his hand stroking her hair comfortingly.

"You don't have to go on," Colton said, taking her hand.

Rheia shook her head. "I can go on. Penny lived it, I'm only telling you about it. I can be no less brave than she has been."

Colton raised her hand and kissed her fingers gently. She took comfort in that small action.

"Radek knew the couple had been paranormal, so he called Athan to pick Penny up. They brought her to me, knowing I would never turn her away." She paused and looked around. "You see, I was adopted when I was a little girl, too. My father was the town sheriff at the time; he found me much the same way Radek found Penny, except both of my parents were alive, they were just too high to feed and take care of me. Daddy took me home, the same home where I was living when Penny came to me." She smiled. "He didn't have to forge any paperwork like we did, he just stubbornly refused to give me up. Eventually, the judge awarded them custody. You can't do something like that anymore though."

"For the first six months Penny was with me, she was practically catatonic, completely non-responsive. It took me nearly a year to get her to the point where she was communicating with nods, head shakes, and thumbs up signs. Her smiling today was the most beautiful thing I have ever seen." She swallowed hard and wiped the tears from her eyes.

"That's it!" Colton said, his eyes blazing. He stood up and pounded the table with both hands.

Everyone stared at him in shock.

"What in the world?" Rheia asked.

He turned to her, his eyes suspiciously moist. "We're going to motherfucking Disney World! You and Penny have lived through hell. I want to do everything I can to make you smile. You deserve to spend the rest of your life smiling."

Rheia couldn't take her eyes off him. He stood there, green eyes bright, his blond hair glowing in the afternoon sun ,and to Rheia, he looked exactly like she had dreamed Prince Charming would be.

Smiling up at him, she nodded. "Okay, let's do Disney World."

His smile was beatific. He sat back down in his chair and took her hand. "I swear, on my life, to do everything in my power to make you happy."

"Oh, that was just beautiful," Beth said, sighing happily.

Rheia blushed; she wasn't used to such open displays of emotion.

"I want to go to Disney World, too." Meryn said looking up at Aiden with puppy dog eyes.

Aiden shot Colton a nasty look. Colton raised his hands and shrugged.

"It will be a nightmare arranging security." Aiden grumbled.

"Worth it," Colton said, dismissing his friend's concern.

"My brothers would be more than happy to help," Rheia volunteered. In fact, she knew they would jump at the chance to see Penny playing.

"You keep saying brothers, but you were adopted. Are they your biological brothers?" Beth asked.

Rheia shook her head. "Heavens no. I think I mentioned my father was sheriff when he found me. His deputy was Radek Carson. Radek belongs to a small squad of paranormals that monitor Jefferson, the town I'm from. My father, mother, and I discovered they were paranormals by accident when my father returned to the station to berate Radek for not going to the hospital after getting shot while out on a call. My mother had insisted on going with him since she was a nurse and could look at the wound. I went with them because they didn't want to leave me alone and because I loved helping my mother treat people. Daddy walked right into Radek's office just as Levi was healing him with a spell. The door was standing wide open so my mother and I saw as well; I was about eight at the time. They sat us down and explained how squads like theirs existed all over the country to help people. They called themselves the Vanguard.

"The squad in Jefferson consists of Radek Carson, the sheriff, Levi Sorrel is a police detective, Marco Rodriguez is the Fire Marshall, Dax Vi'Eaereson is a firefighter, and Athan Durant is the lead paramedic. They were my best friends growing up and always looked after me. They are the only family I have left."

"Ai-DEN! What the fuck?" Meryn screeched.

Aiden looked at her, puzzled. "What?"

"What? What do you mean what?" she asked, standing.

Seconds later, Ryuu came rushing in with Penny on his hip. "*Denka*, what is the matter? What has he done this time?" he asked, setting Penny down on her feet. She ran over to Colton and climbed into his lap

Aiden glared at him. "Why do you always assume it's me?"

Ryuu glared at him flatly. "Because it usually is." He hurried to Meryn's side and cradled her wrist in his hand. Rheia watched in wonder as an electric blue dragon tattoo on Meryn's arm began to glow. Meryn took a deep breath, but continued to send her mate death glares.

Aiden looked around; the men all shook their heads and shrugged their shoulders. Rheia could see that whatever had set Meryn off, the men were clueless as to what it was.

Ryuu maneuvered Meryn back into her chair. "Now tell me, what exactly has you so upset?"

Meryn pointed a finger at Aiden. "Him! He's been keeping secrets! Secrets that could have helped me months ago!"

"Oh my Gods!" Beth's eyes widened.

Meryn turned to her. "Exactly!"

Aiden rested his head on the table. "I never understand you," his voice was muffled by the table.

"Understand me? Understand *me!*" Meryn yelled, jumping to her feet again.

She turned to Rheia. "You said your brothers are part of this Vanguard squad?" she asked.

Rheia nodded. "Yes."

"You say they're all across the country?" Meryn prompted.

"Yes, I've heard them talk about many different cities."

"So like, maybe, I don't know, five or ten squads?" Meryn asked.

Rheia shook her head. "More than that, at least one per state, for sure."

"Aiden!" Meryn turned back to Aiden and picked up a fork. "I'm going to fucking stab you!"

Aiden jumped back as Ryuu brought his arms up under Meryn to keep her from stabbing her mate.

"Meryn, you need to calm down and tell us why you're so upset!" Aiden said, concern etched over every inch of his face.

"You all can't be that thick." Beth declared, turning an angry look to her mate.

Gavriel shook his head. "We would never knowingly upset either of you, my love."

"Let me stab him. Just once!" Meryn yelled. "Just four tiny holes!"

"Can someone please explain?" Aiden boomed.

"You want an explanation? Fine! How about this for an explanation? Lycaonia is slowly being invaded by ferals; we've been attacked not once, but twice. Manpower is so scarce, I had to restructure your entire training system just to get rookie trainees distributed, to speed up the training process, and you mean to tell me you have hundreds, fucking *hundreds* of trained unit warriors around the country that you haven't told me about?" Meryn gasped for air. She glared at him for two seconds before bursting into tears.

Aiden moved forward, waving his hands around his mate, not knowing what to do. "Baby, please calm down, you'll make yourself sick." Ryuu released her and Meryn collapsed into Aiden's arms. "I didn't deliberately keep it from you, to be honest, I forgot all about them until Radek called me last night, they don't report to me. The Vanguard project was never sanctioned by the council, so it was all volunteer based. Instead of cycling from active duty to retirement, we had unit warriors establish identities outside of Lycaonia to provide quicker assistance to families living outside the four pillar cities. Instead of retiring, they were put in an inactive status until they returned. They aren't even on our rosters anymore. For all intents and purposes, they are doing this on their own time."

"Please tell me you have a list somewhere. Please tell me you've been keeping track of their names and locations," Beth pleaded.

Aiden looked at Colton and Gavriel. Both men shook their heads.

"Unbelievable." Beth closed her eyes and leaned back in her chair.

Aiden pulled Meryn into his lap; she had calmed down enough that she was just sniffling. "You have to keep in mind, this project was never approved, and it technically doesn't exist. As one warrior would return, another one would go out. If a warrior wanted rest and relaxation, he would put out feelers in a low-crime area. If they wanted sunny weather and the beach, he would check with coastal squads to see if they had an opening. These men go into an inactive status when they leave. They pretty much run things themselves with Radek being the point of contact for all the squads. He might have more information, but then again, he lives outside of Lycaonia and doesn't have to worry about paperwork being found in an audit."

"Don't blow smoke, Aiden." Beth said, her eyes opening. A small grin tugged at the corners of her mouth. "I saw the state of your office before we redecorated, you weren't worried about an audit."

Aiden had the decency to blush.

Colton leaned back in his chair and threaded his fingers behind his head. "Radek is still with Vanguard, huh? That sneaky bastard, he owes me five bucks."

Everyone turned to face him. Rheia knew that his offhanded comment made it seem like the missing five dollars was Colton's only concern, but she saw it for what it was: comic relief. Sure enough when she looked around everyone was smiling.

"I can call him for you. I'm sure he'd be very interested to hear you're my mate." Rheia teased.

Colton's chair landed on all fours and he looked at her, not blinking. "Fuck! I've mated Radek Carson's little sister."

"Actually, he calls me his *baby* sister. That probably doesn't make a difference though." Rheia laughed at Colton's morose expression; it tickled her.

"You talk about him like you know him," Beth said.

The men all nodded.

"He's good enough to be in Alpha, he could have had my position if he had wanted it. But the idea of leaving Lycaonia was too tempting," Colton explained.

"We need an accurate count of all Vanguard warriors and their locations. Then we need to be able to get in contact with them and mobilize them if need be. We have to make sure that they are either up to speed on current human technology or get a sixth man out to them to run their command centers." Meryn began listing everything that needed to be done.

Beth stood. "First things first, your wellness checkup. I'm sure that Rheia would love to see our recently renovated clinic."

Meryn stood, her eyes and nose red. "Okay." All the spunk seemed to have been drained from her during her outburst.

"I'm sorry, baby, if I had remembered, I would have told you sooner." Aiden nuzzled her cheek gently.

Meryn sighed. "It's just that Beth and I worry about you guys all the time. You're always outnumbered, the ferals seem to be breeding like rabbits," she turned to Beth, "no offense." Beth rolled her eyes. Meryn continued. "We've been doing everything we can think of to help you. If even half the Vanguard returned, we could easily triple our numbers. We never know which routine patrol will be the one where one of you doesn't return and it eats us up inside."

The men fell silent.

Rheia stood and stretched. "Nothing in life is guaranteed, not even tomorrow. I learned that early in life. You have to do what you can, when you can, like wellness appointments or Disney World." She smiled at Colton. "What you can't do is live in fear. It will leech every moment of joy out of the time that you do have, and that's no life at all." She turned to Penny. "What do we do when we're afraid of something?" she asked the little girl.

Penny stuck her tongue out and blew a loud raspberry. Rheia nodded. "That's right, baby girl. You give it the ole two finger salute and you keep moving forward because backward isn't an option."

Gavriel shook his head ruefully. "Human's lives are so short, but the wisdom you acquire stuns me at times."

Rheia looked at him. "It's because our lives are so short that we have to learn quickly." She turned to Beth. "Ready when you are, but who'll watch Penny?"

Colton spoke up quickly. "We can watch her," he said, pointing to the men.

Rheia looked around, the men wore varying expressions, ranging from neutral to anxious. "Are you sure?"

Colton nodded. "Absolutely! We got this."

Beth and Meryn walked around the table heading toward the doorway, Ryuu following behind them.

Rheia kissed Penny on the forehead. "Same rules with Papa as when Uncle Radek and your other uncles watch you, okay?"

Penny nodded and reached under the table to retrieve the small backpack Rheia used to carry her most favorite toys and snacks. Penny pulled out a cell phone.

Rheia smiled. "Good girl."

"Wait, what rules?" Colton asked as she walked out of the room.

"Never mind. Have fun." She waved goodbye.

In the foyer, Beth eyed her scrubs. "Are you sure you don't want to change?"

Rheia looked Beth up and down, taking in her outfit. "You're a clothes person, aren't you?"

Meryn chuckled. "You have no idea."

Rheia pointed to her fresh scrubs and shook her head. "No thanks, I like my scrubs."

Beth shuddered.

"Ladies, your coats." Ryuu held three coats over one arm and handed them out, one by one.

Meryn arranged her scarf and Rheia could have sworn it moved on its own. Blinking she looked again and it was still.

"Okay, let's blow this popsicle stand," Meryn said, heading out the door.

Rheia followed eager to see somewhere familiar.
I can't wait to get to the clinic and normalcy.

CHAPTER FOUR

Colton bundled Penny up before they took her outside. The construction crew building the trainee's new barracks had moved the dumpsters yesterday, giving them back the grassy area they used for drills. Penny stood calmly at his side holding his hand.

"Are you sure this is a good idea? Having her outside during training?" Colton asked Aiden. The men were all staring at the little girl as if they had never seen a child before.

His friend turned to him. "Why not? She can't be inside all by herself, she could trip and fall or choke or drown in a bathtub. You heard your mate; she knows how to cut pieces off without killing us. Do you really want to risk something happening to our little angel here?"

Colton's brows furrowed. "Why would she be in the bathtub?"

Aiden rub his hands over his face. "I don't know, but I remember doing a lot of stuff when we were cubs that didn't make sense."

"Good point." Colton looked down at Penny. "No bathtubs, okay?" Penny nodded and gave a thumbs up, her tiny hand encased in a mitten.

Colton's heart was a melted pile of goo in his chest. He scooped her up and kissed her cheek. "You're so damn cute!"

"Ah, sir? What's with the kid?" Graham, the Delta Unit leader asked.

Aiden thought about it for a second then smiled. "So glad you asked." He walked over to Colton and Penny. "Penny, are you good at hiding?" She nodded. "Are you fast?" She nodded again.

Colton felt a growl crawl up the back of his throat. He turned his body so Penny was away from Aiden. "What in the hell are you thinking?" he demanded.

Aiden looked hurt for a moment before he reached out and cuffed Colton in the back of the head.

"Ow, dammit!"

"Do you really think I would do anything to put her or any child in danger? You're like a brother to me Colton; I would never hurt my own niece," Aiden grumbled.

Colton was instantly contrite. "I'm sorry, Aiden. My wolf is really at the surface, any perceived threat and he loses his mind."

"Apology accepted." Aiden nodded his head and turned to walk towards the group.

"Especially since I was going to ask you to be her *Athair*," Colton yelled to Aiden's back.

Colton had known all his life that if he had any children, Aiden would be their *Athair*.

Aiden turned back around to face him and looked dumbstruck. Colton turned to Penny. "Penny, do you know what an *Athair* is?" She shook her head. "An *Athair* is someone very special in the life of a child. If anything were to happen to me or your mommy, Aiden would take over raising you and he would see to your protection and care." Penny's arms tightened around his neck. "Nothing is going to happen, I promise."

"Did you mean it?" Aiden asked quietly.

"Of course I did, you idiot. I chose you to be my children's *Athair* when we were pups."

"Thank you for the honor, I will help protect her with my life," Aiden said, sounding choked up. The damn bear had always been sentimental.

"Congratulations, Aiden, we know you'll be a wonderful *Athair*." Sascha clapped Aiden on the back.

Aiden winked at Penny and nodded at Colton before turning to face the men. "We have a new little cadet with us today. She assures me that she is great at hiding and is very fast. We'll be dividing up into units; the goal of this drill is to protect your bell tower from this stealthy assassin," Aiden said, pointing at Penny. Colton was surprised to see her put on a pretty scary "game face", but he was even more surprised to see two of the warriors step back from her. He leaned in. "Did your Uncle Radek teach you that?" he whispered. She nodded. "Not bad, kiddo." She held up a mitten-covered hand and Colton gave her a high five.

"Any unit that cannot defend their tower will have extra laps and will be put on the list as available babysitters for one afternoon." Aiden looked at his clipboard. "Trainees, your jobs will be to distract your unit, giving our angel opportunities to ring those bells. Alpha trainees, your job will be to record how many times each bell is rung. Any questions?" Aiden asked looking up.

"What will the Alpha Unit be doing?" Sascha asked, pointing out the fact that they only had three bell towers, one each for Gamma, Delta, and Beta. The two absent units were running patrols.

"We'll be making sure nothing happens to Penny. Let's get something straight men, I love all of you like brothers, but if anything happens to my niece, I will happily turn you over to her mother, and trust me, she is not a woman to be trifled with, understood?" Aiden gave the men dark looks.

"Yes, sir!" Male voices rang out.

Aiden walked over. "Okay, Penny, it's up to you now. Do you think you can take these puffed up warriors down a peg or two?" he asked.

Penny nodded and wiggled. Colton put her down and stepped back. Penny removed her coat and mittens. Like all shifter children, her temperature ran warm. They were usually bundled up if they weren't going to be moving much, but since Penny was going to be moving around a lot, her jeans and fleece shirt would do just fine.

"Go easy on us, baby girl," Quinn called from the field, his tone almost teasing.

Penny turned and looked him in the eye, never changing expression. Wordlessly, she reached down, picked up some mud, and covered her face.

"Oh, fuck!" Quinn and the rest of the men stared at her.

"What are you two idiots waiting for? Get those barrels of hay up to block the tower," Sascha barked. Suddenly, the men were a lot more serious about this drill.

Colton knelt down next to Penny. "Take your time. It will be a lot more fun watching them panic if they can't see you than if you manage to ring the bell but they saw you coming." Penny nodded and spread her feet apart to stretch.

Colton stood and frowned down at his daughter. "Remind me to call Radek and ask him what he taught my daughter."

Aiden nodded. "No kidding." He turned to Penny. "Hey angel, if you manage to get all three bell towers, I will buy you whatever dessert you want after dinner for a whole week."

Penny stopped stretching and held up two fingers.

Aiden laughed. "Two weeks, huh? You drive a hard bargain, but you have yourself a deal."

Colton shook his head. "I have the best kid in the history of kids, including the time we were kids."

Aiden nodded again. "Agreed. Okay men close your eyes; let's give her a thirty second head start."

When Colton turned to see what Penny would do, she was already gone.

Best. Kid. Ever.

"Adam, Aiden's brother, runs the clinic. They're just wrapping up some much needed renovations, so you'll have to excuse the mess," Beth explained as they got out of the car. Ryuu held the car door open for Meryn.

"I've probably seen worse," Rheia assured her.

They walked through a heavy set of metal double doors and down a long hallway. From top to bottom, the entire building looked brand new. The smell of paint and cut lumber was thick in the air. Rheia walked behind Meryn, Beth and Ryuu, peeking into rooms. She saw box after box piled together, covered in plastic. It looked as if none of the imaging machines had been unpacked yet. They turned down another hall that opened up to a large waiting room area. Beth pulled out her cell phone. After a few seconds, she spoke.

"We're here. Okay, see you in a second." Beth smiled at Rheia and put the phone away.

A minute later, a tall, dark haired man emerged from behind a set of double doors at the end of the hallway. Without even asking, Rheia knew this was Adam; he looked just like his brother.

"Adam, I would like you to meet Rheia. She's only just arrived this morning, and it looks like she'll be here for a while. She is Colton's mate and a doctor," Beth informed him.

Adam's face broke out in a smile. "Welcome! I could really use your help here at the clinic. Between an unexpected baby boom and feral attacks, we don't have the personnel to deal with everything."

Rheia smiled up at him. "I'm actually relieved. I didn't think a paranormal city would even have doctors, considering how quickly you heal."

Adam's eyebrows shot up "You have experience treating paranormals?" he asked eagerly.

She nodded. "As a child, I helped my mother treat the squad of paranormals that lived in our town. Since becoming a doctor, I've continued to treat them."

"I must have done something right; the Gods are smiling down on me. First, my wonderful sister Meryn tricks the council members into renovating and upgrading the clinic, and now Fate herself has sent me a doctor with experience in treating paranormals. I may actually get a few hours sleep this week after all."

"When would you need me?" she asked.

"Would starting tomorrow be too soon?" he asked hopefully.

"That shouldn't be a problem; I'll have to make sure someone can watch my daughter."

Adam blinked. "You have a daughter?"

"Yes. Will that be a problem?" she asked frowning. He didn't seem like he was a man to judge.

Adam shook his head smiling wide. "No, not at all. That means Colton is a father. I can't wait to congratulate him."

"We're still figuring things out, but he seems like he'll make a good father," she admitted.

"Anyone who can grow up around Aiden and keep his sense of humor can't be all bad," Adam teased.

Meryn turned to Adam. "Speaking of your brother, where on his body would be a safe place to stab him with a fork? Where it would be painful, but wouldn't take long to heal?"

Adam brought his hand up to his chin and tapped his finger on his lips as he thought about his answer. "Why don't you tell me, Adair, and Ben what he's done and we'll take care of it. After all, that's what brothers are for," he offered.

Rheia had to admit, he handled Meryn fairly well. It was highly unlikely that his brothers would stab Aiden.

"He forgot to tell me about the two hundred plus warriors living out amongst humans in an inactive status," Meryn said sourly.

Adam stared at Meryn in disbelief. He blinked and then shook his head. "Outer thigh."

So much for brotherly love.

"Okay enough about my baby brother, I'd rather talk about my baby niece or nephew. Let's head to my office, it'll be more comfortable."

Adam led the way to a small office painted in a butter cream color. Rheia and Beth sat down on the office sofa while Ryuu stood outside the door. Meryn took the chair in front of Adam's desk.

He pulled out a folder and began reading the contents. Rheia knew from experience the news would not be good. Doctors always knew the contents of those folders cover to cover before the patient even stepped into the room. He was pretending to look over the contents of the folder to gather his thoughts.

"Am I allowed to speak freely in front of everyone in this room?" he asked.

Meryn frowned and nodded.

"Okay then, to be honest Meryn, your test results worry me. The anemia hasn't gotten any better and if you didn't have Ryuu tending to you, I would seriously doubt you were taking your vitamins." He closed the folder and put it on his desk.

"But I've cut back on my coffee!" Meryn twisted her hands anxiously.

Rheia noticed Beth was on the verge of standing to go to her friend when the door opened. Ryuu walked in and placed a comforting hand on Meryn's back.

"What more can we do?" he asked Adam. Rheia noticed he didn't even try to hide that fact that he had been eavesdropping.

Adam took out a pad and began writing. "I'm recommending iron supplements to take in addition to the pre-natal vitamins I prescribed during your last visit. As I told you, human and shifters can have babies, but it may be a rough pregnancy. No caffeine, in any form, and a diet with lean meats and lots of dark green leafy vegetables should help. No more long nights without sleep. You have to start thinking of your baby, Meryn." His voice was gentle, but firm.

"I'll do whatever it takes; I'm going to be a good mom," Meryn said, her voice trembling.

Beth shot off the couch and wrapped a supportive arm around Meryn's shoulders. "Of course, you are. Whatever you need, we'll get it."

Ryuu was already on his phone. The way his finger moved rapidly over its surface, Rheia was willing to bet he had already ordered the iron supplements and was planning new menus.

Adam stood and walked around his desk to kneel down in front of Meryn. "I won't let anything happen to my niece or nephew."

"It's a girl. I keep telling Aiden we're having Meryn 2.0," Meryn said smiling.

Adam's eyes crinkled at the corners when he smiled. "Then I will help Meryn 2.0 into this world because she has a lot of people already waiting to meet her." Adam stood. "Okay, I'll put you down for more blood work in about three weeks and then you can come back in for your three month check-up." He walked back around to his chair and sat down.

Rheia frowned. "Aren't you going to do a pelvic exam?" Four sets of eyes turned to her.

Adam turned red. "Normally yes, but given the circumstances..."

Rheia stood, exasperated. "Men! Meryn, would you feel comfortable if I did it?"

Meryn nodded rapidly. Adam sat back in his chair, relief pouring from him. "Thank you, Gods!"

Rheia turned to him. "Do you have a room we could use? It shouldn't take too long."

Adam practically leapt from his chair. "I'll show you."

"Ryuu and I will wait here," Beth said.

"Be right back." Meryn waved.

Rheia and Meryn followed behind Adam. He opened a door to one of the smaller room and stood to one side. "Everything you need should be in here. I'll go wait with Beth and Ryuu." He shut the door, and they heard him practically race away.

Meryn turned to her. "I'm so glad you're here."

Laughing, Rheia pointed to the paper-covered table. "Have you ever had a pelvic exam before?" She opened the first cabinet and was pleasantly surprised to find the examination gowns.

"I started getting them in college as part of my yearly physicals."

"Good, then you know the drill. Normally, I would step out of the room while you undress, but to save time, I'll just be over here assembling the needed supplies, if that's okay with you?" Rheia handed her the paper gown.

"Fine by me, I'm just glad it's you looking up my hoo-ha and not Adam. Can you imagine how awkward that would have made family holidays?" Meryn asked.

Rheia snorted and started opening the other cabinets. She found a speculum and the lubricant and lined them up side by side on the metal tray. Looking around, she found an assortment of non-latex gloves by the sink. She put on a pair and turned to find Meryn playing around with the blood pressure cuff.

"Ready?" she asked sliding the tray in her direction.

Meryn nodded and tried getting on the table but it was too high. They found the small metal step stool, and she hopped up on the table.

"What do you guys listen for when you use that thing, anyway?" Meryn asked, pointing to the cuff.

"Your heartbeat, now lay back and get comfortable."

Meryn reclined back.

Rheia pulled out the stirrups from either side of the table. "Okay, scoot down to the edge of the table."

Meryn wiggled down and Rheia helped place her heels on the stirrups.

"Okay, while I do this, you can tell me about this mating. To be honest with you, everything feels like it's moving too fast for me," Rheia said, starting the exam.

"Well, being mated to a paranormal is way different than being with a human. It's as if you've been slipped this really cool happy drug that makes all your defenses come down and bam, you're exposed. But you realize it's okay, because no matter how crazy or broken or unworthy you think you are, your mate loves and wants you just the way you are. And just when you're about to freak out that this stranger can see right to your heart, you realize his walls are down, too. Before you know it, your souls are reaching out for one another and you feel incomplete without him. You look at this man you just met and know that no other will ever compare. Plus, the sex is really hot, hence my current condition."

Rheia finished the exam and helped Meryn sit up. "You're a nut, you know that, right?"

Meryn nodded. "Yeah, but I can be nutty and crazy, immature and brilliant. And it doesn't matter, because Aiden loves me no matter what, even after I accidentally shot him, so everyone else who can't take a joke can fuck off."

Rheia took off her gloves and washed her hands. "I'll step out so you can clean up, I'll wait for you outside."

"Okie dokie."

Rheia handed Meryn a box of tissues, opened the door, and stepped out into the hallway. A couple minutes later, a dressed Meryn emerged. "So is everything kosher down in lady town?"

Rheia laughed. "Yes, everything is fine."

"Good. I have enough problems with functioning with no caffeine in my life and having low iron."

"The supplements should help a lot."

"Thanks. Hey, can I ask you something?" Meryn stopped.

"Sure."

"Why doesn't Penny talk?"

Rheia shook her head. "I don't know. She wasn't physically injured during the attack that killed her parents, so it has to be psychological. When I asked around at the hospital, to get a recommended course of action, they all said to institutionalize her. There's no way I was going to do that to her, so I decided to let her go at her own pace. When she's ready to talk, she will."

"That's cool; I just didn't want to put my foot in it, in case it was something specific. I do that a lot," Meryn admitted.

"You?" Rheia asked, feigning surprise.

"You're so funny." Meryn smiled. "She's a really neat kid. I've never met another Whovian who was so young before."

"It was the only thing that caught her interest after I got her."

Meryn made a face. "I'm not judging, because I think that's a dick thing to do, but as much as I love the Doctor, do you think it's appropriate for a little kid?"

"Trust me; I know exactly what you're talking about. I tried every cartoon in existence, even the annoying singing ones, but she would stare at me then turn off the television."

"Some of the bad guys can be pretty scary."

"She's seen real monsters; I don't think much scares her anymore."

"I've seen them, too," Meryn said quietly.

"Meryn, be honest with me. How safe is it here? The things that attacked my house, they were like rabid dogs." Rheia shuddered at the memory.

"It's safe, but it isn't."

"That's helpful."

"It's safe because we're surrounded by unit warriors. They do patrols at all hours to guard the city's perimeter. It isn't safe because the ferals know where to find us."

"There's no way to keep them out?" Rheia asked.

"The men are working on it." Meryn resumed walking, heading back to Adam's office.

Rheia opened the office door and they walked in.

Adam stood. "So, everything okay?"

"She's fine. If you hand me her chart, I'll make notes." Rheia held out her hand.

"Good to hear." Adam walked over and handed her the folder.

Rheia made her notes and handed it back to him. "What hours are you thinking of for me?"

"How does a typical nine to five sound? We can rotate nighttime on-call hours," Adam offered.

"Sounds heavenly compared to my old schedule. Did you need help setting up the machines?"

"Yes, please. Beth tried to help, but she didn't know what the machines did, so some of the room set ups aren't very logical."

Beth grimaced. "Sorry, Adam. You're right, though, knowing what the machines are and what they do would make the difference."

"Don't be sorry, your organization of patient files and data input saved me weeks of work; it's not your fault you don't know what the machines do." He turned to Rheia. "The machines are heavy, so I'll see if I can get some volunteers to help with the heavy lifting."

"If you can't find anyone, let Aiden know. He can check to see if one of the units can help," Meryn offered.

"Thanks, Meryn." Adam kissed her cheek.

Meryn turned to Ryuu and Beth. "You guys ready to go?"

"Yes, I'm ready." Beth stood and everyone walked to the door.

"Bye, Adam!" Meryn waved.

"Bye, hun." He turned and went back into his office.

"Let's go check on the men," Rheia said.

Beth frowned. "Don't you mean check on Penny?"

Rheia grinned. "Nope."

Beth sighed. "Oh, dear."

Ding!

Colton collapsed against Aiden, laughing.

"Motherfucker!" Quinn exclaimed.

Aiden snapped upright. "Quinn! Language! I know it's hard to believe, because she's kicking your butt, but there's a toddler on the field."

Quinn blushed. "Sorry Aiden, Colton." He turned back to his defensive position in front of the Gamma bell tower.

Ding!

In the middle of the field, the Delta bell tower chimed.

Graham shook a finger at Aiden and Colton. "Y'all are cheating by using magic!"

Grinning broadly, Colton shook his head. "Sorry, but my baby girl is just that good."

Aiden turned to him. "Has she hit the Beta tower yet?"

Colton shook his head. Beta had done an excellent job of creating high partitions to keep out the small four-year old.

Aiden looked down at his watch. "Two-minute warning!" he bellowed.

The field grew louder as the trainees stomped, yelled, and waved their arms trying to distract their assigned units. Colton looked at Aiden to see if he noticed. Aiden nodded. No bells had gone off after the two-minute warning.

"She's going for Beta." Colton whispered.

"If she gets them, I'll buy her an entire cake." Aiden whispered back. Both of them stared at the Beta bell tower.

Aiden looked down at his watch. "Thirty seconds!"

Lorcan Ariav, the Beta Unit leader, bowed to them looking smug.

"She has ten seconds." Aiden stared down at his watch.

"Five, four, three, two..."

Ding!

"Sonofabitch! Impossible!" Lorcan turned around to see his bell swaying back and forth.

Aiden and Colton whooped and yelled, dancing jigs, and laughing their heads off.

"Penny, come out, come out where ever you are," Keelan sang.

"Oh, shit!" Colton heard Darian yell.

Colton turned and Penny was sitting on top of the bell tower. Instead of going after the well-defended rope, she had gone for the bell itself. She was currently trying to get down, but looked stuck.

"Penny!" The men all raced around the bell tower.

"Keelan, do something! Float her off!" Colton ordered.

"I'm trying, but she's an animate object, it's a bit tricky," Keelan snapped back, sweat running down his face.

One second she was trying to swing her leg over the rail and the next she was falling.

"Darian! Leg up!" Colton yelled and ran towards the fae warrior. Darian knelt down and cupped his hands. Colton stepped into his fingers and Darian flung him in the air. Colton flew up and wrapped his arms around Penny's body. He turned, but didn't have enough time to land on his feet. Holding her tight, they hit the ground, and he rolled them. When they came to a stop, Colton sat up with her in his lap.

"Is she bleeding? Is she broken? I can't tell! Keelan, can you do something about the mud!" Colton yelled frantically.

Between Keelan and Quinn, Penny's face and clothes became spotless and her hair tucked back in a perfect ponytail.

Penny beamed up at him, her eyes lit up in excitement.

"Oh Gods, I think she's okay." Colton felt weak with relief. Hands helped him up, and he walked back with her to the front of the training grounds. Penny pointed from bell tower to bell tower excitedly showing them the path she had taken. At the end, she stuck her tongue out at Lorcan and flexed her arms.

The men erupted into boisterous laughter. Colton was the first to collapse to the ground equal parts exhausted from worry and relief. Around him, the rest of the men sank down and rested against each other; it had been a long afternoon.

Penny went up to Aiden and held up two fingers. Opening one eye, he nodded. "I promised, didn't I? We'll start your two weeks tomorrow. Tonight, I'll let you choose from my stash of snack cakes." He winked at her. Hopping up and down, Penny threw her tiny arms in the air.

The sound of tires crunching gravel had all the men turning to see that Meryn, Beth, Ryuu and Rheia had returned from the clinic.

"Men, not a word," Aiden growled.

"Do we look stupid?" Sascha asked incredulously.

The women walked up, frowning. Penny ran up to her mother, bouncing up and down happily. Rheia's face transformed from worry to sheer joy at the sight of her daughter's exuberance.

"What did you do while we were gone?" Rheia asked Penny. Penny stopped bouncing and looked over her shoulder to the men. Meryn, Beth, Rheia, and Ryuu stared at them. Colton knew that the men looked wrecked. Penny looked at the ground and then shrugged.

"Bless that baby's heart," Quinn whispered. Around him, the men all nodded.

Rheia eyed them all carefully. "You know what? I don't want to know. Come on, Pumpkin Dumpling, I think I have some Teddy Grahams leftover in my purse. Let's go in for a snack." Rheia took Penny's hand and the women headed for the house.

Rheia stopped at the door, allowing Ryuu to open it. She picked Penny up and kissed her on the head, then frowned. "It's so strange; you've never been so clean after playing outside. You even smell clean. How did you stay so clean?"

Colton held his breath. The ladies walked in and Ryuu turned to them, smiling slyly. "Must be magic," he said simply and went in after them, closing the door.

Colton, Aiden, Keelan, and the rest of the men lay on the ground breathing hard.

"How old is she?" Graham asked.

"Four. She's four," Colton answered.

"Ninety-six more years until she's considered an adult and you don't have to worry about her," he said.

Colton turned his head. "Do you really think I'll ever stop worrying about her?"

Graham shook his head. "I probably won't stop either. You have one hell of a kid, Colton."

"Yeah, yeah, I do."

"Hey Aiden, you weren't really serious about babysitting right?" Quinn asked nervously.

Aiden just smiled.

"Aiden? Uhh, sir?" Quinn pleaded.

"We're so fucked," Sascha said sounding depressed. All around the field, the men groaned.

Penny, one. Beta, Delta and Gamma Units, zero.

Colton chuckled and stared up at the blue sky.

"What a wonderful day!" He sat up and looked at Aiden. "I feel like some Teddy Grahams."

Aiden waved him on.

He got to his feet and headed toward the front door, whistling. He opened the door and went looking for his family.

CHAPTER FIVE

Rheia watched as Colton and Penny played at the table.

"See this teddy? This is Sascha; he is outflanking that group of teddies, which are the Beta Unit. He's moving in." Colton set up a mock battle on their paper plate.

"And we captured this one," he said handing the small snack to Penny. She popped it in her mouth.

"We're not taking prisoners, eh? Good. Oh no! He tripped. Silly Sascha!" Colton said, making one teddy spin on the paper plate. Penny covered her mouth, her eyes laughing.

"Okay, he's back up. Look, he's tricked them all and captured all of the Beta Unit. Hurray!" Colton made the teddy dance. Penny bounced around in her seat.

Rheia was shocked at the dramatic difference between the solemn little girl she'd known living in Jefferson and this happy child.

"Okay Mom, all the teddies have been eaten," Colton announced.

Rheia smiled and picked up Penny's learning backpack. "Okay, Penny, quiet time." Penny hopped down and took her hand. Rheia led her to the family room and sat down next to the coffee table. She laid out all of Penny's favorite books along with her tracing paper and letter book.

"Practice your letters until the big hand is pointed down," Rheia said, pointing to the clock over the fireplace. "When you're done with your letters you can watch Doctor Who until dinner time. Meryn's set up the TV in here so that when you turn it on, it's already on Netflix." Penny nodded. Rheia stood and watched as the little girl pulled out her favorite pencil and meticulously began tracing her letters.

"I'll be in the dining room if you need me, baby, okay?" Rheia asked, almost wishing she was needed.

Penny simply nodded, without even looking up.

Sighing, Rheia turned and walked back with Colton to the dining room. Colton shut the door.

"Okay, what's wrong?" he asked wrapping his arms loosely around her waist. He wasn't being pushy or trying for sex; if he had, she could have easily shot him down. The look of concern on his face was genuine and his arms comforting.

"A couple months ago, Radek asked if I was still comfortable raising Penny. He knew how hard it was being a single mother. He offered to look for shifter parents who may want to adopt her. I told him she was mine, and I didn't want to give her up. However, seeing her here, with you all, in this environment, she's getting better by the hour. I can't help but think I was being selfish keeping her with me," Rheia said, admitting her fear.

Colton pulled her close, and she rested her head on his broad chest. It had been so long since she had felt like it was okay to let go, that if she fell apart, someone would be there to not only watch Penny, but to help pick up the pieces.

"There's no way to prove Penny getting better is linked to coming to Lycaonia. It's probably all your months of working with her paying off and you just happen to be here. It could be that she feels safe. She knows she's living with unit warriors. All shifters teach their children from a young age that unit warriors are to be trusted, and if they are ever in trouble to seek us out. She may not remember her parents teaching her this, but I bet they did. Wanting to keep her with you isn't being selfish; it's being a good mother. If it makes you feel any better, I have asked Aiden to be Penny's *Athair*; she has another layer of protection in our world," Colton said and pulled back to she could see the sincerity in his eyes.

"What is *Athair*?"

Colton paused. "It's sort of like an uncle, only more. If anything happens to us, he'll be there to protect her and make sure nothing happens to her. Among paranormals, the child's father chooses the *Athair*, someone they trust above all others," he explained.

"In the human world we call that a godfather. I wish you'd asked me about it first; she has uncles on my side, you know."

"I'm sorry I didn't ask. I've known since about Penny's age that I knew I was going to ask Aiden to be *Athair* for my children, I didn't even think twice when the situation presented itself. You couldn't ask for a better *Athair* than Aiden. He hasn't known her long and he would already tear the world apart for her. Of course, he's a huge marshmallow when it comes to the softer sex, but don't tell him I said that."

Rheia smiled. "Your secret is safe with me. So, what did you all do today?" she asked.

Colton eyed her carefully. "I thought you didn't want to know."

"I didn't, not until I saw how relieved everyone was that I didn't want to know. So now I want to know."

"I will tell you, I promise, but how about six months from now?" he said, trying to negotiate.

"Why six months from now?"

"Because by then you'll be head over heels in love with me and you will be less apt to cut off pieces of me we both may need later."

Rheia sighed; she knew it had been dangerous. "Did she have fun?"

Colton nodded breaking out into a huge smile. "She is something else! She outsmarted three units! She's like a tiny master ninja. She's great at hiding and stealth."

"It's how she survived, remember?" she reminded him gently.

She watched as all the color drained from his face. "Oh, Gods! You don't think we traumatized her, do you? I'm such an idiot!" His voice grew more panicky.

"She's fine. She was happy, smiling, and dancing around. Whatever you did, helped." She rested both hands on his chest; she could feel his heart beating wildly. You couldn't fake this. He was genuinely upset he might have hurt Penny.

"Meryn said that when you find your mate, it's like your defenses come down, but that it's okay, because your mate's defenses are down as well and it helps your souls to meet. She said that's why it's so easy to fall in love so quickly, because there's nothing left to hide."

Colton nodded slowly. "Sounds about right."

"What do you think it's like?"

"I asked my dad the same thing when I was younger. I was obsessed with finding my mate. He would laugh and say I would find you when I was ready. But I still remember what he said. He said that finding your mate is like buying a new pair of shoes."

Rheia wrinkled up her nose. "Shoes?"

Colton leaned in and kissed the tip of her nose. She blushed and he laughed. "Yes, now hush. He said it was like buying a new pair of shoes. You get the excitement of having something new, something you've always wanted. Normally, when you buy a pair of shoes, it's bittersweet. They're new, but you have to break them in, and that can be painful. He said mating is like finding a pair of new shoes that go with everything and you never have to break them in. They're the most comfortable things you have ever worn, fit perfectly, and because they go with everything, you never have to look for another pair of shoes again."

"It sounds lovely. I hate new shoes," Rheia admitted.

"Me, too. That's why paranormal males are so protective of their mates; we only get one perfect fit. It's also why matings tend to develop rapidly. If you have the perfect pair of shoes, why waste time on another pair?" He leaned down and ran the tip of his nose up and down the side of her neck.

"Because sometimes change is scary. You want to keep wearing your old pair of shoes, because, even if they don't fit quite right, you know what to expect. Because nothing is worse than building up your hopes and dreams, thinking you found the perfect pair of shoes, only to have them give you a blister." Rheia fisted Colton's shirt in both hands.

Colton stepped back and cupped her face with both of his hands. "I can't promise you I'll never give you a blister, but if I rub you the wrong way, tell me, and I'll stop before I cause you any more pain. Then I'll carry you until you're better."

Rheia felt tears running down her cheeks and realized it was because she was crying. Meryn was right; there were moments when your souls really did touch.

Colton wiped away her tears with his thumbs and slowly leaned forward. She knew he was giving her every opportunity to turn away, but she couldn't. If he didn't kiss her in the next couple of seconds, she would forget how to breathe.

When his lips finally touched hers, she expected him to devour her, but he didn't. Ever so gently, he nipped, nibbled, and kissed her lower lip, from one side to the other. Then he started on her upper lip. Always teasing, never demanding, she soon found herself frustrated. She wanted more. Reaching up, she buried both hands in his hair and pulled his face closer. She forced his mouth to open and took what she wanted. She found his tongue and slid hers alongside it.

Groaning, he wrapped his arms around her, welding their bodies together. She could feel his arousal and her knees almost gave out. It had been so long since she felt she could just give in, too long since she had been with someone she trusted completely. In that moment, she realized she trusted him. She might not know him completely, but she did trust him, with her daughter, with her body, and even her heart.

She stepped back, breaking their kiss, both of them breathing hard. When she looked up, she was startled to see his normally green eyes were yellow. When he grinned, his canines peeked out from under his lip, giving him a devilish look.

"You're a danger to all women," she said, trying to get her breathing under control. Her daughter was in the next room for goodness sakes!

"No, just you," he corrected. He closed his eyes and let his head drop back on his shoulders. When he opened them again, his eyes were back to green.

She shook her head. He would be the death of her.

"Too bad you don't like blonds, huh?" he asked, wistfully.

Her mouth dropped. Whistling, he threaded his fingers behind his head. "I wonder if Penny is done with her letters yet; I could go for some *Doctor Who*." He walked out of the dining room, leaving her a confused and aroused mess.

"Damn blond wolf shoes!" she rambled incoherently.

She heard him chuckle from the hallway. Smiling, she followed him so they could all watch the Doctor together.

"Ryuu, I'm so sorry. I forgot to mention how picky she is." Colton watched as Rheia apologized for the third time.

"Don't worry about it. I just wish I knew what she liked so I could prepare it for her," Ryuu assured her.

Rheia picked up a fork with a piece of baked chicken on it. "Come on, baby. Just one bite."

Penny shook her head and crossed her arms over her chest.

Colton stood. "Hold on angel, be right back." He walked out of the dining room and into the kitchen. It didn't take him long to assemble all the ingredients for his special sandwich. He made two, knowing how much running around Penny had done that afternoon, then one for him. He put everything away, carried the plate out to the table, and set it in front of Penny. She looked up at him questioningly before leaning in and sniffing the sandwich. Her eyes widened in surprise before she picked up the sandwich and took a huge bite.

Rheia turned to him, disbelief on her face. "What on earth is that?"

"My specialty: beef jerky, pickle, peanut butter, mayonnaise, and cheese sandwich," Colton announced proudly.

Everyone stared at him, the silence uncomfortable.

"Ah, an oldie but goodie. I love that sandwich," Aiden said, taking a bite of his chicken.

"Everything a growing pup needs. It was my favorite when I was a kid," Colton said, picking up his fork.

Everyone looked from him to Aiden and back again.

Darian shook his head. "When you were a kid? You just happened to have all the ingredients on hand and knew where they were?" he teased.

"Okay, okay you got me. I had one yesterday," Colton admitted.

Aiden looked up a hurt look on his face. "Without me?"

"You like it?" Meryn asked, swallowing hard.

"Don't knock it, till you try it, short stuff." Colton waved his fork at her.

Aiden shrugged. "One day, when we were cubs, I was playing over at his house and his mom went to visit his grandmother. We got hungry, so Colton said he'd make us sandwiches. Since we liked all the ingredients separately, we figured we'd like them all mixed together. We were right."

Penny picked up her second sandwich and dug in.

Rheia shook her head and turned to her own food. "I don't care how crazy it is, if she likes it and is willing to eat it, she can have it."

"I will have to learn about 'kid' food," Ryuu admitted, watching Penny carefully.

Meryn sat back smiling. "My favorite was always mac and cheese with cut up hot dogs in it, covered with barbecue sauce."

Beth licked her lips. "My odd food is tuna fish, made with mayonnaise and spring vegetable sour cream mix, served with Andy's Hot Fries."

Meryn's eyes widened. "That sounds amazing."

Beth nodded, "I know, right?"

A tiny sigh of contentment had everyone looking at Penny. She sat back in her chair patting her belly like an old man. Everyone burst out laughing.

"Glad you liked it, angel," Colton said, before ruffling her hair.

Yawning, she surprised the hell out of him when she climbed into his lap, popped her thumb in her mouth, and snuggled up next to his chest. Colton stared down.

"What do I do?" he mouthed to Rheia.

Laughing, she pointed to his full plate. "Good luck and welcome to parenthood."

Colton carefully maneuvered his fork, taking small bites so that nothing would drop on his daughter's head.

Aiden chuckled at his discomfort. Colton flipped him off.

His friend took a huge bite of chicken and licked his lips, teasing him. Colton nearly woke Penny when Meryn elbowed her mate, causing Aiden to choke slightly on the huge bite he had taken. Meryn winked at him.

Aiden cleared his throat. "The contractors said they'll be with done with the addition by tomorrow. Meryn, what did Jaxon and Noah say about moving out?"

"They want to stay here, close to Command Central. Jaxon brought up a good point, too. He said that as I get further along with my pregnancy, it might be a good idea to have them nearby. I may need their help walking and getting up, that sort of thing."

Aiden frowned. "You're kidding right?"

Meryn rubbed her belly. "Look at me, then look at you. I'll be lucky if I'm not on bed rest the last months of my pregnancy. I'm already having problems with anemia."

Colton frowned, feeling concerned for his friends. As much as Aiden was a brother to him, Meryn had become the bratty kid sister he'd never had; he didn't want to see anything happen to her.

Aiden stared at his mate. "I thought humans had babies all the time?"

Rheia spoke up. "We do, Aiden. I have a feeling that, after today, I will be Meryn's attending physician. I can tell you that if your baby is as big as I think it will be, I will be classifying Meryn as a high-risk pregnancy."

Colton reached over and placed a supporting hand on Rheia's shoulder. She smiled at him gratefully.

Aiden paled and pulled Meryn into his lap. "What does that mean exactly?"

"It means I'll have to have a C-section for sure. I'll be cut from here," she pointed to one side then dragged her finger horizontally across her midsection, "to here."

"My poor mate," Aiden said sounding slightly ill.

"That's right, buddy, I may not be able to have chocolate, but you owe me desserts and lots of them." Meryn said, snuggling close.

Colton noticed that Rheia had to look away to hide her smile. Poor Aiden.

Colton frowned when suddenly something very warm spilled across his lap and down his legs. He looked down and Penny had a blissful expression on her face. Stirring, she opened her eyes and blinked. He knew the exact second that she realized what she'd done. Her tiny face contorted into silent tears and she reached out for Rheia.

"What happened?" Rheia demanded.

Colton winced, looking down. "I think we might have had an accident."

Penny's small frame shook with sobs as she hid her face in embarrassment.

"Shh, baby, it's okay. Look, Colton doesn't mind, do you?" she asked giving him a look.

Colton scooted over until he was in Penny's old seat next to Rheia.

"Of course, I don't mind. Look at it this way, kiddo, you marked me, now you have to keep me," he said, rubbing her back.

When Penny looked up, her bottom lip trembled. He took her tiny hand and kissed it. "Accidents happen; it's nothing a little water won't fix. I'm not mad at all and no one minds. Everyone's had accidents before, right guys?" Colton asked giving everyone a look identical to the one he'd just gotten from Rheia.

A chorus of agreements sounded off around the table. Penny sniffled, but didn't hide her face again.

Rheia turned to Colton. "Can you do me a huge favor and run to the store to get her some pull-ups for nights? We've had a lot of excitement and scary things happen in the past couple days, and she's in an unfamiliar place, so I'd rather be safe than sorry. I think she'll be back to normal after she adjusts."

"Sure I can get some, no problem," Colton said.

Relief filled his mate's eyes. He could tell this was the first time she had someone around to ask for help. He couldn't imagine the hardships she'd faced over the past year raising Penny alone.

Rheia stood. "Come on, doodlebug, let's get you washed up, and ready for bed."

Penny turned and stared at Aiden. He nodded. "I didn't forget. I'm going to the store with Colton and I'll pick you up something special. Get ready for bed and if your mommy says you can, maybe you can have it for breakfast in the morning," he promised.

Penny nodded and rested her head on Rheia's shoulder. Rheia turned to Aiden. "If you promised her sweets, she can have small powdered donuts for breakfast. How's that pumpkin?"

Penny nodded and popped her thumb back in her mouth. Rheia started to walk past Colton then paused. She leaned down and kissed him on the lips. "Thank you," she whispered and left with Penny.

Aiden stood. "Come on men, this time Colton needs our help."

"Gods, I hope Bart is working tonight," Darian muttered.

Colton stood and followed the men out to the foyer.

"Colton, I thought you might need these," Ryuu said, holding out a wet washcloth and clean pair of sweatpants.

"You are a lifesaver!" Colton dropped his pants right there in the foyer and quickly washed up with the washcloth.

"See, I told you he had a great ass." Colton heard Meryn say.

He turned slowly and saw that Meryn and Beth were watching them with huge smiles on their faces. Grinning, he strutted a bit. He heard their growls only seconds before Aiden and Gavriel dragged him backward out into the cold, in his underwear and barefoot. They threw him in the SUV and dropped his shoes and pants on his head before closing the door. Colton quickly got dressed and into his seat.

When everyone was inside, he spoke up. "Okay, I lied. I have no idea what in the hell pull-ups are."

Aiden started the SUV. "Okay Keelan, look them up on the Google."

86   ALANEA ALDER

Keelan swallowed hard. "Do I have to? Human stuff is scary. I'm still having nightmares about lamb's stomachs exploding all over my..." The men turned to look at him. "Never mind."

"Please, Keelan? It's for baby girl," Colton said, pulling no punches.

Keelan sighed and pulled out his phone. About a minute later, he was smiling. "Guys, I think we're safe this time; they look like they're diapers for humans."

Darian relaxed back in his seat. "Thank the Gods."

Gavriel smiled. "Diapers don't sound too bad."

Colton grinned at his friends. "We're buying diapers for my baby girl. I have a daughter."

The men chuckled.

Keelan turned off his phone and looked around. "Who would have thought a few months ago that we'd be buying diapers now? It's funny how finding mates has made everything more fun."

Feeling confident, Colton joked with the men all the way to the Duck In. When they arrived, everyone climbed out. This time, it was Aiden reaching for the gun.

He looked at Colton. "You had my back when I had to get those important items for Meryn; I could do no less for you."

Colton nodded. "Thank you, old friend."

Aiden lifted the shotgun then the AR-15. "I'm leaning toward the AR-15, what do you think?"

The men nodded.

"Good." Aiden slipped the gun on his back and locked the SUV.

"Let's go."

When they walked through the door, they heard a familiar voice almost instantly.

"Lord have mercy, you boys are back. I'm almost afraid to ask," Bart chuckled.

The men gathered around the older man's register.

"Tonight, we are after *pull-ups*," Colton said slowly.

Bart blinked. "Say again?"

"Pull-ups," Colton repeated.

Bart frowned. "Yes, that's what I thought you said. Boy, do you know what pull-ups are?"

Colton nodded. "I think so. They're like diapers."

Bart eyed him carefully. "Why do you boys need diapers?"

Colton puffed out his chest. "I have a baby girl, now. I didn't even have to use condoms to get one," he said, elbowing the older man in a conspiratorial way.

"Well, if you didn't use condoms, I guess you would end up with a baby. A girl, you say?" Bart's face softened. "Baby girls are miracles from God boy; you better do right by her. How long have you been seeing her mama?"

Colton thought about it for a moment and looked around at the men. "About what, twelve hours, give or take?" The men all nodded.

"You sure that baby girl is yours?" Bart asked seriously.

Colton nodded. "Yeah, she's mine. She even has my eyes."

"But you just met her mama?" Bart asked.

"Yes, sir." Colton nodded.

"Son, I don't think you understand how some things work." Bart frowned in concern.

"I'm not sure how everything is decided either, but I'm the luckiest bastard alive to have those two angels in my life." Colton smiled.

Bart shook his head. "I guess that's all that matters, though, I have to say, I worry about you boys."

Aiden clapped the older man on the shoulder. "Thank you for your concern, but we have everything under control." He patted the gun on his back. Colton thought it was touching that Bart was worried about their safety.

Bart's eyes widened when he noticed the gun on Aiden's broad back. "You boys are staying out of trouble, aren't you?"

"Yes, sir," Keelan nodded.

"Right. Okay, well boys, pull-ups are near the aisle you found the feminine products on, time before last." Bart nodded to the center of the store.

"Many thanks, friend," Colton said, and they made their way to the aisle.

"Okay men, let's grab a box and go," Aiden ordered.

They turned and looked at the huge wall of boxes in front of them.

"Look! Tiny bottles and toys!" Keelan pointed to the display that held what looked to be baby items. "This isn't so scary."

"Aiden, which box?" Colton asked looking from floor to ceiling.

"Box? Which wall?" Darian pointed out that the diaper selection extended almost the full length of the store.

"The babies on this package look quite happy," Gavriel said, pointing to a box on the left.

"Yeah, but so do these." Darian pointed to the one on the right.

Colton frowned. "They all look happy."

They all continued to stare.

"Okay, this one has stars on it. Rheia did say they were for nighttime," Keelan said, pointing out a purple box.

"Good job, Keelan!" Colton said, reaching for the box. He stopped when he saw something he didn't understand. He read the box closely and put it back.

"What was wrong with that one?" Aiden asked.

"It has something called 'Cool Touch'. If the baby wets the diaper, there is this gel that turns cold; it's to alert the child that they went to the bathroom. It sounds uncomfortable; I don't want anything cold on Penny," Colton shuddered.

"I think it's a miracle humans have survived this long," Darian whispered.

They all nodded.

"Okay, how about this one?" Darian said pointing to another purple box, but this one didn't have the 'Cool Touch' feature.

"Looks good." Colton went to pick up a box and noticed that some of them had different sizes.

He turned to the men. "These things come in sizes!"

"How do we know which size Penny takes?" Aiden asked.

Colton shrugged and looked at the size chart. The weights were useless because he didn't know how much she weighed; to him she seemed as light as a feather.

"Colton this one says for three and up. It should be okay, right?" Keelan asked.

Colton frowned. "What if it doesn't fit? What if it's too tight and hurts her? This thing will be covering baby girl's important parts; we can't get this wrong, gentlemen!"

The men paled and turned to study the boxes again. Suddenly, Colton had a brilliant idea. He took the box that Keelan found and opened it up. He held a pull-up out to Keelan. "Put it on."

Keelan blinked. "Excuse me?"

"You're the smallest here; we can use your frame as a point of reference. Now, put it on," Colton ordered.

"Hell no!" Keelan began to back away and bumped into Darian, who shrugged before securing the witch's arms.

"Sorry, Kee, but this is for Penny."

Keelan began to thrash around.

Colton knelt down and undid the sticky tabs. "Quit moving Keelan, you're making this difficult."

"Damn right, I am!" Keelan said, turning crimson.

Colton managed to get the diaper between Keelan's legs and fastened. The pull-up actually stretched quite far.

"Oh my goodness!" they heard a female's voice gasp. They turned to see one of the pretty female cashiers standing at the end of the aisle. "I'm so sorry, I didn't mean to interrupt, I don't judge lifestyles, I... oh dear!" she rambled. Blushing, she hurried away. The men looked at each other and realized what the scene she witnessed might look like to someone else.

"Oh Gods! She thinks we're into fetish play and Keelan is our baby," Darian whispered, horrified.

Keelan collapsed to his knees. "That was my mate," he groaned.

Colton dropped to the floor beside Keelan. "I'm so sorry, I'll go explain."

Keelan shook his head. "I'll do it." He stood and looked down before removing the pull-up. "They're quite comfortable; I'd go with the one that has princesses on it for Penny." He dropped the pull-up and sprinted to the front of the store.

Colton wished the floor would open up and swallow him whole. He had just humiliated his fellow unit brother in front of his mate! Aiden, Colton, and Darian glanced at each other. Colton was about to follow Keelan when he heard a wheezing sound. They all turned to find Gavriel on the floor, his arms wrapped around his stomach; his entire body was trembling and shaking.

"Has he been poisoned?" Aiden demanded. He dropped to his knees and turned his second in command over onto his back. The vampire that they now knew to be the Dark Prince was laughing so hard he had tears running down his face. His eyes were bulging slightly and he couldn't seem to breathe. Aiden whacked him on the back a few times. Gavriel simply rolled around and began to laugh out loud.

"Oh Gods! Never in all my years!" Gavriel laughed uproariously.

Aiden sat back on his heels and looked up at Colton. Colton looked at Darian. Then Darian's mouth twitched. That was all it took. Colton wiped his eyes. "Can you imagine what we must have looked like?" he asked. His question brought a round of fresh laughter.

Gavriel reached for Aiden and made cooing sounds. "Change me, Daddy, I am wet," he joked.

"Perverts!"

The men froze and looked down the aisle. Ethel, the judgmental, older woman they had encountered on their previous trip to the Duck In, scowled at them, before shuffling to the front of the store, calling for Bart. It was another couple of minutes before any of them could breathe again.

Colton looked up at the fluorescent lights, grinning. Before Rheia and Penny, before any of the mates, they had never laughed like this. They heard the sounds of footsteps before Bart appeared over them frowning.

"Ok boys, get on up. I say this because, obviously, you have a baby in the house now. Drugs, like that wacky tobacco, don't do a body good. Y'all need to stay away from it," he warned.

The men fought to hide their smiles as they stood and brushed each other off.

"I can assure you, we do not indulge in that disgusting vice," Aiden said, walking alongside Bart.

Colton grabbed the opened box and then grabbed a second one for good measure. While Aiden convinced Bart they weren't drug addicts, Colton went to the register where Keelan stood with a pretty brunette. She blushed when he approached.

"I'm sorry for thinking y'all were up to no good." She smiled at him shyly.

"And I'm sorry for embarrassing you. We're normally not quite so exuberant. I was very lucky that Keelan was willing to help me. I've never shopped for my daughter before," Colton said, trying to place the blame for the entire episode on his shoulders.

The brunette raised an eyebrow. "He didn't exactly look willing," she chided.

Colton looked at her nametag. Anne. "No, he didn't, did he Anne? But he's an amazing sport and didn't get mad at me for humiliating him. I couldn't ask for a better friend." Colton nodded at Keelan who nodded back.

Anne rang up his boxes. "How old is your daughter?"

Colton smiled. "She's four. Her mother thinks that the recent excitement we've had caused tonight's little accident, so we're getting these to be on the safe side."

Anne nodded and told him the total. "Backsliding happens a lot with toddlers, especially after a stressful event. My little cousin was almost hit by a car; he wet the bed for a solid month after that."

He handed Anne his money and turned to Keelan. They both knew his poor baby girl had had nothing but stress in the past twenty-four hours.

Keelan cleared his throat. "Anne is a nurse. She just graduated at the top of her class."

"Congratulations," Colton said.

She blushed again. "Thank you, here's your change." She handed him his change and his receipt.

"Maybe we'll see you around," Colton said.

"I'd like that," Keelan chimed in, making her blush again.

Keelan was still waving when they walked out of the store. When everyone had climbed into the SUV and the doors closed, the men sighed as one.

"Is it just me, or are these store runs getting more and more complicated?" Darian asked.

Aiden reached back and handed him a bag. "That's for sure."

Colton eyed the bag. "What's this?"

Aiden started the car. "Penny's donuts. Bart seemed especially concerned when I told him I was getting them for your daughter because she had excelled in our training drills; he kept looking from my gun to your box of pull-ups. I wonder what he was thinking?"

Gavriel shook his head. "No telling, humans are odd creatures."

Darian nodded. "You can say that again."

Colton looked out the window. He couldn't wait to get back to his own confusing human.

CHAPTER SIX

Colton walked into his bedroom to find Rheia reading Penny a bedtime story. They looked up, and both smiled at him. Colton knew his world had narrowed and now revolved around these two beautiful angels.

"Did you find them okay?" Rheia asked.

Colton smiled and shut the door behind him. "Yes, though I may have to end up paying for Keelan's therapy sessions. I accidentally embarrassed him in front of his newly found mate," he confessed.

"Poor Keelan." Rheia shook her head and looked down at Penny. "Did you need my help?"

Penny shook her head and got out of bed. She walked over to him and held her hand out. He stared down at her and realized she was waiting for a pull-up. He reached into the box he'd opened and pulled one out. "I chose the ones with the princesses on them." Penny nodded. Colton leaned in, "I decided against that 'cool' feature, it looked uncomfortable." Penny nodded emphatically. Colton felt like he conquered the world. He handed her the pull-up, and she went to the bathroom.

"Thank you for going," Rheia said softly, leaning against the headboard. He noticed she had changed into a T-shirt and he could see the outline of her breasts against the soft material. He went to his dresser and stacked the boxes up beside it.

"It was no problem. That's what mates do, support each other." When he looked back, he noticed the blanket had slipped down even farther. He shifted from foot to foot trying to alleviate the pain his jeans were causing him. She wasn't even trying, and he was as hard as nails.

The sound of the bathroom door had him turning, and he watched Penny race across the room, her tiny, bare feet creating a rapid staccato as she ran. Without even stopping, she jumped on the bed and wiggled in close to Rheia.

Colton let out a relieved breath. The appearance of his baby girl had helped his growing jeans problem. He frowned as a thought struck him. What if he and his mate had to wait until Penny was grown to have sex? He quickly looked over at the bed; both Rheia and Penny were yawning and settling in for the night. He stood there frozen. If he got into bed as a man, what would happen if he woke up with morning wood next to Penny? Colton brought a hand to his mouth feeling ill.

"Colton, are you alright? You don't look well." Rheia asked, leaning up on one elbow.

"Yup!" he answered quickly his voice cracking. The look she gave him clearly communicated that she didn't believe him.

"Really. I'm going to go change." He turned toward the bathroom.

"Into a wolf again?" she asked.

Ab-so-fucking-lutely as a wolf!

"I think we'll all be more comfortable that way, more room." He gave her his most charming smile. She rolled her eyes, not buying a bit of it. His mate was starting to read him already. Feeling buoyant, he went into the bathroom and shifted. Rheia reached over to the nightstand and turned off the lamp.

He jumped up and settled in next to Penny. Immediately, she rolled over and practically put him in a stranglehold, but he didn't dare move. She looked so peaceful. He crossed his front paws and rested his head on them.

He felt a hand gently stroke his fur and opened one eye. Rheia was smiling at him as she lazily petted his fur.

"Thank you. Thank you for not pressuring me, for being amazing with Penny, and for putting her needs first." Her head disappeared as she got comfortable for the night.

He sighed. He was never going to be able to claim his mate.

The next morning Rheia woke to an empty bed again, only this time there was no panic. She knew that Colton would take care of Penny. Smiling, she stretched out and enjoyed the feeling of having the bed to herself. It was a wonderful feeling, knowing Colton was watching Penny, letting her have some precious time alone. If he kept this up, she might actually come to love mornings.

Twenty minutes later, she got out of the bed, her bladder winning the war against laziness. She grabbed her toiletries out of her suitcase and headed to the bathroom. She showered quickly, deliberately using his soap and shampoo. Whatever this mating thing was, it was really starting to get to her. She walked on edge, almost desperate for his touch. Only Penny's presence had kept her from throwing herself at Colton the night before when she caught a glimpse of the erection straining at his jeans.

She reached for a towel and stopped. The material in her hands was decadent. Eagerly, she wrapped her body in the towel and savored the way the fabric felt. He might not have spent a lot of money on frills, but he didn't skimp on creature comforts and the things that made him feel good. His sheets and linens had been just as warm and cozy. She'd slept wonderfully despite being in a strange bed with a wolf.

She towel dried her hair, applied her normal bare minimum make-up and lotion regimen, and got dressed. She looked down at her blue scrubs and wished she had something more feminine to wear. Maybe she could ask Beth to take her shopping later. Feeling better about the day, she pulled her hair back in her normal ponytail, grabbed her utilitarian 'mom' bag, and headed downstairs, ready to start her new job at the clinic.

When she walked into the dining room, the men stood. Surprised, she stared at them; they had done this the day before, but she didn't know why.

"It's a guy thing, from way back to whenever, come sit down," Meryn explained.

Rheia sat down next to Penny and the men sat back down. She felt Colton's warm arm stretch across her back. She leaned back rubbing her head back and forth on his arm and smiled at him. His answering smile reminded her of a sunrise. She leaned over and kissed Penny on the forehead. Penny looked up, both cheeks puffed out as she continued to cram chocolate chip pancakes into her white powder-rimmed mouth. It looked like someone had already gotten into her donuts. Rheia shrugged; as long as she was eating, she couldn't care less what it was. Penny ate healthfully for the most part, but lately it seemed almost impossible to find something she liked.

"I ordered your coffee for you," Colton said.

She smiled at him. "Thank you and thank you for letting me sleep in. I can't remember waking up feeling so rested. I almost feel human," she smiled.

Keelan frowned. "What else would you be?"

Rheia blinked at him then realized what she said.

Meryn took the liberty of answering for her. "Human women have the capability to go for days without food or sleep before we have to rest. However, in order to do so, we need coffee. If we don't get it, we can get evil. Like, set you on fire evil."

Keelan gulped. "Is that a physical condition, like stretch marks?" he asked.

Meryn looked at Rheia nervously and nodded at Keelan.

Rheia looked between the two. "What about stretch marks?"

Keelan turned to her, eyes as wide as saucers. "Meryn said that when human women grow from childhood to womanhood, their skin can sometimes rip causing tiny scar lines. She said things like that make human women stronger than human men."

Rheia stared at Keelan and then swung her gaze to Meryn who fidgeted in her chair. Ryuu walked in and handed Rheia her coffee before he started to pick up empty platters. She took a sip and sighed happily. She turned to Keelan and nodded. "She's absolutely right. When I was working at the hospital, I would treat five to ten stretch mark cases a week; ghastly process." She took another sip of coffee before setting her cup down. She looked across the table at Meryn who was smiling wide at her. There was no telling what the nutty woman had told the men, but she knew one thing, she wouldn't be the one to tell them otherwise.

Colton turned to her looking a bit pale. "Does your womb turn inside out monthly as well?"

Inside out?

Rheia nodded without looking at Meryn. She put on a tragic expression before looking up at Colton. "It's a miracle we live through such pain." She had to look away quickly to keep from laughing when Colton swallowed hard.

"Don't worry, Rheia; Aiden and the guys bought practically every tampon the local store had for me last month, I can share," Meryn offered.

"Thanks, I'll probably have to take you up on that." Rheia looked at the assortment of pancakes Ryuu had made. She speared two blueberry ones and looked around for the syrup. Colton handed her a small bottle and she drenched her stack with the sweet amber liquid. She cut off a piece and took a bite. They were perfect. As she continued to eat, she listened as the men made plans for the day.

Colton turned to Keelan. "Did you make arrangements to see your mate again?

Keelan nodded. "She's staying with her aunt and uncle in Madison while she interviews for a job. I asked her out, we're going to go see the *Hobbit* marathon Saturday. The small theater downtown is running all three movies back to back to back. I've been dying to see the third one again."

Beth scrunched up her face. "They didn't have anything romantic playing?

"There's romance!" Keelan protested then thought about it. "Well, up until the end when..."

"La la la la la! No spoilers!" Meryn put her hands over her ears.

"Okay, okay. Why haven't you seen it yet? It's been out for a while?" Keelan asked.

Meryn just gave him a look and pointed at Aiden. "Overprotective, paranoid mate."

Keelan winced. "Sorry."

Colton looked over at Aiden. "Okay, today is Tuesday, so we have drills with Epsilon today. Did you want to continue with blind drills?" Colton asked.

Rheia was about to take another bite when a thought struck her. She turned to Aiden. "Do you always have drills with Epsilon on Tuesday?" Aiden nodded. Rheia sat back as a knot began to form in her stomach. "What about Wednesdays?"

"Wednesdays we train with Beta," Darian answered.

"Do you keep a schedule posted somewhere?" she asked.

The men shook their heads. Colton turned to her. "We maintain the same routines to cut back on confusion."

Rheia looked around and gave the men an acerbic expression. "So you've been using the same routine for quite some time?"

They all nodded.

"So if the ferals have been paying attention at all, they know exactly who will be where at any given point throughout the week?"

The men all nodded and then stopped mid-nod. Their expressions changed from smiling, to horror-stricken, to ill.

"Dear Gods, she is right," Gavriel whispered.

Aiden sank back in his chair. "Thank Fate for you women. You see things differently than we do, question things we don't even think about anymore." He looked over at Colton. "Call all the units, tell them we have a mandatory meeting, including the trainees, first thing this morning," he said, before standing and kissing Meryn on the forehead.

Colton turned to Meryn and Beth. "We had planned on watching Penny again, but I don't think today is a good day for it. Is there any chance you two can watch her?"

Meryn and Beth eyed each other then turned to look at Penny. Meryn shrugged. "Why not?"

Colton stood. "Thank you, ladies." He ruffled Penny's hair and walked around her chair to stand next to Rheia. He leaned down and kissed her gently. "Get my cell phone number from Meryn and text me later."

"I will. Have fun today."

Colton rolled his eyes. "Aiden always gets so grumpy when he realizes he's made a mistake, he'll be an absolute bear to be around." He wagged his eyebrows at her. Both she and Meryn laughed.

"Colton, get your mangy ass out here!" Aiden bellowed from the foyer.

"I am loved after all; he missed me." Colton laughed and waved goodbye.

"Goofball," Rheia said and resumed eating her pancakes.

"A lovable goofball," Beth said.

"Sexy even," Meryn chimed in.

"Will you two be okay watching Penny?" Rheia asked.

Meryn looked at Beth. "I had no younger siblings and never babysat. You?"

Beth grimaced. "I was the youngest person in Noctem Falls for close to twenty years."

"We can help," A light male voice said from the doorway. Rheia looked up to see two young men come into the room. She was shocked to see one of them in a wheelchair. As far as she knew paranormals could heal from just about anything, she had never heard of one having to use a wheelchair before.

"Jaxon, Noah! Perfect timing. Meet Rheia and Penny. Rheia is Colton's mate and Penny is her daughter," Meryn said introducing them. The men smiled at her and waved. "We have five other trainees you haven't met yet. They've been helping the construction crew with their barracks. They'll spend the day moving in after the meeting Aiden just called. These two are my minions. Noah is the cutie with blond hair and Jaxon is my hell on wheels!" Jaxon laughed and Beth shook her head.

"Keelan filled us in on about Penny yesterday, we'll be happy to help," Jaxon said, meeting Rheia's eyes. She could tell he knew about Penny's past, the sympathy was in his eyes.

Rheia looked down at the chair and Jaxon chuckled.

"I bet you've never seen a shifter in a wheelchair before." He guessed.

"No, I haven't. What happened?"

"I had an accident when I was a child that left me paralyzed, before I was able to shift. The injury has kept me from shifting to heal, it's a catch twenty-two." He explained.

"Sorry to hear that." Rheia said sympathetically. Jaxon shrugged.

Noah took Colton's empty seat next to Penny. "So what do you want to do today?"

Penny rummaged around her bag, pulled out a box of crayons, and held them up.

"Perfect! We're going to be working in Aiden's office today tracking down some older files to get an accurate Vanguard count, we'll set you up," Noah promised.

"See, no problem. Once a kid can walk and communicate, it's smooth sailing. It's the tiny ones that cause trouble." Meryn said rubbing her belly.

Beth sighed. "At least you're not calling her 'Larvae' or 'Spawn' anymore."

Meryn laughed. "I only did it to irritate Aiden. He gets the cutest little eye tick when I say stuff like that. It's adorable."

Beth stood. "You may make him the first shifter in history to suffer from high blood pressure."

Meryn shrugged and stood. They walked around the table and Meryn held her hand out to Penny. Penny turned and got up on her knees in the chair to give Rheia a kiss. Rheia gave her a tight hug before letting her hop down to join Meryn. Meryn promptly picked Penny up and put her in Jaxon's lap for a ride.

"Be good," Rheia called after them.

Meryn turned scowling. "Why does everyone always say that to me?"

Rheia chuckled. "I was talking to Penny, but if it applies..."

Meryn blushed. "I knew that. Have fun doing your medical thing." She turned to leave and then spun back around. "What's your number? I told Colton I'd give you his number so you could text him later." Meryn pulled out her phone and waited.

Rheia rattled off her phone number.

Meryn typed, her tiny fingers moving quickly. "Okay, I just texted you Colton's number, Aiden's number, and the house phone number. You're officially hooked up."

"Thanks, Meryn," Rheia said as her phone buzzed from her bag.

"Later gator." Meryn wiggled her fingers at her and breezed out the door.

Rheia just stared at the open doorway; suddenly the room was much bigger and felt empty.

"She has a presence that seems to take over everything around her, doesn't she?" Ryuu asked, walking in from the kitchen.

"Yeah, she does. How long have you been with her?"

"Just a few months, but it seems longer. In a good way." Ryuu started stacking plates.

Rheia ate her last bite and picked up her coffee cup. "Could I ask a favor?" She turned the cup in her hand nervously.

Ryuu gave a half bow. "Of course."

"Could you see if Penny has any relatives in Lycaonia? Her last name is Carmichael and her mother's name was Elena." Rheia was afraid to find out if Penny had family, but she owed it to the little girl to find out. It hadn't been safe to alert others that Penny had survived while they lived in Jefferson.

However, they lived in Lycaonia now; there was no reason to keep her from her family.

"I'll contact Marius Steward; he is the squire to Aiden's mother, Adelaide. He knows just about everyone in the city and if he needs further information, he can easily ask Aiden's father, Byron. Byron is the shifter Elder here in Lycaonia," he explained.

"Thank you." She took one final sip and set her cup down.

"Was there anything else you needed? Adjusting to this world can be difficult, even for those who have known about paranormals their entire lives." His dark eyes were filled with warmth.

"I think I'm okay for now. As long as Penny is happy, that's the most important thing. Is my car still parked out front?" she asked, standing.

He nodded. "I think they left it there for you to get to the clinic."

"Perfect. What time is lunch? I'd like to eat with Penny?"

"Noon. I used the internet and looked up child-friendly foods. We will be having different types of sandwiches. Hopefully, I can discern her likes and dislikes based on her choices," he said, frowning.

"I know Penny will love it. Thank you again, Ryuu."

"My pleasure. Don't forget your coat."

"I won't," she promised and went to the closet in the main hall. She grabbed her coat and headed to the clinic.

"Thanks, Oron, there's no way I could have gotten these set up, even if I'd had a forklift. What do they feed you guys anyway? All the fae I know are huge," Rheia said before she sat down in one of the patient chairs they'd just carried.

Oron smiled. "We've always been the largest of all the paranormals, although no one knows why. I'm glad I could help. Doc always takes good care of us. We do heal, but he helps us heal faster and with less pain."

"I'm not sure how much I'll be able to assist, but I'll help any way I can. I've got some catching up to do when it comes to shifter's accelerated healing."

"We're glad to have you. We were all hoping Colton would find his mate soon; the nightmares he was having changed him," Oron said, leaning against the examination table.

"Changed? What do you mean?" Rheia asked concerned.

"You've only seen him as he is now, and that's how he usually is, joking and carefree. He's the kinda guy that would give you the shirt off his back if you needed it, then walk around flexing, acting like you did him a favor." Rheia smiled and shook her head at the image. That definitely sounded like the Colton she had come to know.

Oron smiled and then got quiet. "The past couple weeks though, when he was dreaming of you, he was withdrawn, quiet, depressed. I don't think we all realized how much we counted on him to keep us upbeat and to balance out Aiden's grumpy nature. Drills have been exceedingly dry and almost painful without Colton's usual antics to liven things up."

Rheia suddenly wanted to talk to Colton; it was as if she had to know he was okay. She didn't realize she was clutching her chest until Oron bent down in front of her, a panicked look of concern on his face.

"I didn't mean to upset you. I just figured, as a human, it might be hard to accept a mate since they don't exist in your world. I wanted to let you know that you lucked out; Colton is one of the good ones, you know?"

Even with Oron bending down, she had to look up at him. "Thank you. I think I'm starting to see how lucky I am, but don't tell him that. It would probably take weeks to deflate him."

Oron stood and laughed loudly. "You *are* getting to know him."

"Yeah, I am."

"Take good care of our boy, and if you need any more help, just let the commander know," Oron offered.

"Thanks, I will."

He waved goodbye and the door shut behind him.

Rheia looked at the clock; there was still another hour until lunchtime. She stood and went to find Adam.

She found him cussing at a stack of papers at his desk.

"I know administrative work when I see it." Rheia walked in and sat in the chair across from him.

Adam growled. "Since the businessmen put up the money for the renovations, they want weekly reports. What am I supposed to tell them? Sorry, no one nearly died today. I almost want to put Aiden in traction just so I have something to give them."

"How many warriors do you have?" she asked.

Adam sat back. "We have thirty at each level. Thirty full-fledged unit warriors, trainees and cadets, so there are ninety altogether."

"That's not including mates, right?"

"No, just the men. Why?"

"Well you have me here, now," she started.

"You mean you'll do the reports for me?" he asked hopefully.

"No. But what I can do is give the guys their yearly physicals. If each unit had two men report per week for a yearly physical, in addition to the wellness checkups for the pregnant women and their babies, that's a pretty full report right there," she explained.

"But paranormals don't get physicals."

"They do now," she smiled widely.

Adam leaned back in his chair grinning from ear to ear. "I like the way you think. I'll call Aiden; we can start tomorrow."

"What are we going to do until then?"

"You and Oron got all the rooms set up already?" He looked down at his watch and then up at her.

"Yeah, that guy was like a one man moving team. It should have been physically impossible for him to lift some of those machines." She frowned, remembering how easily he maneuvered the X-ray machine.

Adam smiled. "You missed his belt."

"His belt?"

Adam nodded. "I saw a charm hanging from his belt, probably done by Quinn, Gamma's witch. I bet that enabled him to lift more weight than normal. That way only one person missed drills. From what I caught from the conversation with Aiden this morning, they have to completely revamp all of their training schedules."

Rheia winced. "That may have been my fault," she explained the conversation they had at breakfast.

"Gods, you know I never thought of that either; no wonder he was in such a foul mood. Good thing Colton is back to normal, otherwise we'd probably have a full waiting room of men complaining that they'd pulled a muscle just to get away from them both."

"Was he really depressed?"

Adam nodded. "I was on the verge of pulling him in here for a chat when you showed up."

"Why wasn't I affected?"

Adam raised an eyebrow. "Weren't you?"

Rheia shook her head then stopped. She remembered her reaction to hearing his voice in her dreams. It hadn't been sexual; she would have dismissed that for what it was: the result of a dry spell. No, his voice had made her feel complete, as if she had everything she ever wanted. Somehow, in her dream she'd known that no matter what, the faceless voice would be there for her. When she'd woken up, she'd been relieved the nightmare was over, but at the same time, she'd wept because he wasn't real. Each night when she went to sleep, she'd been torn; she knew that with the terror came the knowledge that she wasn't alone. She'd been willing to suffer through one to get to the other.

"I take it from the look on your face that he affected you as well?"

"I didn't realize it until now, but in my nightmares, he was always there."

"There you go. Matings affect people differently. For some it's a grand passion, dramatic and lusty. For other's it's the quiet, simple, small things, like your mate knowing your favorite tea, or remembering that you always forget your keys. No two couples ever come together in the same way."

"Meryn said for her it was like getting a roofie," Rheia said, looking up at Adam.

Adam's mouth dropped before he began to laugh. "Fate had her work cut out for her with those two. It probably would've been easier to drug them. Did she tell you that she beat Aiden unconscious with the back of his toilet?" he smirked.

"No! Little, itty, bitty Meryn took Aiden down? Are you sure she didn't drug him?"

Adam shook his head. "She's a force of nature. She threatened every single unit warrior with a revolver smaller than my shoe. What's even more unbelievable is that she had them shaken. I have learned there are no half measures with Menace. Either she loves you or she hates you. If she loves you, she hugs you; if she hates you, she shoots you. There's a measure of comfort in that type of honesty."

"She is stable though, right? She's watching Penny."

"They'll be fine. Meryn's rough around the edges, but she isn't stupid. Everything makes perfect sense... to her," he winked.

"Okay, now I really need a project. If I sit here and think about what could be happening, I'll lose it." Rheia rose.

Adam thought for a moment. "I have the perfect project for you, come on." He opened the door and headed down the hallway.

"Where are we going?" she asked, jogging to keep up with his long stride.

"The morgue."

Peachy.

CHAPTER SEVEN

"What is that?" Rheia asked, pointing to the body lying on the gurney.

"This, this is my enigma. He came in as one of the ferals killed during the attack of the Alpha estate, except he hasn't started decomposing like regular ferals, much less dead ones. In fact, if I didn't know better, I'd say this wasn't a feral at all since he's decomposing like a regular paranormal." Adam pulled back the sheet to reveal a plain looking man with nondescript brown hair and average build.

"When you say 'decomposing like a regular paranormal', what do you mean?" she asked stepping closer.

"Paranormals have a naturally regenerating cellular structure; it's why we age so much slower than humans. The same is true after death; the cells take a long time to break down. Ferals, on the other hand, begin to decay while they're still alive. That's why this man's appearance is such a mystery. Not only do ferals have visible signs of decay while alive, once killed, they practically rot in front of us."

"Did you take samples?" she asked.

"Of course. I have samples from a living paranormal, from this charming character, and from a dead feral. They're in that locked cabinet. One of the keys I gave you should unlock it. I've been keeping them in a small travel sleeve with the portable microscope. It made it easier to take it all home for homework."

"Sounds like a challenge." Rheia was already heading to the cabinet.

"I'll leave you to it then." Adam gave a salute and left.

She pulled out the slender leather slide case, set it on the counter, and turned back to the body. Visibly he was no different from any other corpse she'd ever seen. She turned to the counter and pulled out a pair of gloves and mask. There was no 'Y' incision, meaning there had been no autopsy. She wondered if Adam had deliberately delayed the procedure or if that just wasn't a common practice with paranormals. She'd have to ask before she proceeded. She was about to head to the door to ask Adam for permission to proceed when she noticed a flicker out of the corner of her eye. She stared and then blinked. Why had they left a necklace on the body? She walked around to the long counter and pulled out a drawer. She found a pair of scissors and returned to the body, carefully cutting the leather thong and pulling the necklace free.

Instantly, the smell of sickness and death overwhelmed her. She watched in horror as the body began to decompose right before her eyes. The once average corpse was becoming the thing of nightmares.

"Adam! Adam!" she screamed backing up toward the door.

Moments later, the door burst open and Adam barreled in, canines descended. He stopped abruptly and covered his face with his hand.

"What in the hell happened?" he demanded grabbing her arm and pulling her into the hallway.

Coughing, she had to rip the mask away, before dropping to her knees to retch on the immaculate new tile floor.

"Shh, honey it's okay. Just get it all up." Adam rubbed her back with one hand and fumbled with his phone with the other. Seconds later, she heard him talking to Aiden.

"I need you and Colton at the clinic now," he coughed.

"Are you hurt?" she heard Aiden demand. In the background, she heard Colton's voice.

"Is Rheia okay? Dammit, Aiden! Is she hurt?" She was secretly pleased to hear that Colton sounded angry and concerned.

"Adam, answer us!" Aiden yelled.

Adam cleared his throat and swallowed hard. "We're fine; I just need you down here. There's been a development with our mystery man."

"On our way," Aiden said and ended the call.

"Your mate sounded concerned," Adam joked as he helped her to stand. Together they walked to the water fountain. They each took a turn rinsing out their mouths. When they were done, they each looked at the other and sat down on the floor leaning against the wall. The smell had literally knocked them on their asses. Rheia's stomach was still trying to climb up the back of her throat when Colton and Aiden rounded the corner at a dead run.

"Gods! Rheia, are you okay?" Colton skidded to a stop and dropped down in front of her.

She nodded. "Just tossed my cookies. I didn't even do that when I was a med student. That is one foul bastard in there." Colton pulled Rheia to her feet and wrapped a steadying arm around her waist.

Aiden helped Adam to stand. "I thought this one wasn't like the others."

Adam shook his head. "He wasn't. At least, he wasn't when I left the room. What happened, Rheia?"

Colton stepped in front of her. "She didn't do anything wrong."

Adam looked at Colton. "I know. But something changed from the time I left until she called me back in."

Rheia held up the necklace that was still in her hand. "All I did was remove this from the body."

Adam frowned. "There wasn't anything on the body, it had been completely stripped."

"I didn't see it at first. Then there was a flicker and when I looked straight at him, I could see it. The second the necklace was off the body, it started to decompose right before my eyes. I mean cheesy B-rated Syfy Saturday graphics kinda shit. It was like he was melting and rotting at the same time, and don't get me started on the smell." Rheia brought a hand up to her mouth.

Aiden took the necklace and examined it. "This is the first one we've taken intact. The feral that attacked Meryn had a necklace as well. Only Meryn could see it then, too, but unlike this guy, we couldn't see the body until the necklace had been removed."

Adam leaned in to look over Aiden's shoulder. "So only humans can see the necklaces?"

Aiden nodded. "Looks that way. The necklace masks the smell of ferals to make them undetectable. I need to report this to the council."

Colton pulled her closer to his body. "I'm taking Rheia home for a break. It's almost lunch time anyway."

Rheia put a hand on her stomach. She hoped once she was out of the clinic her appetite would return. She stepped back and Colton looked down at her.

"We need to take another sample," she said, pointing back to the room.

Adam rubbed the back of his neck looking tired. "That's a good idea. I need to go with Aiden for this report since I've been studying the corpse longer. Don't worry about the mess in the hall; I'll take care of it. Just open the window and air the room out, I should be back after lunch."

"I am definitely opening a window." Rheia turned and headed back to the morgue, Colton right on her heels.

When they got to the doorway, they both hesitated, looking at each other. She held her breath and immediately walked to the windows. She and Colton opened all three of the room's windows, letting in the icy, fresh December air.

Rheia took a deep breath. "It's going to snow," she predicted.

Colton sniffed the air and nodded. "This evening."

She turned to the cabinets and prepped two new slides. Carefully, she labeled them and added them to the travel case. She tucked the small leather case into her lab coat pocket and looked at the body.

"I think as long as it wasn't decomposing, it was okay out on the gurney, but now..." She had to turn her head as a section of skin slid down off the ribs.

Colton swallowed hard. "I think having the windows open will make it pretty cold in here. Let's just shut the door and let Adam deal with it when he gets back," he suggested.

Rheia felt a momentary pang of guilt before nodding her head. "Let's get out of here."

Colton grabbed her hand, and they practically ran from the room. When they got outside to her car, they looked at each other and started laughing.

"Some unit warrior I am, running from a dead body." Colton climbed into the passenger side.

"What about me? I'm a doctor for crying out loud," Rheia pointed out closing the driver's side door behind her.

"But he was..." Colton paused.

"Gooey," Rheia finished.

"I think that's what did me in," Colton admitted.

"Me, too." Rheia felt a thousand percent better now that she was away from the smell and heading down the lone road back to the estate. By the time they pulled into the driveway, she was actually starting to get hungry.

"Is it wrong to be hungry?" she asked.

"I hope not because I'm starved." Colton licked his lips. "Ryuu always makes the best lunches."

"I hope Penny behaved," Rheia said following Colton into the house.

Colton took her hand and again she felt her stomach flip. "I'm more worried about Meryn behaving."

After hanging up their coats in the hall closet, they walked into the office and Rheia saw that

Meryn, Beth, Jaxon, and Noah were hard at work behind their computers. She had been anxious for nothing. Looking around the room, she frowned.

"Where's Penny?" she asked. The four looked up from their computers and pointed to the wall next to Aiden's desk. Penny sat on the floor, crayons out, drawing on the lower two feet of the wall.

"Penny! Honey, you can't do that." Rheia dropped Colton's hand and rushed over. Penny looked up at her and pointed to Meryn.

Meryn shrugged. "We didn't have any of that kid construction paper and ever since we went digital we stopped buying printer paper. The lined legal paper sucks for drawing; I hated it as a kid. The only other option was Post It Notes, so I told her she could color on the wall, but she had to stay on that section. She's actually pretty good."

Rheia looked down and had to agree. Penny had drawn a picture of her and Colton smiling and holding Penny between them. Off to one side, she had drawn almost everyone else she knew. Her uncles from Jefferson and many the unit members she had just met.

Colton scooped Penny up and looked down at her work. "Not bad, kiddo."

"Why is everyone in my office?" Aiden asked from the doorway.

Colton turned. "That was quick. I thought you had to call the council."

Aiden shrugged. "We did. I left Adam in his office explaining the medical stuff. There wasn't much for me to add." He frowned and his eyes widened when he saw his wall. His eyes went from Penny to Meryn and back to Penny.

Penny hid her face in Colton's neck. Rheia saw how gentle Colton was holding her and never would have guessed he wasn't her real father. The bond forming between the two was genuine and strong.

"Look, Aiden, Penny drew you a present," Colton said cheerfully, however his eyes narrowed at his friend, daring him to make an issue of it.

Aiden stepped forward. "Is that what this is? For me?"

Penny peeked out and nodded.

Aiden smiled and looked down at the picture. "I love it. You're very talented Penny; I can easily tell who is who." He pointed to the picture that was clearly meant to be Colton. "This little piggy is just adorable."

Penny clapped both hands over her mouth, her eyes dancing.

Colton growled at his friend. "That is me."

Aiden pretended to be shocked. "Oh my! Colton, you make such a cute little piggy."

Rheia watched as Penny shook with laughter in Colton's arms. Chuckling at Colton's expression, she stepped forward and took Penny from him. "Time for lunch, kiddo." Penny smiled.

Colton sniffed and turned dramatically. "I need sustenance."

Meryn snorted. "You always need sustenance; I think both of your legs are hollow."

Rheia carried Penny to the dining room where Ryuu had already set the table. Plates stacked high with different types of sandwiches filled the middle of the long dining table. Rheia picked up a plate and walked down the table, treating it like a buffet. She let Penny pick out her favorites and grabbed a turkey on wheat for herself.

She sat down and helped Penny get situated with her napkin and her milk cup. Penny had opted for a peanut butter and jelly and a tuna fish sandwich. Rheia watched as Penny took a bite of one sandwich then the other.

She looked past Penny to see that Colton was doing something similar. He had chosen the chicken salad sandwich and pulled pork barbecue and was alternating his bites between sandwiches as well.

"Is it a shifter thing?" she asked.

Colton looked up, his mouth full. "Is what a shifter thing?" was his muffled reply.

"Conflicting flavor combinations." She pointed at him and then at Penny.

"I think it's just those two. I don't like it when the flavors of one sandwich threaten to overwhelm the flavors of another," Beth offered.

"I don't like it, either," Jaxon agreed.

"Do the two of you normally eat here?" she asked.

Noah nodded. "We've been busy all week helping with the barracks so we've been eating with the other trainees. It's nice to get Ryuu's cooking again, though, I don't think he meant for the sandwiches to be paired like that." Noah swallowed hard as he watched Penny take another bite of her tuna fish sandwich.

Colton looked down at Penny and they both shrugged. Rheia was thankful Aiden didn't bring up the mysterious body over lunch. She was able to eat her entire lunch without feeling sick. When she finished her sandwich, she looked down to see if Penny was done. She frowned as she watched something she didn't understand.

Penny was smiling and holding out pieces of crust with jelly on it. For a second, the crust would hover in mid-air and then disappear. Rheia blinked.

"Uh, Colton." There must have been an edge to her voice because he looked up immediately.

His eyes went to Penny and he smiled. "She's just feeding Felix. He's a sprite that adopted Meryn. Not everyone can see them, but from the one time I saw him, I have to say, he's a cute little guy."

The air in front of Penny shimmered for a second and a small, red haired fairy-like creature appeared. He looked young with slightly rounded cheeks and bright green eyes. His wings beat lazily, keeping him aloft. He smiled at her and waved. Then his hands moved to his necklace and, a second later, he was gone again.

"Right. Sprites. Of course." Rheia had grown up knowing about shifters, vampires, witches, and fae. She should have known there would be more to the world than that.

"He likes Penny; they've been playing together all day," Meryn said, smiling at Penny.

Rheia turned to the strange, yet brilliant woman. "You can see him?"

Meryn nodded. "Yup. I met Felix in Vivian's garden. A whole colony of sprites live there."

Penny clapped happily and spun her finger around in circles. Coming here had been a good thing. Rheia turned to Ryuu who was standing by the kitchen doorway. "Any news?"

Colton turned to her. "What news?"

"I asked Ryuu to see if Penny had any relatives in Lycaonia. I thought she might want to visit and get to know them," she explained.

Ryuu bowed. "Marius and Byron are working on it. I believe they have located Penny's maternal grandparents. Unfortunately, since they were estranged from their daughter, they have had to break the news to them about what happened."

Penny stopped playing with Felix and scooted closer to her. Rheia wrapped an arm around her small frame. "What wonderful news, Penny, you have family here." She kissed the top of the girl's head.

Colton leaned in and ruffled Penny's hair. "As soon as they're open to it, I'll take you both for a visit. Won't that be fun?"

Penny's face had returned to the one that Rheia knew best. Penny's eyes looked flat and lifeless, her expression solemn. Colton looked at Rheia with concern in his eyes. Rheia shook her head. They had to let Penny process this news without their interference. Rheia looked down into Penny's face. "If you don't like them, we won't visit again. But I do want you to at least meet with them once, deal?"

Penny stared at her for a long moment then nodded. Rheia kissed her face repeatedly until the girl squirmed away and practically jumped into Colton's lap. Colton scooted his chair back and easily lifted her up over his head. He brought her down and began his own kissy-face assault. Penny was smiling when he set her back in her own chair between them.

Rheia stood. "Okay, I'm going to head back to the clinic to help wrap up that mess," she made a face, remembering that awful smell.

Colton stood. "I'll go with you."

Rheia couldn't think of a possible thing he could assist with, but she kept her mouth shut. She wanted him next to her. The idea of spending the afternoon with him left her feeling giddy. He stretched his hand out between them. Smiling, she took it and squeezed tight. He had a questioning look on his face but didn't say anything. They both said goodbye to Penny and headed to the hall. They grabbed their coats from the closet and went out to her car.

During the drive back to the clinic, a comfortable silence filled the car. On the console between them, Colton never let go of her hand. She pulled her hand out of his to park, but reached for him once the car was turned off. They sat there not saying a word.

"Everything okay?" he finally asked.

"No. But I think it'd be scarier if I was okay. I've only been here a little over a day, but needed to be with you this afternoon. My body... no, my heart craved it. There are moments when you're with Penny that threaten to overwhelm me because the two of you together is so beautiful. The core of who I am is being pulled toward you, but my mind is confused." She looked down, afraid to see the disappointment in his eyes.

She felt soft, warm lips on her hand, and she looked over at him. His eyes were gentle as he raised her hand to his cheek. He closed his eyes and sighed happily. He stayed that way for a moment before opening his eyes.

"Before we met, I dreamt of you. At first, all I could see were your eyes, then your face. You were always worried, so anxious and sad. You would look into the distance and I could see the pain you were trying to bury. I remember how hot my tears were when I begged Fate for just once chance to be with you, just one chance to hold you in my arms and tell you everything would be okay."

Rheia swallowed hard and tried to keep the tears from falling. How many times had she wanted just that? Not sex, not Valentine's Day gifts or date nights, just someone to be there at the end of the day, a set of open arms she could collapse into and not have to worry about hitting the floor.

"Do you know how blessed I am?" he asked, tracing her hand with his thumb. She shook her head.

He continued. "Fate not only granted my wish, but gave me so much more. I have you by my side and you have given me the gift of a daughter. Overnight, I have a family of my own. I know that this may seem impossible to you, but it's not to me. If you're ever in doubt, lean on me; let my faith support us both. We can take this at your pace, sweetness, because as long as you're beside me, I'm the luckiest and happiest man on the planet."

"Shut up," she choked out, tears streaming unchecked down her cheeks. He looked at her, a painful expression in his face. "Shut up and kiss me," she said already reaching for him.

Colton didn't hesitate. Both hands came up to frame her face, pulling her as close as the console would allow. The second his lips touched hers, a shiver raced down her spine. The smell and the taste of him was exactly what she wanted. She sucked on his tongue and buried her fingers in his hair; every erogenous zone was screaming for attention. She turned and, in an attempt to get closer, was brought back to reality when she got wedged between the steering wheel and her seat.

She pulled back and saw Colton's eyes had changed from his normal bright green to a dull yellow.

"Gods, I want to eat you up," he growled.

She whimpered. She wanted nothing more than to be at his mercy. Colton turned his head toward the road. Some unit warriors were jogging by on their way to the Alpha estate for afternoon drills. He sat back and closed his eyes. Breathing hard, she began to sit back in her seat but found she was stuck. The leather case that held the slides had shifted in her pocket to wedge itself in the steering wheel.

"Colton."

"Just give me one second, sweetness." He winced and shifted his weight in his seat.

"I'm stuck."

His eyes opened and he turned to her. "Say what?"

"I'm stuck. That damn case in my pocket is stuck in the wheel and I can't move."

Colton reached between her and the steering wheel and dislodged the case. She turned and collapsed back into her seat. She looked over at him; he had a thoughtful look on his face.

"What are you thinking about?"

"Bench seats."

"I'm sorry?"

"I'm buying a truck with bench seats."

She gaped at him and then realized what he was talking about. "If we had a truck, where would Penny sit? She needs a car seat."

"It'll be our special date night truck."

"You're having a fantasy right now about fucking me in a truck aren't you?"

Colton raised an eyebrow at her. "Did you really have to ask that question?"

"I guess not."

"Can I interpret your silence as consent for a later date when I have said truck?"

She looked at him, frowning. "You're going to wait until you have that truck?"

Colton leered at her. "Well, if you put it like that..."

She opened her door and got out. "Come on, Balto."

Colton got out and closed his door. "Technically, Balto was a dog."

Rheia shrugged. "Close enough."

"No seriously, there's a huge difference. I'm not a dog."

"But you're so fluffy and cute," she protested.

Colton grimaced. "Please, never, ever say that in front of the guys."

"I make no promises," she teased.

Colton opened the clinic door, and they walked down the long hallway.

"Seriously Rheia, those guys have memories like elephants. We're still giving Sascha shit about the time his horse kept running from him because it hadn't been broken in to ride paranormals. I think he has a complex."

"When was that?"

"Not long, maybe like three hundred years ago, give or take."

She stopped and turned to face him. "Three hundred years?"

Colton nodded emphatically. "And we still crack jokes about it."

Rheia started walking, making a left down the hall that led toward the morgue. "I thought you said he had a complex?"

"And?" Colton asked before he stopped dead in his tracks. He grabbed her arm and pushed her against the wall.

"Colton?" she asked confused.

Colton stood with his back to her, looking up and down the hall. He reached into his pocket and pulled out a cell phone. "Aiden, I need units Alpha, Gamma, and Beta at the clinic, ferals are here and I'm by myself with Rheia."

"On our way. Any way you can get out?" she heard Aiden ask.

"No, their stench is all around us; I don't want to walk into a trap. We're in the hallway down from the morgue."

"My brother?"

"No sign of him, he may have gone to your parent's house for lunch. You may want to give them a call to make sure he's okay."

"Calling now. ETA is less than five minutes. Don't die," Aiden commanded.

"Now that's an order I'll happily follow." Colton ended the call and pulled out his sidearm, constantly scanning the halls.

"Are they here?" she whispered.

"I don't think so, but I'm not taking any chances with you."

Rheia grabbed the back of his coat and buried her face between his shoulder blades.

"We should have stopped to have car sex," she muttered.

"Don't distract me," he said. She lifted her head and peeked around his shoulder. He was grinning from ear to ear.

It seemed like forever before they heard the sound of heavy boots running toward them.

Aiden and Gavriel stealthily approached the morgue doorway from both sides. Aiden signaled to Sascha and Gavriel before they flooded the room. Gamma and Beta units moved carefully, doing a full sweep of the clinic, while Darian and Keelan helped Colton guard her.

Aiden and Gavriel came out of the morgue frowning. Rheia stepped from around Colton. "Well?"

Gavriel looked at her. "The body is gone and the entire place has been trashed."

Aiden turned to them. "Get her home."

Colton wrapped an arm around her shoulders. "Adam?"

"On his way, you were right; he was at my parent's house."

She felt Colton release a relieved breath.

He looked down at her. "Come on, Rheia; let's head back so these guys can concentrate on collecting evidence."

Rheia looked around and realized that every man in the hallway had subconsciously positioned his body to protect her. She was about to start walking when a question struck her.

" Colton, why would they want the body now, after all this time?"

"I don't know, but whatever the reason, it can't be good."

CHAPTER EIGHT

The afternoon was crawling by for Rheia. Colton dropped her off and headed back to the clinic. His parting kiss had scorched her, sending shivers of excitement through her. Grinning like an idiot, he got back in the car and drove off, leaving her to feel frustrated and on edge.

She was relaxing with Meryn and Beth in the family room as Penny worked on her letters when the doorbell rang. Looking at each other, they all got up and followed Meryn out into the foyer. Meryn opened the door and an irate stranger shouldered his way inside.

"Where is it? Where is this necklace that was found?" he demanded.

Beth stepped closer. "Elder Evreux, how nice to see you again."

The Elder nodded at Beth and then his eyes traveled downward until he was looking at Penny. His lip curled. "How disturbing. Children like her always make me nauseous." Penny edged behind her as Rheia glared at the odious man.

Meryn stepped forward. "Elder, I'm afraid the necklace isn't here. Aiden has it with him at the clinic."

Elder Evreux looked down at Meryn and sneered. "I heard you were breeding. Gods only know why the world would want another version of you running around. You probably won't be able to carry to term you know; most human-shifter pregnancies are dangerous."

Meryn's eyes filled with tears and she stepped back, placing her hands over her stomach. Without even thinking, Rheia reared back and punched the man as hard as she could, aiming for his nose. When she heard a crunching sound, she smiled.

The Elder spun around and hissed at her. He took a step forward and was brought up by an incandescent Ryuu. The squire had a faint blue glow surrounding him. He placed his body directly between the Elder and the women.

"Elder, I suggest that you leave. I will let the Unit Commander know that you were inquiring about the necklace. But for future visits, please call ahead and make arrangements with me, personally." Ryuu seemed to swell, his presence filling the foyer.

"Elder McKenzie will hear about this!" he said threateningly. When it seemed that Ryuu was about to step toward him, the Elder turned and left.

"I am not going to lose my baby!" Meryn wailed.

Rheia turned to her. "Of course, you aren't. I'm here now and I don't make it a habit of losing patients."

Beth took out her cell phone and lifted it to her ear. She didn't even give the person on the line a chance to say hello.

"Uncle, you will probably be getting a phone call from Elder Evreux about an assault charge. Don't even bother listening to his drivel; he completely deserved it. In fact, he's lucky I didn't hit him myself! No, I don't care about his station. You shorten his choke collar, Uncle, or I will!" Beth stabbed her finger at her phone, ending the call, her normally creamy cheeks flushed pink.

Ryuu steered Meryn and Beth into Aiden's office. "Why don't you two work on your projects? That should take your minds off things. I'll bring in some tea later."

Penny pointed to her wall and Rheia nodded.

Meryn sniffled as she turned on her laptop. "Fucking douchebag."

After all the afternoon's excitement, Rheia didn't know what to do with herself. Satisfied that Penny was happily occupied she soon found herself in the kitchen. At home when she'd felt discombobulated, she'd done the dishes. She looked around the kitchen and sighed, it was immaculate, and every surface gleamed.

Ryuu walked in from a back room holding a pad and pen. He looked surprised to see her in his domain.

"Was there something I could help you with?"

Rheia shrugged. "I'm feeling out of sorts and was hoping to find some dishes to wash so I could feel useful, but it looks like you clean just as well as you cook."

His expression softened. "Why don't you sit down, I'll make us some tea." He pointed to a small table that held five chairs.

She sat down. "Why is there a table in here if everyone eats in the dining room?"

Ryuu put a kettle on to boil. "Because less than two months ago, only five men lived in this house. First Aiden found Meryn, or I should say Meryn crash landed in his life," he smiled. "Then Beth came. After Beth, we got Jaxon and Noah, then you and Penny. This family is growing exponentially," he said smugly.

"You seem pleased with the idea."

Ryuu nodded. "The last family I served, I was with them until the last of their line drew breath. Then I found myself banned from my own country. I came to Lycaonia thinking this would be a good place to die. My kind, what I am, we are bound to service. Without a family to serve, I grow weak and begin to fade away. The larger this household is, the more mates and children that live here, the better."

"Don't you ever get tired of taking care of everyone?" she asked, curious.

Ryuu shook his head. "It pleases me to serve others, especially someone as special as my *denka*."

Rheia had to grin, Meryn sure was special all right. "Thank you for all your help with Penny's family."

"Family is important." He lifted the kettle, poured the hot water into a simple cream teapot, and the smell of jasmine filled the air. He carefully poured two cups and set them on the table. He sat down next to her and took the second cup for himself.

"Do you believe finding your mate results in an instant love?" she asked. She'd been battling her feelings for Colton all day. Her body and her heart wanted him, craved him like a drug. Her mind, however, kept rejecting the idea that what she felt was love. It shouldn't be so easy or happen so quickly.

Ryuu sipped his tea. "I believe that matings induce the feelings one experiences when one falls in love. That rush one feels at the thought of seeing their mate, the overwhelming desire to touch and be touched, the realization that no one else in the entire world will ever suit them as perfectly is enhanced. These are all things humans experience over a certain amount of time when finding a life partner. For paranormals, these feelings herald the knowledge that the person they are with is their predestined mate. The person that they barely know will be the only person they will be with for the rest of their long lives."

He paused, taking another sip of tea. "The feelings are real, but they aren't true."

She was about to ask him what he meant when, smiling, he held up a finger.

"What you feel, the impatience, the desire, those feelings are real, but they aren't manifestations of a true love, that takes time. However, by the time the first flushes of the mating heat subside, you are truly in love with your mate. That is when the true heat begins. What you feel for them will intensify a thousand fold over the years, before the two of you move on to the next world.

"So what you feel is real, but it isn't love, not yet. For those who don't fight the mating heat at all, love can develop quickly. However, for someone like you, someone who is used to working with facts and science, I have a feeling that it will be a defining moment. Now, if I can offer you two pieces of advice?" he asked. Rheia nodded spinning her teacup in her hands.

"Don't doubt Colton's feelings for you. He didn't fight the mating at all and I am almost one hundred percent certain that he is head over heels in love with you and your child already, that's just how he is."

Rheia took a deep breath. She had suspected as much; his sincerity and intensity were hard to fake. "What's the other piece of advice?"

Ryuu set his cup of tea down and allowed himself to relax against the back of the chair. "Don't doubt yourself. You're a very intelligent woman; don't doubt your inner voice. Your biggest battle won't be falling in love with Colton; I think that battle is half lost as it is."

Rheia snorted in agreement.

Ryuu chuckled, then sobered. "No, the biggest battle you will face will be admitting to yourself that you love him."

"Well, damn." She set her cup down and sighed.

Ryuu took one final sip of tea and stood. "It's time for me to start dinner. Please, don't feel like I am expelling you from the kitchen. Quite the contrary, I find that I have enjoyed having tea with you." Smiling, he gave her a half bow. "Thank you, Rheia."

Rheia stood and gathered up her teacup. "So you won't mind if I invade your kitchen every once in a while? At home, it was my place of solace." She carried the cup to the sink and set it down carefully. She would have washed it herself, but didn't want to step on Ryuu's toes. She was still finding her place in this crazy family.

"I will even save you a dish or two to wash," Ryuu teased.

"Speaking of dishes, I have a tea set that's very precious to me; it was my mother's. If I'm to live here, I'd like to find a safe place for it."

"Bring it down and I will care for it personally," Ryuu promised.

"Thank you, Ryuu."

"Anytime."

She walked out of the kitchen feeling better, but she knew she still had some things to work out for herself before she could give Colton any kind of definitive answer. She walked upstairs to Colton's room and closed the door. Fighting a wave of homesickness, she grabbed the cream knit throw from the bench at the end of the bed and wrapped herself in it. Padding over to the soft, light brown wingback chair by the window, she sat down and stared out into the distance.

What was she going to do?

Colton scoured every inch of the clinic with Aiden; they determined the ferals entered through the open windows of the morgue. The more they found out about this convoluted mess, the less they knew.

His wolf was constantly at the surface now. He would never tell Rheia how desperate he was to claim her. She was having a hard enough time accepting the fact they were mates. Even now, his wolf was torn between wanting to track down the threat to his family and his overwhelming desire to return to the estate and claim Rheia as his. He knew Aiden would never allow him to hunt alone and he had only known Rheia for about a day; it looked like he wasn't going to do either.

"Colton, why don't you head home? There's not much else to do here. We'll wrap up and be right behind you," Aiden said, walking up behind him.

"Are you sure?"

"Yes. Go to your mate, you haven't had a lot of time together. Go get to know her." Aiden gave him a not so gentle push toward the exit.

"See you at dinner." Colton gave him a salute and practically ran for the door.

The entire drive home all he could think about was Rheia. The kiss earlier had relaxed her quite a bit and her true, teasing personality had started to shine through. Colton wanted to peel away the layers until he found the Rheia she kept hidden.

Once at the house, he parked her car out front where she could see it later. When he walked through the front door, he looked around and

listened carefully. He could hear Meryn, Beth, Jaxon, and Noah in the office. The question was now whether Penny with them or her mother?

Colton peeked his head into the office and saw Penny hard at work decorating Aiden's wall. If he had his way, Aiden would never paint over her drawings. He wanted to keep them forever. She looked adorable sitting cross-legged on the floor, her tongue sticking out as she concentrated on her artwork.

"Hey, Colton, if you're looking for Rheia, I think she went upstairs," Noah said looking up from his laptop.

"Thanks, Noah." He turned and was about to leave when Jaxon called out to him.

"Hey, Colton. We know you haven't had, umm, time alone with your mate. So if Rheia's comfortable with it, Penny can have a sleepover with Noah and me tonight," Jaxon offered.

Colton felt his heart skip a beat; these two might be his new best friends. Colton looked over at

Penny. "What do you think, princess? Would you like to have a sleepover with Jaxon and Noah?" Penny looked at the two young men who were smiling at her and nodded. Colton wanted to jump up in the air and click his heels. "Okay, darlin', I'll let your mother know." He turned to Jaxon. "Thank you."

Jaxon blushed slightly though his grin was knowing. "We may be young, but we're not monks."

Colton laughed. "I hear that. Okay, I'm going to go find my mate."

"Toodles! Don't do the things I wouldn't do if they're boring," Meryn called out. Colton nodded then stopped.

Don't do...

He turned back to her. "What?"

"Have fun," Beth said, nudging Meryn.

Colton winked at them and jogged up the stairs.

Colton walked in and saw Rheia was sitting in his reading nook by the window. Wrapped up in his large throw, she looked small and vulnerable. He didn't like the serious look on her face.

"Is everything okay?" he asked. He walked over and sat down in the other wingback chair next to the window. He loved the fact she had gravitated to his favorite spot in the room and wrapped herself in a blanket covered in his scent.

She turned to him, her blue eyes thoughtful. "I'm really going to have to move here, aren't I?"

The sad look in her eyes hurt his heart. He would do anything to make her happy, even give up the

Alpha Unit and move away, but that wouldn't keep her or Penny safe.

"Yes. It's no longer safe for you outside of Lycaonia. To be honest, I'm not sure how safe it is here since the ferals have decided to learn new tricks. At least here we have the other units to fall back on." He scooted his chair closer to hers so he could reach out and take her hand. She smiled and gripped his hand like a lifeline.

"I'll call Radek tomorrow and tell him to start boxing up my stuff. I never thought I would ever leave that house. It's the last tie I have to my parents." She dashed a tear from her cheek and looked at him, her bottom lip trembling. "I'm being silly, aren't I?" It broke Colton's heart that she was trying so hard to appear strong, when he was the one person who could be strong for her. He was overwhelmed with the sudden need to show her how good they could be together.

Without saying word, he stood, scooped her up in his arms, and carried her to the bed.

He looked down at her and let what he was feeling show on his face. When her pupils dilated, and he caught the faint scent of her arousal, he nearly groaned aloud. Breathing hard, he pressed his forehead to hers. "Tell me to stop and I will, but if you don't, I am going to do my damnedest to show you how I feel. I know you're giving up a lot to stay here with me. Let me show you it will be worth it."

Her arms came up and circled his neck. She pulled back and looked up at him, eyes hesitant. Whatever she was about to say, she wasn't sure of his reaction. Colton wanted to drive away every trace of doubt; he needed to prove to her that he was hers, no matter what.

He smiled and nudged her nose with his. "Whatever you want to say, just say it. Nothing you say or feel can be wrong."

She took a deep breath. "I do want you to show me how good it can be between us, but I don't think I'm ready to be claimed yet," she confessed.

Colton kept his smile frozen on his face. His wolf was already chomping at the bit to claim her, but he had a feeling if he pushed the issue, she would just pull back even farther.

"You're mad, aren't you?" she asked. The scent of her arousal began to diminish.

Colton shook his head. "No, it's just that..." He paused, trying to figure out the best way to phrase what he wanted to say. Somehow, he knew, 'I may accidentally fuck you to death in an effort not to claim you.' probably wouldn't go over very well. "Without claiming you, the sex may be a little wild."

Her eyes widened and his heart stopped when she gave him a sultry smile.

"Challenge accepted," she said and leaned forward before biting his chest.

Growling, he tossed her onto the bed. His canines burst through his gums and he knew without looking his eyes would be the yellow color of his wolf.

"Strip," he ordered, reaching for his own shirt.

Startled, she gasped before she quickly undressed. He was completely nude by the time she was down to her bra and panties. She hesitated and looked up at him. When her eyes landed on his groin, she subconsciously licked her lips and he growled low in approval.

"Do you want to suck my cock, baby?" he asked as he started to stroke himself.

Her eyes followed his hand. She nodded, completely mesmerized by his movements.

"Let me see your body, baby; show me how wet you are, and I'll give you a treat."

Rheia raised a brow at him. Without breaking eye contact, she reached behind her back and unsnapped her bra, letting the material fall away before she threw it over the side of the bed. Colton had to grip the base of his dick tight to keep from coming; her breasts were perfect. They weren't high and perky like those fake human commercials. She was rounded and completely natural. He knew he could spend hours between her breasts and never tire of them. When she shimmied out of her panties, he nearly came undone.

Without hesitation, she opened her legs wide, separating her tender folds. He could see that she was already dripping wet. When he looked up, he saw that she was biting her lip. Despite the sex kitten act, she was nervous; she was the best of both worlds.

"Do you have any idea what you do to me?" he asked. He watched her shiver at his deep bass-filled voice. His wolf was truly at the surface now.

"Please, Colton, make me forget, even if it's just for a little while. I just want it to be you and me," she pleaded.

He crawled onto the bed, moving slowly, until he was kneeling between her legs. "Then I can do nothing less than give my mate what she wants. Now turn over and get on all fours."

She looked at him, uncertain.

"It will help me not claim you, sweetheart," he explained.

Understanding filled her eyes. Grinning, she turned over and raised her ass in the air. Unable to help himself, he leaned forward and buried his nose against her slit.

"Gods, baby, you smell like heaven. Later, when we have more time, I am going to tongue fuck you until you beg me to stop, but I don't think either of us wants that right now, do we?" He reached forward and lightly traced her opening with two fingers. She moaned and pushed back against his hand.

"So eager." He leaned forward and nipped her right cheek. She yelped, but he noticed that the scent of her arousal got muskier. Groaning, he did the same to the other cheek.

"Colton," she moaned his name.

"It's gonna be fast and hard, baby." He couldn't wait another second. He reached down, lined up the head of his cock, and thrust hard. He placed his hand on her lower back for control and set a merciless pace. Beneath him, she gasped for breath and groaned his name over and over again.

With his canines fully extended, he wanted with every fiber of his being to lean over her and bury his teeth into the soft flesh of her neck, welding them together for all eternity. However, he'd made her a promise; they would take this at her pace. The thought of breaking her trust was the only thing holding him back.

He felt his balls draw up and knew that he was close. Leaning forward slightly, he reached around her hip and snaked his hand down to dip between her folds. He found her clit and fingered it roughly.

She went wild, and he felt her body clench around him. It was enough to send him over the edge. Crying out, he emptied himself deep inside of her.

Colton shook his head to focus; he had never come so hard in his life. Slowly, he pulled out of her and she slumped down onto the bed, she was gulping air. He slid off the bed and headed to the bathroom.

When he caught a glimpse of himself in the mirror, he was shocked. His eyes remained yellow and his canines dangerously low. He ran the water in the sink until it was warm and splashed some on his face. He took several deep breaths and looked back up. His eyes were back to their normal color. He washed himself off and rinsed out the washcloth.

He chuckled when he saw that Rheia hadn't moved an inch from where he'd left her. Walking to the foot of the bed, he started to get hard again watching his seed drip down the back of her legs. Gently, he cleaned between her legs before placing a soft kiss over his two bite marks on her delectable ass.

He walked back to the bathroom, tossed the washcloth in the sink, and returned to his mate. She was still on her stomach, face down in the covers. He pulled her onto her side and into the curve of his body.

"That was amazing. I've never come like that before. Claiming me can't get better than that." Rheia said, turning her head slightly to look back at him.

He leaned down and whispered into her ear. "Challenge accepted."

When Colton and Rheia ended up being a no-show for lunch and dinner, Meryn and Beth sat the little girl between them during meal times. Meryn was afraid at first that Penny would be nervous without her mother, but she was soaking up the attention that Aiden and the rest of Alpha Unit heaped on her. It looked like she was used to being the center of attention when it came to her uncles. Aiden had even taken her upstairs to introduce her to his fish, Jaws.

After dinner, they all retired to the family room to wind down before bed. Noah and Jaxon were absorbed in their X-Box game. Normally, Meryn would be right there with them, but she wanted to work on the personnel list before tomorrow.

"I can't believe y'all are teaching a four year old to play poker," Beth said in disbelief.

Meryn looked up from her laptop to see what shenanigans the men were up to. They'd set up a table in the family room and were currently explaining different hands to Penny. The men decided to play for candy and snacks instead of money, for Penny's sake.

Meryn watched the girl's eyes go from the cards to each of the men, before nodding. When she neatly stacked her 'money' into piles, Meryn had to hide her smile.

"So we'll play one hand to practice, okay?" Keelan asked. Penny nodded.

Meryn shook her head; they'd figure it out eventually.

"Wow, look guys, Penny won that hand. Way to go, baby girl!" Aiden announced proudly.

Meryn looked up and saw Penny on her knees, raking the candy pile over to her.

Meryn smiled and reviewed the short list of Vanguard warriors Aiden and Gavriel had compiled from memory. She'd have to get with Radek soon to get a more complete list.

"Look at that, she won again. She's too cute," Keelan said as Penny arranged her winnings in order from hard candy to chocolate.

Beth walked over holding the novel she'd been reading. Frowning, she sat next to Meryn.

She nodded her head in Penny's direction. "She..."

"Probably, yeah." Meryn nodded.

"Do they realize..."

"Nope."

"Are you going to tell them?" Beth asked, her eyes now filled with amusement.

Meryn turned to her and just stared blankly.

Beth sat back in her chair and lifted her book up. "Yeah, me either."

About a half an hour later Meryn heard the men mumbling is disbelief.

"Okay that's the eighth hand in a row; that can't be beginner's luck," Darian grumbled as Penny packed half her winnings away in her backpack, making room for more candy on the table.

The men stared at Penny who expertly shuffled the deck before dealing.

Aiden cleared his throat. "Penny, darlin, do you know how to play poker?"

Penny looked up and nodded and the men groaned.

Darian sat forward, a devilish look on his face. "Okay sweetie, gloves are off. You're going down."

Not even fifteen minutes later, Meryn and Beth watched on as Gavriel and Penny faced off as the last two remaining players, staring at each other across the table without blinking.

Meryn held up her pen like a microphone. "We're down to the professionals folks."

"Hey!" Aiden, Darian, and Keelan protested.

Meryn ignored them. "On this side of the table we have the epic vampire legend of the past two millennia and on the other, the stoic toddler." Beth and Meryn giggled.

"I believe she is bluffing," Gavriel announced. "I call."

Without changing expression, Penny laid her cards on the table. The men crowded around, their jaws dropping. Groaning, Gavriel dropped his head to the table.

"She swept the table," Noah whispered in awe.

"How old is she again?" Jaxon asked.

The men all looked up and answered as one. "Four!"

CHAPTER NINE

When Rheia turned over in bed, it immediately registered that she was alone. She opened her eyes and rolled onto her back. Sex with Colton had been the hottest experience of her life, but she couldn't forget the look in his eyes when she'd told him that she wasn't ready to be claimed. She wasn't sure if she could ever explain it in a way he would understand; for that level of commitment, she needed to be sure. She knew she was close to saying yes, but she needed more time.

He was a shifter, he'd grown up with the knowledge that, one day, if he was lucky, he would find the one person meant just for him. Growing up human, she knew there was no guarantee for her. She had fully expected to marry another surgeon, have a late-in-life baby, divorce five years later and live out the rest of her life as a single parent.

Now, the rest of her life was looking like it would last much longer than she had ever anticipated. She ran her hand over the indention his body had left in the mattress. What was with him always waking up and getting out of bed before she was awake? Feeling grumpy, she got out of bed and got ready for her day.

She was still kinda pissed when she went downstairs in search of Penny and Colton. She paused at the doorway of the dining room and glared at Colton, who was completely unaware that she was there. Keelan saw her first and stood, the rest of the men following suit. When Colton turned and saw her expression, his face dropped. She walked over and pulled his face down to hers. The taste of him was more potent than coffee. Sighing, she stepped back and had to hide her smile at his dazed expression.

"I don't like waking up alone," she grumbled.

"You may have to explain that to me again," he teased.

Ignoring him, she walked past his chair and sat down next to Penny. "Did you have fun with Jaxon and Noah last night?"

Penny nodded and reached for her backpack as Colton and the rest of the men sat down. She opened it up and Rheia saw that the inside of the bag was filled with candy and small individually wrapped cakes. She looked around the table. "Where did this come from?"

The men looked down with sheepish expressions. Rheia's eyes narrowed and she turned back to Penny. "Penelope Carmichael, did you hustle these men playing poker to get snacks?"

Penny shrugged one small shoulder and turned back to her breakfast. Rheia was about to scold her when she noticed what the girl was eating. "Are those cinnamon rolls?"

Ryuu walked in carrying a cup. "I thought I heard you come down. Here's your coffee and yes, those are homemade cinnamon rolls, fresh from the oven. It was one of the many recipes I received as a housewarming gift from the Alpha Unit."

Rheia reached for the plate and snagged two with her fork. "Looks like everyone can benefit from a present like that." She lifted the warm, sticky pastry and took a bite. She couldn't stop the moan that came from her. "Oh God!" Her head fell back on her shoulders, and she closed her eyes. To her right, she heard a low rumble. When she turned to look at Colton, he was growling at Ryuu, who completely ignored him as he walked around the table refilling water glasses.

"I thought you had a man crush on him, too?" she asked, surprised at his reaction.

"I do, but damn, baby, I should be the only one who sees that expression," Colton said pouting.

Rheia looked down at Penny. "They never grow up. Remember that." Penny nodded.

Winking at Penny, Colton simply grabbed an entire pan of cinnamon rolls and put it on his plate. Penny's eyes widened. "I'm a mighty wolf, I need my energy."

"You're adorable."

"My puppy."

"You are cute," Rheia, Meryn, and Beth said at the same time, then looked at each other, before smiling. The men around the table burst out laughing.

"Cute wittle puppy," Aiden teased.

Meryn elbowed him. "I wouldn't say anything; I prefer his wolf to your bear."

Aiden's mouth dropped. "I can't believe you just said that."

Meryn turned to him. "Have you seen a shaved bear, they are fugly! If that's what you look like under your pouffy fur, it's gross," she shuddered.

"What's fugly?" Aiden demanded.

"Fucking. Ugly," Colton said, barely able to get the words out he was laughing so hard.

Aiden's face was like a thundercloud. "I am not fugly!"

"I didn't say you were; I said a shaved bear was. When you're all pouffy, you're my teddy bear," Meryn assured him.

"I don't think that's better," Keelan muttered.

"Shut up, Keelan," Aiden growled.

Meryn whacked him again. "Be nice to Keelan."

Rheia turned to Penny. "I'll let you keep half those snacks. You don't need that much sugar." Rheia sipped her coffee. "So besides poker, what else did you do yesterday?"

"Wait, she plays poker? Did you teach her?" Colton asked her, his eyes sparkling.

"Nope, that's all Radek's doing. The guys used to babysit on nights I had to work the graveyard shift. They taught her how to play; evidently, she has a knack for it. Marco plans to take her to Vegas on her twenty-first birthday."

Gavriel, Aiden, Keelan, and Darian stared at Penny.

Gavriel shook his head. "She is the perfect little card shark."

Penny grinned and pointed to Aiden. Rheia looked up. "You did something with Aiden yesterday?"

Aiden frowned for a second then brightened. "I introduced her to my fish; his name is Jaws."

"What is he, a piranha?"

Meryn snorted. "No, he's a clownfish like on *Finding Nemo*."

"Did you know that clownfish are hermaphrodites? That movie, if it had been based on science, would be about Nemo's father changing sexes to female, since the dominant female, Nemo's mother, was killed. He then, in turn, would try to reproduce with the only other male, which would have been Nemo," Rheia explained, munching away on her cinnamon roll. When she noticed how quiet it had gotten she looked up to find everyone staring at her. "What? That's science."

Aiden looked horrified and actually had a fine sheen to his eyes. He stood and started to walk out of the room.

"Aiden, where are you going?" Meryn called after him.

He turned and held up a cell phone. "I'm ordering Jaws a girlfriend," he said, then walked away.

Ryuu clucked his tongue. "His day is not starting off well."

Beside her, Colton began to choke. He quickly swallowed the cinnamon roll he'd been chewing, and laughter burst from him like water from a dam.

"Oh Gods!" he wheezed.

Across the table, Meryn was giggling. "He loves that little fish," she cackled.

"Poor Aiden," Beth murmured, but Rheia could see the light of laughter in her eyes as well.

"I wonder if I should apologize," Rheia mused.

Gavriel shook his head. "He will be fine. I think maybe Jaws was due for a girlfriend anyway."

Colton collapsed against the back of his chair looking exhausted. "Okay, I'm done for the day. It won't get any better than this."

"Guess I'm not coming home for lunch then," Rheia teased.

Colton turned to look at her so quickly his neck popped. "What time?"

"I have a couple of physicals to do today and probably some more work on the slides, but I should be able to get back here by noon again."

Colton turned to Meryn and Beth, giving them puppy dog eyes.

"Of course, we'll watch Penny." Beth said smiling.

"You better hope Aiden lets us have lunch today, you know how he gets when he's in a bad mood," Darian reminded him.

Colton winced. "I'll talk him around; the men need lunch after all."

Rheia was about to respond when Aiden walked back in, a serious look on his face.

Gavriel sat up straight in his chair. "What? What is it?"

"Rheia, I just got off the phone with my father. The Carmichaels, Penny's grandparents, they're petitioning the council for custody," he said gently.

"What!" Rheia stood, knocking over her chair. She scooped her daughter up, who immediately wrapped her arms and legs around her in a death grip. "No! She's mine! I'm not giving her up!" Colton was at her side before she could blink. He pulled them close, giving her something solid to lean against. Penny stretched out a small hand and gripped his shirt tightly.

When Rheia turned to Colton, she was shocked at the simmering rage she saw in his eyes.

Colton turned to his childhood friend. "They can't break up my family," he growled.

Aiden held up his hands. "Colt, you know Father is doing everything he can to keep her here with us. But he said it will be difficult since neither you, nor Rheia have a blood tie to Penny, and they do," Aiden explained.

Rheia felt her world spinning out of control. When she felt hot tears on her neck, she knew she had to pull her shit together. Penny would always come before her own pain. She ran a hand over the girl's hair. "Shh, Pumpkin Dumpling, everything will be just fine. I'm sure, when they see what a wonderful family me, you, and Colton are, they will reconsider. I think that they are so happy to have a granddaughter; they want you all to themselves. They must care about you a lot," she said soothingly.

Penny pulled her head away from her shoulder and looked at her. Rheia could see the fear in her eyes. Colton rubbed Penny's back. "You're needed here, baby girl, someone needs to teach me how to play poker." Penny smiled at him sadly and nodded.

Rheia set her down. "Tell you what; we're not going to worry about this. We won't let this destroy all the fun we're going to have today, right Penny?" she said in an upbeat manner. Until a decision was made, Rheia knew the best thing for Penny was to keep things as normal as possible, which meant she had to return to work at the clinic, despite not wanting to let her daughter out of her sight.

Colton knelt down in front of Penny. "I'm going to be hanging out with your mom today, but when we get home, we'll do something together," he promised.

Penny held up her pinky and Colton didn't miss a beat. He hooked his pinky with hers and they shook on it.

Meryn and Beth walked around the table and Meryn wrapped an arm around Penny. "Come on EGIT time to get to work. Jaxon and Noah are already waiting for us in Command Central. They woke up early and snagged two pans of cinnamon rolls for breakfast and decided to get a jump on the day. I bet they can give you some good ideas for stuff to do with your mom and dad later."

Colton stood and they both looked at Meryn. Rheia had to ask. "What is EGIT?"

Beth sighed. "Evil. Genius. In. Training."

Colton looked at Meryn. "Don't infect my daughter with ..." he motioned to Meryn's whole body.

Meryn grinned. "You just gestured to all of me."

Colton laughed and they gave each other high fives. Behind Meryn, both Aiden and Ryuu groaned.

Rheia looked at Colton. "Why does that sound familiar?"

Ryuu grumbled under his breath. "It's from *How To Train Your Dragon*. Meryn and Colton have been watching it non-stop for the past two weeks."

Penny began to hop up and down. Rheia looked down. "Is that what you want to do later? Watch that movie?"

Penny nodded and continued to bounce up and down.

Ryuu's sigh was long and heavy. "If it's for the baby, I guess I'll allow it."

"Allow it?" Rheia asked.

Meryn laughed. "He banned it. He said that the movie in no way depicted real dragons, therefore wasn't worth the time it took to watch. I mean, what does Ryuu know about dragons? It's not like they're real or anything." Rheia noticed the sly look on Meryn's face.

Ryuu on the other hand was looking more and more agitated. "I'll prepare refreshments later for the movie," he said shortly and headed to the kitchen.

Meryn's grin was decidedly evil. Rheia looked at the smaller woman. "Did I miss something?"

Meryn shook her head. "Nope, just my squire thinking he's clever. Occasionally, I have to remind him I'm not stupid. Anyway! Come on, petite commando, let's go see what trouble we can get into today." Meryn took Penny's hand and led her from the room. Beth leaned over and kissed Gavriel, picked up her cup, downed its contents and headed for the door.

Aiden smiled at Beth in commiseration as she walked by him. "Thank the Gods for you, Beth." She winked up at him and walked away.

Rheia put a hand to her stomach. It had taken everything in her to send Penny out and about for the day. What she really wanted to do was scoop her up and run back to Jefferson.

"It'll be okay, Rheia. We're not going to lose her," Colton said, pulling her in for a hug.

"I want to take her away from here, take her back home. It's all my fault for looking for her family." She buried her face in his chest.

"You are home, sweetheart," he reminded her softly. "And don't blame yourself for this. If you hadn't contacted them, they would have found out soon enough. Lycaonia isn't that big. We would have had to face this eventually."

Rheia looked up into his eyes and saw the hurt her casual comments had caused. "I'm sorry, Colton, I didn't mean that I didn't want to be with you, or that this wasn't home. I'm just scared, and my parents' house in Jefferson has always been a safe haven to me."

Colton kissed her forehead. "I know."

Aiden cleared his throat. When she and Colton turned to him, she noticed that Gavriel, Darian, and Keelan were standing with him at the door. "We're going to start drills. Colton, why don't you stay with Rheia today? Adam contacted me yesterday, saying something about physicals, so I'm sending Keelan along for one and I've scheduled Gamma to get theirs today as well, since they're the ones assigned to guard the clinic."

Rheia let out a deep breath. She was surprised how relieved she felt knowing that Colton would be with her today. But if she and Colton were at the clinic, what would happen if someone came for Penny? She looked past Aiden and bit her lower lip. "What if someone comes for Penny?"

Aiden's face hardened. "Then they'll just have to wait for you two to get back here. No one is taking her away, Rheia, not without you and Colton here," he promised.

"Thank you, Aiden," she said gratefully.

Aiden blushed. "She just grows on you. She already has all the unit warriors wrapped around her tiny finger," he admitted gruffly.

"She's very special," Rheia said leaning into Colton.

Colton turned to Aiden. "You guys head out. I think I want some more cinnamon rolls."

"Call us if you need us," Aiden said, and the men left.

Rheia turned to Colton. "You can't possibly still be hungry."

He shook his head. "I'm not, but you should eat some more."

"I don't think I could eat right now, I'd probably throw it up."

"Just one more, you haven't eaten much," he pointed to her half eaten cinnamon roll.

Rheia popped the half-eaten roll into her mouth and chugged her coffee. She wiped her mouth with a napkin and turned to Colton. "Okay, ready."

Colton walked past her and placed three cinnamon rolls in a napkin.

"Colton, I'm fine."

"It's for my snack later, but since you're my mate, if you get hungry, I'll share with you." His eyes were filled with sincerity.

Rheia accepted it for the act of affection it was. She knew that if Colton was willing to share his food, his feelings for her were real.

Colton sat between Keelan and Sascha in the waiting area. Rheia was getting things set up in one of the examination rooms and said she would be calling the men back one at a time.

Colton leaned closer to Keelan. "What's a physical anyway?"

Keelan's face became thoughtful. "You know, I don't know. I just thought she'd take some blood or something, but if that were the case, we wouldn't need an examination room." Keelan took out his phone and started tapping away at it.

Sascha leaned back and extended his legs out in front of him. "Maybe that's just how she's used to doing things."

They heard banging and movement coming from down the hall where Rheia was straightening the room after the ferals trashed it.

"Rheia, you okay?" Colton called out.

"Yeah! Just moving this cabinet; be done in a second," she yelled back.

Colton smiled and sat back. He knew his mate was on edge about Penny. He was determined to take her mind off her worries later. Even though she hadn't allowed him to claim her, the previous night had shaken him. He'd never had such an intense orgasm in his life; he was practically salivating at the thought of making her his.

"Umm... Colton," Keelan whispered, his face bright red.

"Yeah?"

"I don't think this is right." Keelan's voice squeaked.

Colton noticed that the area around Keelan's mouth had become pale.

"What is it, buddy?" he asked.

Just then, Rheia stepped into the waiting area. "Okay Keelan, you're first."

Colton was shocked when Keelan actually whimpered and looked at him with stark fear in his eyes. Slowly, the witch got to his feet and walked toward Rheia as if he was going to his death. When they disappeared around the corner, Colton started to feel uneasy.

He turned to Sasha. "Do you have your phone on you?"

"Yeah, why?"

"Look up what a physical is."

Sascha shrugged and pulled out his phone. After a few moments, his cheeks were tinged pink.

Colton felt his mouth go dry. "What?"

Sascha turned and placed a steadying hand on Colton's shoulder. "Remember Colton, your mate is a doctor, she probably does this sort of thing all the time."

"What sort of thing?" he demanded.

Sascha opened his mouth to explain and then shut it. Wordlessly, he handed Colton his phone. Colton began to skim the article before he read something that made his canines surge through his gums. He threw Sascha's phone at him. "I'll kill him!" he growled and stood.

Sascha grabbed his shoulder. "It isn't personal, Colton; she's just doing her job."

Colton walked down the hall toward the examination room practically dragging Sascha along behind him. They were almost to the door when they could hear the voices from inside the room.

"I don't think it's going to go in," Keelan said. Colton could hear the worry in his voice.

"Of course it will; that's what it's designed for."

Colton and Sascha froze then leaned in closer to the door. Colton held his breath as images of medical devices floated through his mind.

"I think it's too big. Do you have anything that will grease it up?"

Colton turned to Sascha whose horrified expression matched his own. What was his mate doing to Keelan?

"Okay, it's going in, just don't force it," Keelan said, sounding relieved.

"I've done this before; I know what I'm doing."

"Okay, I think something's wrong, it feels off."

"Seems okay to me."

"Ow! Dammit!" Keelan's sharp exclamation had Colton and Sascha jumping back.

"There, it's all the way in," Rheia said.

"That hurt," Keelan said, sounding dejected.

"It wasn't that bad."

"I have to admit, it looks a lot better. It will probably work a lot better, too."

"I hope so; I plan to get a lot of use out of it."

Colton stared at the door as her words registered. He stepped back and kicked the door in. "Like fucking hell you will!" He snarled at Keelan, taking satisfaction in the way the blood drained from his face.

When he stepped into the room and looked around, he realized he had made a terrible mistake. Keelan was fully dressed, sucking on his finger and his mate was standing next to a cabinet, testing the top drawer by pulling it in and out. She hadn't been performing an exam; she had been fixing the drawer.

Fuck!

Keelan took one look at him and Colton could see the dawning realization as to what his conversation with Rheia must have sounded like. Without a word, he raised the window and jumped out. Since they were on the ground floor Keelan didn't have very far to jump. Colton could see him running around to the front of the building and away from him as fast as he could.

Rheia turned to him shock and disbelief on her face. "What in the everloving fuck was that?"

Colton stepped back to stand next to Sascha; they looked at each other then turned to look at Rheia.

"Nothing," they said together.

"You can't be here if you do stuff like this, Colton. I need to be able to do my job. Go back to the waiting room and eat your cinnamon rolls," she ordered. She then looked at Sascha. "You're next."

Sascha turned to Colton with a huge shit-eating grin. "Sure Doc, you can fix me up, too."

Without even blinking, Colton punched him in the nose.

"Colton! Don't break them! I have to fix them!" she admonished with her hands on her hips.

Colton shrugged and glared at Sascha who was holding his bleeding nose and tilting his head back.

Sascha held up his other hand in surrender. "I deserved that one, Doc," he admitted, sounding nasally.

"Men! You!" she pointed at Colton. "Waiting room. Now. You need to be far enough away so that you can't hear what's being discussed. Haven't you ever heard of HIPAA?"

"Now that's being mean, baby, I know Sascha's a big boy, but he's a tiger, not a hippo," Colton said, grinning.

"Out!" she yelled, pointing to the door.

Colton turned and leaned in close to the Gamma Unit leader. "You touch her, I'll kill you."

"I won't be touching her, pup; she'll be touching me," Sascha teased.

Colton growled and walked out of the examination room. The bastard flipped him off and slammed the door in his face.

Grumbling, he stalked back to the front and threw himself into a chair. Without saying anything to the men staring at him, he picked up his snack from Rheia's bag and started munching on his cinnamon rolls.

"Um, Colton..." Colton looked up to see Keelan standing near the front entrance. He waved him over and when he sat down, offered him one of his cinnamon rolls.

"Sorry I growled at you."

"No worries, it must have sounded terrible from your side," Keelan admitted.

"It did."

They sat in silence eating their rolls.

Colton kept turning his head and staring down the hallway. He knew Rheia would never betray him, but the idea of her touching other males made his skin crawl. Savagely, he bit into his last roll. The more he thought about Sascha's satisfied smirk the more pissed he became. Again, he knew Sascha would never even think about making a pass at Rheia, but he was in there with his mate, had her undivided attention, and she was touching him.

"Colton, you're growling again," Keelan whispered.

Colton looked over at Keelan and an idea began to form. He looked up and saw that most of the Gamma Unit were patiently waiting for their leader to come out, so that they could resume their patrol around the clinic.

"Hey, Keelan."

"Yeah?"

"Have any good revenge ideas?" Colton asked, his eyes flicking to Quinn, then down the hall to where Sascha was.

Keelan's eyes grew bright, and he nodded, his own eyes turning to look at Quinn.

Colton knew that Quinn and Sascha were the ones responsible for turning the young witch purple right after Beth moved in. It looked like it was time Gamma was reminded why he and Keelan were in the Alpha Unit.

CHAPTER TEN

"Okay, you're free to go. Try not to antagonize Colton on your way out."

Sascha grinned. "I make no promises. See ya later, Doc." He hopped off the examination table and left the room.

Rheia shook her head. After Colton left, Sascha had become the epitome of a perfect gentleman. It was good to know that the unit warriors in Lycaonia were as close as her brothers were at home. Thinking of Radek and the others, she pulled out her cell phone and dialed his number.

"Rei?" Radek answered on the first ring.

"Hey, Radek."

"Where in the fuck have you been? I have been waiting for a phone call for days!" he shouted.

Rheia pulled the phone away from her ear. She had meant to call him sooner, but it had been a hectic couple of days.

"I'm sorry, Radek, I found myself running for my life with my child to an unknown paranormal city where I discover I'm mated to a wolf of all things. Then there was a break-in here at the clinic, and now, Penny's grandparents want custody, so I am really fucking sorry I didn't call sooner. My mind is still playing catch up," Rheia ranted.

"You're mated to a wolf?" the disdain in his voice was clear.

"That's all you heard?"

"No, I heard everything else, of course, and we'll get to that in a second, but first, I want to know who thinks they're good enough to be your mate."

"Colton Albright." Even saying his name made her smile.

"Shit, you've already fallen for him," Radek chuckled.

Rheia's mouth dropped. "What makes you say that?" she demanded.

"You should hear the way you say his name; you're a goner. We'll have to visit soon so I can show that pup exactly how loved you are and tell him exactly what will happen to him if he hurts you," he grumbled.

"She's mated to Colton?" she heard Levi ask in the background. Evidently, Radek had put her on speaker.

"Yup," Radek answered.

"I thought for sure she'd end up with a vampire," Marco chimed in.

"Guys, quiet!" Radek boomed. When he came back to her, his voice was gentle. "Now, what is this about Penny?"

Rheia felt her throat close. "Oh Radek, I think I've made a horrible mistake. I wanted Penny to meet her family, if she had any here in Lycaonia, now they want custody." She made the mistake of sniffling.

"We can be there in five hours. Just say the word, Rei," Radek promised.

"It takes at least eight to drive down here," she reminded him.

"No, it takes *you* eight hours to drive down there. It would take Athan five hours, especially after I tell him the clinic where you work has had a break-in."

"What!" she heard the men's voices break out into chaos in the background. For a moment, the men were talking all at once, mostly saying they were coming to Lycaonia to kick someone's ass. She'd missed this. Suddenly, she wondered how Colton would fit into their small family. She smiled; he was such a jokester, he'd probably drive Radek crazy. It could be fun.

"Guys! I'm okay. Whoever it was, stole a body. There's some crazy stuff happening here, I feel like I walked into the middle of something huge, but I don't have all the pieces to make heads or tails of it. It's frustrating," she confessed.

"Back to Penny. Unfortunately, the paperwork we forged is only valid in the human world, you're in Lycaonia now; her grandparents will have the upper hand. What's Colton doing about it? How is he with our Penny?" Radek asked.

"Colton's wonderful with her. You wouldn't recognize her, Radek; she's smiling and bouncing around, and really coming out of her shell. I know it's because of Colton. He didn't hesitate for even a second to accept her as his own. He'll be just as devastated if we lose Penny," she swallowed hard, feeling a knot in her throat. She took a breath and continued. "He's letting Aiden's father deal with it; I think he may be important here."

There was silence on the other end of the phone. "Did you say Aiden's father, as in Byron McKenzie?" Radek asked.

"Yeah, Colton and Aiden are childhood friends, Colton asked Aiden to be Penny's *Athair*, so Byron's doing everything he can for Aiden, if that makes sense."

"Holy shit! The McKenzie's are the closest thing you can get to shifter royalty, if we had royalty. She couldn't have better men looking out for her." Radek's voice sounded awestruck.

"You sound unusually impressed, Radek."

"It's because of Commander McKenzie, the older one," Levi called out in the background.

"Older one?" she asked thoroughly confused.

"Byron McKenzie, Aiden's father, used to be the Unit Commander before his son took over. Most of us who volunteered to be in Vanguard served under him," Radek said.

"So what do you know about Colton?" She felt bad about asking, but she valued their opinions.

"If Aiden is the crown prince, Colton would be the court jester," Marco called out, laughing.

Radek chuckled. "There's more to that wolf than meets the eye. He acts like the laid back Lothario so most people drop their defenses around him. I think he's played the good cop to Aiden's bad cop for so long he doesn't even realize he does it anymore. But I will tell you this, he's good, very good. He's the second highest ranked shifter in all the units for a reason."

Rheia knew what Radek said was true; she had caught enough glimpses of Colton's wolf behind his eyes to know he wasn't as easygoing as he let on.

"You got quiet, kiddo. All jokes aside, is he treating you right?" Radek asked.

Rheia answered without hesitation. "Yes. He's even agreed to wait to claim me."

"Ouch." Radek hissed.

"What?"

"Rheia, honey, I'm sure he didn't tell you, but that will be very hard for him. Every instinct in his body is screaming at him to claim you. He must have extraordinary self-control." There was a new degree of admiration in Radek's voice.

"Wait, I'm causing him pain?" Rheia felt ill.

Radek hesitated. "Yes and no. You have every right to ask him to wait, but in honoring that request, Colton is under a certain amount of mental and physical duress. Whatever you do, don't sleep with him."

"Why?" she asked suspiciously.

"Shit, you've slept with him already, haven't you?"

"Yes. I can't seem to keep my hands off him," she admitted.

"Poor bastard," Dax murmured in the background.

"What? What did I do?" Rheia asked frantically.

Radek exhaled loudly. She could just imagine him pinching the bridge of his nose. "Pumpkin Dumpling, having sex with you and not claiming you would be like teasing someone for hours on end and not letting them orgasm."

"He had an orgasm," she protested.

"It's not physical; basically, you gave his heart and soul the worst case of blue balls in the history of mankind."

"Oh, my God," she whispered.

"So tell me what's wrong with him. What is it about him that you don't like?" Radek asked.

Rheia felt her defenses go up. "There's nothing wrong with him! I've never been with anyone who was as selfless and as considerate as Colton. I know that he'd do anything to keep Penny and me safe and happy." Rheia stumbled as her thoughts collided in her mind. She knew, with unwavering conviction, that Colton would die before hurting her, and that he lived to see her smile. In an instant, she knew. She loved him.

"Caught ya, didn't I?" Radek chuckled.

"Ryuu said it would be a defining moment. He wasn't kidding."

"Who's Ryuu?" Levi asked.

"He's the house squire and makes the best damn food and coffee I've ever had." She couldn't keep the smile off her face remembering the cinnamon rolls.

"Must be nice having a squire," Levi said longingly.

Rheia heard footsteps by the door. "Listen guys, I gotta run. I'll call you back later with updates."

"We miss you. Take care of your wolf," Athan said in goodbye.

"I miss all of you, too. Stay safe."

"You too, Pumpkin Dumpling." Rheia ended the call and stared at her phone. There was no reason not to mate with Colton. She felt her body tightening in anticipation. Considering how off the charts last night had been, she couldn't help but wonder about the claiming process.

Rheia saw a figure moving outside the door. She was about to call out and tell them that they could come in, when the smell hit her. It was faint, not nearly as strong as what she had experienced in the morgue, but it was the exact same smell from her dream, from the attack on her house, and from the corpse.

Shaking uncontrollably, she quietly lifted the window and jumped out as Keelan had. She ran as fast as she could and turned the corner of the brick building. She burst through the front doors and stood in the middle of the waiting room, shaking.

Colton and Sascha looked up from their conversation and froze. Her teeth were chattering so hard she couldn't speak, she just pointed down the hall.

"Keelan, protect her," Colton whispered harshly before he and Sascha took off with the rest of the Gamma Unit down the hall. When she blinked, Keelan was at her side, murmuring low. Slowly, she was enveloped in a warm bubble.

In the distance, Rheia heard the sounds of men's shouts and gunfire.

Colton!

She started to run toward the fight when Keelan grabbed her.

He shook his head. "Stay here. When they give the all clear, then you can go check if anyone needs help."

Adam came running toward them from the direction of his office. "What the hell is going on?"

"Ferals are in the clinic," Keelan answered.

Adam dropped his head back and roared. His chest expanded and his canines appeared over his lower lip. He reached behind him, under his lab coat and pulled out a nine millimeter running toward the sound of gunfire.

Keelan turned to her, smiling. "He's pretty cool, huh? Everyone always forgets he was a unit warrior before he gave it up to learn about healing."

Rheia just nodded. Adam's bear-like war cry made her bones shake. "They would have to be completely unhinged to stand up against him," she said trying to shake off her fear.

After a few minutes, a group of men poured in from behind them, including the Alpha Unit.

Keelan breathed a sigh of relief. "Someone called in back up. Thank the Gods! My phone never seems to work when I'm actively using magic."

Gavriel took up a position right outside their small bubble and kept guard.

Once the sound of gunfire stopped, Rheia watched the hallway, waiting for Colton to appear. Each minute that passed when he didn't, made the acid rise up the back of her throat.

One by one, the men filed by nodding at her and Keelan, heading to other parts of the clinic or outside to set up a perimeter. Thirty minutes later, she heard the men shout 'All clear'. It was only then that Colton emerged from the hallway. When he walked over to them, Keelan dropped the bubble.

Rheia knew she was angry because she was worried. She even knew that it wasn't his fault, but seeing him walk up smiling made her snap.

"Where in the fuck have you been?" she screeched.

Colton stopped in his tracks, looking stunned. With a confused expression, he pointed down the hallway. "Fighting ferals." He looked at her as if she'd lost her mind.

Rheia placed a hand on her stomach. "Is anyone hurt?" she asked, trying to stop her insides from trembling.

Colton shook his head. "Just the enemy."

Rheia nodded absently. "Good. Good."

"Okay baby, we're just going to head out to the car now." Colton said slowly and carefully.

"Quit talking to me like that. I'm a doctor; I know I'm in shock. I just can't stop shaking." She stared at him. "I can't stop shaking." It didn't make any sense to her. She knew what was wrong; she should be able to stop it.

Colton's eyes were full of sympathy. "Oh sweetheart, it's okay."

"I know," she nodded absently.

Colton walked over and placed both hands on her shoulders. "It's okay, Rheia."

"I know, you said no one was hurt."

Colton pulled her close and tucked her head under his chin. "You're not listening baby, it's okay. You can let go now."

It was as if her body had been waiting for his words. Without warning, her knees gave out, and Colton easily lifted her in his arms.

He turned to Keelan. "Tell Aiden and Adam I'm taking her home, she's had too much thrown at her in the past couple of days."

"I'm fine," she protested.

"Sure you are, honey, but I'm going to carry you anyway." He kissed the top of her head and walked out the door.

Rheia rested her head on his chest. "I'm not normally like this. I'm an ER doctor for crying out loud," she murmured.

"I know. But honey, you have to realize, there's a difference between dealing with the aftermath of violence and having that violence directed at you. You're actually holding up extremely well."

Colton set her on her feet and opened the car door.

She looked up into his eyes. "What do they want?"

Colton's face hardened and his jaw clenched. "I don't know, but whatever they're after, I won't let them have it."

Rheia nodded and got into the car.

When they arrived at the Alpha estate, Colton came around the car to carry her, but Rheia held up her hand, shaking her head.

"If you carry me in, it'll scare Penny. Just being near you calmed me down."

Colton's face brightened and seemed to radiate joy. "Now I want to carry you just to keep you in my arms." He held out his hand to help her out of the car.

She let him help her stand and then she took a step forward to wrap her arms around his body. He rested his chin on the top of her head. "I won't let them near you or Penny," he promised.

She looked up and let the confidence she felt in him show in her eyes. "I know. Let's go see what our girl is doing."

Colton cupped her face with both of his hands. "Our girl?"

"You're not going anywhere, right?"

He shook his head. "Of course, not."

"Then I'm yours and she's ours."

Colton sucked in a breath. "Do you mean what I think you mean?"

She turned her head and kissed the center of his palm. "I realized how I felt when I was on the phone with Radek. My feelings became even clearer when I thought we'd never have the chance to be together.

I want you to tie us together in every way you know how, because I'm not letting you go."

Colton captured her mouth and demanded entrance. She felt his tongue slip between her lips and playfully scrape the roof of her mouth. She grabbed his coat with both hands and pulled him forward. She took control of the kiss and took his lower lip between her teeth. When she bit down gently, he moaned low in his throat. When he pulled back, they were both breathing hard.

Colton rested his forehead on hers. "Penny. Gotta check in with Penny, then dinner, then movie. Gods willing, Jaxon and Noah can babysit again."

Rheia felt her heart turn over. According to Radek, the only thing Colton should be thinking about was claiming her, yet here he was being the perfect partner and father. She tilted her head back, which forced him to step back. "I love you, Colton Albright."

Colton jerked her close and buried his face in her neck. "Gods baby, I love you, too. All I can think of right now is how much I want to be inside you and to make you mine forever." He began to nibble up and down the side of her neck.

Rheia tilted her head to give him better access. "I'm buying you that truck with bench seats."

Colton chuckled darkly and gave her neck a final, harder bite. She was shocked at her body's reaction to the sharp pain. It was as if the love bite on her neck was connected to her clit.

Colton brought his lips up to her ear. "I can smell you, sweetheart. I think you like a bit of pain with your pleasure."

"Who knew?" she asked, feeling slightly dazed. If his aim was to distract her from the feral attacks, he had succeeded.

Colton's eyes were wolf yellow when he looked down at her. "We'll find out tonight exactly how much pain you can handle."

Rheia shivered and squeezed her thighs together. She had to take a deep breath to calm her racing heart.

"You're on," she challenged.

Laughing Colton kissed her quickly and took her hand.

What on earth have I gotten myself into?

Noah and Jaxon agreed to watch Penny when Colton asked. They'd even set up a special dinner for her. Currently, the three of them were in the family room playing 'picnic'. Penny looked adorable in her pajamas sitting on a blanket with Jaxon and Noah. She had a feeling the two young men would be more like brothers than uncles to her daughter.

She was never more thankful for a babysitter than she was during dinner. Colton kept turning to her, giving her heated looks that made her squirm in her seat. When his hand 'accidentally' brushed her *inner* thigh for the third time, she was about to excuse herself to the foyer to cool down, when Keelan brought up a topic that cooled her ardor.

"Aiden, were you able to determine why ferals were at the clinic today?" Keelan asked, pushing his food around on his plate with his fork.

"No, and what worries me most is that they didn't go to the morgue or Adam's office, they deliberately went after Rheia." Aiden raised his wine glass and took a sip. Under the table, Colton took her hand.

Gavriel leaned forward. "Could they be trying to recruit Colton in the same manner that they came after me? They are newly mated," Gavriel pointed out.

Aiden nodded. "That could very well be it."

"But I was attacked before I met Colton, remember? It's why I came here to Lycaonia," Rheia reminded them.

"I feel like I'm missing something right under my nose, and it's driving me nuts!" Meryn slumped back in her chair.

"It'll come to you Meryn. You, more than anyone else, have been the one to look at what's happening from an outside perspective. Rheia's also helped us change and become stronger with our new random training schedules. Don't upset yourself. Your most important job is taking care of our future commander," Darian said indicating her stomach.

Aiden smiled. "See love, even Darian thinks we're having a boy."

Beth smiled. "He never said son, Aiden, he said 'commander'. I could easily see a daughter of yours and Meryn's leading the unit warriors."

Gavriel wrapped an arm around Beth, getting comfortable. "That could be interesting," he said smirking.

"No. Just, no. If we have a girl, I'm wrapping her and Penny up in bubble wrap until they are four or five hundred years old, then they can start looking for their mates," Aiden huffed.

Rheia had to laugh. "Can you imagine our Penny with Meryn's daughter?" she asked, turning to Colton.

Colton smiled at first, and then her words began to sink in. His brows came together and he began to frown. He looked over at Aiden. "Do they make tracking devices for children?"

Aiden also looked worried. He shook his head. "How far could they possibly go in Lycaonia?"

Colton looked at him flatly. "You do remember that time you and I wanted to go camping and you fell off the mountain? That was just outside Lycaonia's borders."

Aiden stared at Colton. "Tracking devices, huh? I'll ask my father about them." He looked around the room. "Let's all take the day off tomorrow. Construction on the trainee addition has finally wrapped up. Let's take a day to recover."

Darian snorted. "You just want to keep an eye on Meryn," he joked. Keelan and Colton laughed.

Meryn stuck her tongue out at Darian.

Aiden turned to his mate. "I love you with every breath in my body, but lately you have become more... erratic than normal." Even Rheia could tell that Aiden was worried about his mate.

Colton looked at his oldest friend. "Meryn's adjusting to her new, no caffeine lifestyle. She's also taken on the training of two new intel warriors."

Meryn gave him a thumbs up.

Aiden frowned at him. "Intel warriors?"

Colton shrugged. "That's the phrase Meryn wanted to use. Noah and Jaxon seem to soak up every scrap of confidence she instills in them."

Meryn shrugged. "It sounds badass."

Beth turned to Meryn. "You're going to be an amazing mother."

Colton shook his head. "You mean Ryuu is going to be an amazing mother," he joked.

Aiden shrugged. "Marius played a huge role in raising us; I think it's perfectly natural for Ryuu to help raise our son."

"Daughter. Meryn insists you're having a girl," Keelan said, winking at Colton. Already Aiden's neck was starting to flush. The red stain crept upward to his cheeks.

"We are *not* having a girl. Girls are delicate and fragile. What would we do with a baby girl around here? Penny is enough." Aiden shuddered.

"Well, if your daughter's anything like Meryn, she'll probably blow up the armory." Colton suggested.

Aiden paled. "No! Absolutely not! No girls."

Gavriel shook his head. "This may not be something you can control."

Aiden scowled at Gavriel. "Just you wait. It'll be your turn soon enough, and then I'll sit back and laugh and laugh and laugh. According to Beth, she wants to try to get pregnant next year. What if your daughter takes after Beth?" Aiden asked.

All the men froze and shook their heads.

Colton looked over at the vampire. "We may need to start looking into those large plastic bubbles for children now, just in case your fathers-in-law need time to make modifications," he suggested.

Gavriel sat still as stone. Rheia couldn't even tell if the man was breathing. Without saying a word, he pulled out his cell phone. He put it on speaker and they all listened as the phone rang.

"Hello?" A male voice answered.

"Good evening, Broderick. Listen, how difficult would it be to engineer a large protective plastic bubble for a small child?" Gavriel asked as a greeting.

Beth rolled her eyes.

Over the phone, they heard the man gasp. "Beth cannot be pregnant..."

"No, no, she is not. But she wants to start trying as early as next year. I want to be prepared," Gavriel informed them.

"She *would* want to start right away." Rheia heard another man say.

"True, Caspian. Gavriel, we'll put our heads together here and see what we can come up with," Broderick promised.

"Thank you," Gavriel said and ended the call. The men all breathed a sigh of relief.

Colton looked at the empty plates. "Everyone ready for movie night?"

Ryuu stuck his head into the dining room from the kitchen. "I have already delivered your movie snacks to Jaxon and Noah. If you leave the plates, I'll pick them up momentarily."

Everyone began to stand and head toward the family room.

Keelan stopped, frowning. "If the kid is in a bubble, what happens if they can't get fresh oxygen, won't they suffocate?"

Rheia covered her mouth with her hand.

Wrong thing to say.

Grinning, she and Colton kept walking. Seconds later, she heard Gavriel on the phone with Broderick again.

Never a dull moment.

CHAPTER ELEVEN

They each kissed Penny goodnight twice before making their way up to their room. Rheia knew Colton would never truly hurt her, but she was still nervous about being claimed. She'd never had anyone bite her before. She didn't know whether her body's reaction in the car had been due to the unusual stimuli or because it was Colton. She got undressed on autopilot, as if she was getting ready for bed. She was so distracted by her thoughts, she didn't even realize that Colton was naked and waiting for her. She jumped when she felt a warm thumb rub between her eyebrows.

Colton was standing in front of her, smiling. "You're frowning and thinking too hard. What has you so lost in thought?" She had to take a moment to remember what she'd been thinking. His body was wreaking havoc on her concentration. Her eyes wandered up and down, taking in every golden muscle and dark blond hair. She had only seen bodies like this in magazine ads and on the internet; she had an overwhelming desire to run her hands over every square inch of him.

Shaking her head, she answered. "I was just wondering if my body was responding to your bites because of the pain or because it was you." Unable to resist, she lightly ran her hands down his chest and then down his sides. He jumped a little when she grazed his lower ribs.

"Are you ticklish?" she asked, reaching for him again.

He stepped back. "Nope, not even a little bit."

She took another step toward him. "Then why are you backing up?"

"I don't know what you're talking about," he scoffed.

Her hand darted out and tickled his side making him laugh aloud and convulse. Colton turned and ran for the bed, diving under the covers. She gave chase and jumped on the large lump his body created under the comforter. Colton's head popped out at the top laughing. Delighted, she laughed along with him. "You are ticklish! That is so adorable."

He propped his head up on one hand. "We need to banish the word adorable from your vocabulary."

"You are though, and sweet, and kind. You're only the big bad wolf in your mind." He lifted the covers and she snuggled down close to him. The feel of their naked bodies, skin to skin, was lighting fires everywhere they touched.

"I am a big bad wolf to everyone but my family." He dragged his chin back and forth over her the top of her head.

"Does the claiming part hurt?" she asked. She knew that it involved something other than sex, but she had no idea what it was.

She felt Colton shake his head. "No, it won't hurt. Our souls will entwine, just as our bodies will be, as we're making love. Then they'll split back apart and return to us, carrying a small piece of the other's soul so we'll reside within each other forever."

"Will it change me? Will I sprout fur at the full moon?" she joked.

"No, you disrespectful wench, you won't change," he chuckled. "You'll still be you, but you'll gain my longevity."

"I'll be able to watch Penny really grow up." Rheia felt a deep sense of contentment. She had been so afraid of leaving Penny when she needed her most.

"She'll be driving us crazy for decades to come."

"What about other children? I always wanted a large family," she admitted. She loved her parents growing up, but always wished she had brothers and sisters to play with.

Colton pulled back, his face glowing with happiness. "I want as many children as you can have safely. I was an only child, which is how I ended up hanging out with Aiden so much. I was always jealous that he had so many brothers."

"So you won't mind having girls?" she teased, reminding him of the earlier conversation.

Colton shook his head. "I'm sure Broderick will be able to make as many plastic bubbles as we need."

"We're not putting our kids in bubbles," she laughed.

"Meryn said she ovulates every month, is that the same for you?" he asked, his voice huskier.

She looked up and saw that his eyes had shifted from their normal brilliant green to canine yellow. She nodded slowly.

"Could you become pregnant tonight?" He ran his hands over her lower stomach, caressing her reverently.

Rheia counted back the number of days since her last period and then nodded. "It might be close, but I'm fertile."

Colton growled and before she could blink, he was leaning over her, settling between her legs. She could already feel the throbbing in her clit. She arched her back to grind her body against his.

"I can feel how wet you already are." Colton moved down and took one nipple between his teeth. Lightly, he bit down as a hand moved between her legs. The combination of the sharp pain and pleasure had her throwing her head back.

"I don't have to hold back tonight," he whispered.

"Oh God, please, Colton. I need you so badly." Her throat was already dry from panting to catch her breath.

"I'm going to fill you with my seed and make you mine forever." She felt the head of his cock slowly begin to stretch her. He was well-endowed and knew exactly how to bring her the most pleasure. She thrashed her head from side to side, as he gradually filled her.

He kept up his languid pace until she thought she would lose her mind. Each small thrust was deliberate, as he slid his engorged head over that elusive spot deep inside her.

"I love you, Rheia, I'll love you until the day I pass from this world. Even as my body turns to dust, I will wait at the very veil of existence for you to join me, because heaven would be incomplete without you." He buried his face in her neck and her arms came up to hold him tight. Slowly, he made love to her, showing her with his body exactly what he felt for her in his heart. She was changed forever by his words. He was not only making love to her body, but also to her soul.

"I love you so much, Colton. You're my rock. You don't try to do things for me with your strength; you add your strength to mine. Together, we're more than when we are apart. You gave me the space to make my own decisions and you accepted Penny without question. I couldn't have asked for a better partner or father for my children." She buried both hands in his hair and held him to her, afraid to let go.

Colton pulled up and watched her face as he glided in and out of her body. The slow pace made his eyes on her the single most erotic experience of her life. There was no hiding, and no need to hide. She let her walls come down completely and wasn't afraid to let him see the real her.

He must have seen the surrender in her eyes, because he started to snap his hips at a more frenzied pace, finally giving her what she was aching for. When he slammed inside her as deep as he could go, her orgasm detonated low inside her before spreading throughout her body. Before she could catch her breath, he was above her. Striking quickly, he sunk his teeth deep into her shoulder. Just when she thought she couldn't take any more pleasure, she felt as if she was lifting from her body. Without sight or sound, she floated, moving instinctively toward the warmth just in front of her. When her soul merged with Colton's, for a split second, she was able to see deep into his heart, and what she saw there left her breathless. He was beautiful; his complete selflessness made his soul shine like a beacon, and she was drawn to it, seeking its warmth and shelter. Together they swirled and then slowly separated. When she drifted back down into her body, she carried a piece of him with her and knew she would never be lonely again.

"I'll love you forever," she whispered.

"Still not long enough." He collapsed to one side and pulled her close.

Before sleep claimed her, she realized that she had finally come home.

Rheia and Colton were the last to arrive for breakfast. They'd just sat down when they heard a knock at the door. Rheia looked at Colton; visitors this early in the morning did not bode well.

Her instincts proved correct when a tall, older version of Aiden appeared in the doorway. His eyes were sorrowful as he looked over to where she sat with Penny and Colton.

"Father?" Aiden asked, standing.

"Byron?" Colton also stood, moving his body between the newcomer and Rheia, who sat with their daughter.

"I'm so sorry, Colton, but the council has awarded Wilomina and Gerard Carmichael custody of Penny. I'm to escort her to their home first thing this morning."

Rheia's heart stuttered in her chest. Penny turned to her, fear in her eyes. Rheia had a second to make the decision that would best help Penny adjust to her new family. If she gave in to her feelings and wept, as she wanted to, she knew that it would only traumatize Penny further. Drawing on strength she didn't know she possessed, she put on a brave face.

"Looks like you get to meet your Grandma and Grandpa sooner than we thought. I bet they can tell you all kinds of stories about your Mommy. Won't that be amazing?" She tried as hard as she could to put enthusiasm in her voice.

When she looked up, she could see the battle being fought behind Colton's eyes. After taking a deep breath, he smiled down at Penny, too. "I bet they even have pictures of your Mommy and will show you where she grew up." Even though his voice was even, his eyes glowed a bright yellow. Penny looked between the two of them, fear fading from her eyes a bit.

Rheia turned Penny around to face Byron. "Do you see that man? That is your Uncle Aiden's daddy. He's going to do us a favor and drop you off at your Grandma and Grandpa's so you can meet them. He's not too scary, right?" she asked.

Penny looked from Byron to Aiden and shook her head, grinning. She pointed to Aiden and wrapped her arms around her chest, giving herself a hug.

Rheia nodded. "That's right, he's probably a big ole softie just like your Uncle," she said, smiling. "You will be visiting your Grandma and Grandpa for a bit, while your Papa and I get this legal mumbo jumbo worked out. Run get your backpack, darling." Penny hopped down and ran for the family room. She looked over to Ryuu. "Could you get her suitcase from our room?"

Ryuu bowed. "Of course."

Rheia concentrated on breathing in and out. Colton's hand found hers and they clung to each other as they waited for Penny to return. They heard her quick footsteps as she ran back into the room. Rheia scooped her up and started walking toward the door.

Every step she took, every step that took them closer to the door, she started to feel her control slip. Her soul was disintegrating within her chest. Before she was ready, they were at the door. Byron stood patiently; he made no move to take Penny from her arms.

Ryuu walked down the stairs and handed Byron Penny's suitcase. Rheia clung to her daughter, physically unable to let her go. She repeatedly kissed the top of her head, squeezing her tight. Over Penny's head, her eyes met Colton's. Silently, she begged him to do what she couldn't. Without saying a word, he reached out and took Penny from her. Immediately, her body protested the loss.

"You be a good girl, and if you need anything, anything at all, you call us okay. Day or night, it doesn't matter?" Colton nuzzled her cheek with his nose and kissed her forehead.

"Have fun visiting. Felix says he wants to go with you. He needs a break from all the boring stuff here." Meryn said, her eyes moist.

"Your Uncles Sascha and Quinn and the Beta Unit will be watching out for you at your grandparent's house. You can go to them if you need anything, too." Aiden said reaching forward to ruffle her hair.

Colton turned and passed Penny to Byron. "We will be appealing this," he said his voice sounding deadly.

Byron nodded. "I expected no less and have

already started the paperwork. But until then, Penny can get a good visit in, right princess?" Byron bounced Penny and the little girl grabbed on to his collar to stay upright, smiling.

"I love you, Penny. You be a good girl, my Pumpkin Dumpling. We'll see you very, very soon," Rheia promised.

"I love you, angel," Colton said, and tugged Penny's hair lightly. Penny waved at everyone and Byron left closing the door behind him.

Rheia clutched at her chest and bent over, gasping for breath.

Colton was at side, holding her close. "Hold it in for just a few more seconds, my love, until she's in the car." Colton rubbed her back.

Rheia struggled to breathe. Only when she heard the car leave the driveway did she give in to her body's demands. She wailed. Gut-wrenching sobs shook her body as she collapsed. Colton easily caught her and pulled her close, letting her sag against his body, taking on her weight.

"We'll get her back. I swear it to you, we'll get her back." Colton repeated over and over.

Rheia couldn't think. All she knew was that her heart had been ripped from her chest. Even though she hadn't given birth to Penny, that tiny child was her daughter in every way that mattered.

"I want her back. Please bring her back," she begged, looking up into Colton's face. The pain she saw there made her realize how unfair she was being. "I'm sorry, I didn't mean it," she whispered. Colton pulled her close and rested his forehead on her shoulder. Slowly her sobs turned into a stream of silent tears.

"I'll do whatever I have to do to bring her home. I promise." Under her hands, she felt his body trembling.

"Colton, you and Rheia spend the day together. I will call you with any updates I get from Father," Aiden said, his arm wrapped firmly around Meryn.

Rheia looked up from Colton's neck to see that everyone in the foyer, including Jaxon and Noah, wore identical depressed expressions. Losing Penny had affected them all.

Colton drew a shaky breath and stepped back to face Aiden. "Will Sascha and Quinn be enough to keep her safe?"

"I'm assigning Gamma and Beta Units to the Carmichael's house. They'll rotate and stand guard in shifts."

Meryn sniffled loudly and wiped her eyes on her sleeve. "Plus, she has Felix with her. He'll watch after her."

"I just want my baby back," Rheia whispered.

"Come on, my love, let's go lay down for a bit," Colton suggested, turning her toward the stairs.

"Whatever," Rheia shrugged.

What was the point?

"We'll be down later," she heard Colton say before he gently guided her up the stairs. She blinked and they were in their room. She shook her head. She barely remembered climbing the stairs. She blinked again and Colton was helping her into her pajamas.

She couldn't stop the tears from flowing, so she stopped trying. Colton carried her to their bed and laid her down gently. He curled up behind her, pulling her close to his body. She scooted back as far as she could, not wanting any space between them. She reached behind her and pulled his arm around her body so that she could hold on to it. There was something about his body, his hard muscles and high body temperature that made him something solid and warm to cling to.

"What if we can't get her back?"

Colton kissed the back of her neck. "Then I'll find a way to purchase the house next to the Carmichael's so that we can see her every day. She can visit with us all day long and sleep at their house if they insist on her living with them."

"It won't be the same."

"We'll find a way, Rheia. You and I will explain to the council how much she needs us."

"It won't matter, we're not related, remember? No blood ties," she said, unable to keep the bitterness from her voice.

"Hey, why does that sound like you're not talking about Penny?" Colton asked, turning her around to face him.

"Because I've heard this before. Growing up, my grandmother and grandfather on my mother's side never acknowledged me as my mother's daughter. Not once. I was always 'that child'. Or they'd say, 'Why do you care what happens to her? It's not like she's yours'."

"And now you're hearing the same thing, but from the other side of the equation." Colton gently pushed her hair away from her face. Her tears caused everything to cling to her skin, creating a matted mess.

"And I'm not even a shifter."

"But I am." He tilted her head up with his finger and thumb. "I'll make an appointment with the council for us to plead our case. Penny's wishes have to be taken into consideration."

"I just want her home," Rheia said and buried her face in his chest.

"Me, too," he whispered.

Rheia closed her eyes. With her emotions running so high, she was exhausted. She let the darkness take her, praying that this morning was nothing but a bad dream and that Penny would be home when she woke.

Rheia opened her eyes and rolled over. She was alone in bed as usual. She sat up and looked over to the nightstand. A cup of coffee and a note waited for her. When she felt tears threaten to overtake her, she shook her head. She needed to get her shit together and figure out a way to get her daughter back. Crying in bed wasn't going to do her a damn bit of good. Wiping her eyes, she sat up and leaned against the headboard. She picked up the cup of coffee and took a long sip. It wasn't very hot, which made it the perfect temperature to drink. She grabbed the note.

Sorry I can't be there when you wake up. Aiden needed help testing a new perimeter to keep us safe. See you when you get up. Love you always, Colton.

When she'd finished half the coffee, she walked over to the bench at the foot of the bed where Colton had draped her clothes. She got dressed and picked up her coffee cup. Walking downstairs, she heard voices coming from the family room. Usually Meryn and Beth were in the office this time of the afternoon. When she walked in, she was surprised to

see that Meryn, Beth, Jaxon, Noah, and even Ryuu
were huddled around two of the front windows.

"What's going on?" she asked.

Meryn whirled to face her, grinning ear to ear.
"The men are testing the new perimeter spell Keelan
cast." She turned back and practically pressed her
face to the window. Rheia walked over to stand next
to Meryn and looked out the window. The men were
standing at the property line with their hands on
their hips.

"I wish we could hear what they're saying," Beth
said peeking out from around the curtain.

Smiling, Ryuu snapped his fingers and suddenly
they could hear the men as if they were standing in
the room next to them.

"Keelan you cast the spell, you test it," Aiden
ordered.

They watched as Keelan backed away. "Do I
have to?"

"Yes," Aiden and Colton said together.

"Okay, but I don't like this," Keelan grumbled.
Slowly, Keelan extended his hand, and a second
later, a purple spark exploded, and Keelan dropped
like a rock.

The women gasped and the men laughed.

"You owe me five bucks. I told you he would do
it," Darian said, turning to Aiden.

"They need to leave Keelan alone," Meryn
grumbled.

"Seriously though, men, we need to test to see
how powerful it is. Knocking out Keelan doesn't
really take much. So, which one of you will go
next?" Aiden looked from Gavriel to Colton to
Darian.

"Not it!" Gavriel and Darian called out at the same time.

"Sonofabitch! I hate electricity. I swear I'm still twitching from the time Ryuu shocked me trying to get to you, Gavriel." Colton scowled at his friends.

"Please tell me he's not going to electrocute himself," Rheia said.

"He so is," Meryn chuckled.

They watched as Colton took a deep breath and reached out to the perimeter line. The second his fingertip hit the spell, he went down like a sack of potatoes.

Darian, Gavriel, and Aiden stood over Keelan and Colton's prone bodies. Aiden rubbed his chin. "He has always been susceptible to electricity."

"I bet I don't go down," Darian said slyly.

Aiden and Gavriel eyed the large fae. "I do not know; Keelan did say it would be pretty strong." Gavriel shook his head. "I do not think you can hack it."

Darian frowned and turned to the perimeter. He pulled his arm back and let his fist fly as if he was going to take down the perimeter spell. The second his knuckles crossed the perimeter his body shook, his eyes rolled back in his head, and he landed with a loud thud.

Gavriel and Aiden looked at their fallen brothers, then the perimeter, then each other.

"Oh God, they're going to go for it!" Meryn laughed gleefully.

Beth shook her head. "They're not that stupid."

Ryuu chuckled. "Want to make a wager on that?"

"I have a higher level of immunity to electricity, I will try it next." Gavriel said, rolling up his sleeve.

Beth groaned and covered her eyes with her hands.

Seconds later, the ancient vampire was on the ground next to the others.

"Please, oh please, oh please, do it," Meryn begged under her breath.

Aiden stood, hands on his hips looking down at the men. He looked at the perimeter, then down at the men again.

"I'm a big ole bear; they are weak compared to my manliness. Look how muscular I am, this perimeter can't take me down." Meryn deepened her voice providing a hilarious running commentary to Aiden's thought process.

Aiden took a deep breath and reached out for the perimeter, a flash of purple flared and the Unit Commander was down. Everyone stared in disbelief at the entire Alpha Unit laid out unconscious on the ground. Finally, Beth's laughter set everyone off.

Rheia turned to Meryn who was laughing so hard Ryuu was holding her up with an arm wrapped around her waist.

"Shouldn't we check on them?" Rheia asked.

Jaxon shook his head. "Keelan and Colton are already coming around, looks like it doesn't last long."

"I wish we'd recorded that," Meryn said wistfully.

Grinning, Noah held up his phone. Meryn threw her fist in the air. "Best. Minion. Ever!"

They watched for a few more minutes until all the men were on their feet.

Aiden turned to the men. "Okay Keelan, I think we all have a pretty good idea of how strong it is. Go ahead and take it down, Gamma will be here soon for drills," Aiden said as he, Gavriel and Darian walked around to the side of the house.

Colton lingered back, placing a hand on Keelan's shoulder.

"Want to see if the perimeter is as effective against Gamma?" Colton's voice sounded devilish.

"I do owe Sascha and Quinn for turning me purple," Keelan answered.

"They wouldn't," Beth whispered.

They didn't have long to wait. Soon Gamma Unit was walking up the driveway. Colton placed his elbow on Keelan's shoulder and leaned against him nonchalantly.

"Look Kee, it's hippo." Colton laughed as Sascha's face turned pink.

"I'm not fat; my tiger has a lot of fur," Sascha protested.

Colton nodded. "Of course. Man, I can't wait for dinner. Ryuu said he's making pot roast with carrots and potatoes, hmmm, my favorite." Colton rubbed his belly.

Sascha growled and Quinn frowned at Colton. "You know better than to tease him about food."

"And for dessert I think I heard him say we're having chocolate pie. You know how Ryuu is Kee; I bet he made enough so that we each have our own." Colton nudged Keelan knowingly.

Sascha roared and charged at them, Quinn not too far behind. They both hit the perimeter and flew backward from the shock. Ben, Christoff, and Oron stared, open-mouthed.

Colton and Keelan were laughing and giving each other high fives.

"What the hell is going on?" Aiden bellowed coming around the corner.

Colton turned to Aiden his face a mask of innocence. "Just testing the perimeter with Gamma; I'd say it works perfectly."

Aiden looked over to the unconscious Gamma leader and rubbed his hands over his face. "Keelan, take the perimeter down now. Oron, Ben, help Sascha and Quinn to the drill field. They can join us when they wake up." He turned on his heel and walked back the way he came.

The women watched as Keelan removed a brass key from inside of a dangling brass ring. He looked up. "Okay, it's disarmed now," he called out to the other Gamma unit members.

Shaking their heads, Oron and Ben picked up their two unconscious members, and they all headed to the back. When they all disappeared from sight, the women turned to each other.

"Do they do this kind of thing every day?" Beth asked.

Rheia frowned. "I hope not, that kinda of jolt could cause brain damage."

They all looked at each other and sighed.

Rheia shook her head; this was her life now, and she wouldn't change it for anything. The only thing missing was her daughter.

CHAPTER TWELVE

The rest of the afternoon was uneventful. Rheia sat with Meryn and Beth in Aiden's office as they worked with Noah and Jaxon. She stared at Penny's drawing and smiled. Her eyes wandered over each face until she noticed something odd. One face wasn't smiling back at her; in fact, it looked downright terrifying. She realized she was looking at Penny's nightmare, the scary man that haunted her dreams. The dark figure was outside the house by the window looking in. Rheia shuddered and fought back the urge to paint over the dark figure. If this was what Penny needed to do to face her fears, she couldn't undo it. Still, she couldn't shake the image from her mind. Her daughter was very talented.

"Ladies, gentlemen, dinner is ready," Ryuu announced from the doorway.

"Come on, Rheia, Ryuu's pot roast is amazing," Meryn said, walking up behind her chair. Rheia stood and walked out with Meryn. On the way to the dining room, they passed another group of men.

"Hey, Lennox, what's shaking?" Meryn asked one of the men.

Lennox turned and smiled at them before bumping fists with Noah and Jaxon. "Good evening,

Lady McKenzie. We have been hanging out in the family room playing on the X-Box since ours is not hooked up yet. We are about to head back to the barracks to unpack some more. Lord Ambrosios really went all out for us, the new addition looks like a five star hotel."

Meryn blinked. "Who?"

Beth laughed. "Gavriel."

Meryn grinned. "Oh yeah, I knew that. Lord Ambrosios sounds so swanky. Anyway, I'm glad you like your new digs. I didn't want you guys think we were kicking you out."

The other guys shook their heads. "Lennox is right, that place feels like a spa hotel, we've never had it so good." The smaller of the men smiled.

"That's good to hear, Basil. I'll pass along your thanks to my mate," Beth said, then turned to Rheia. "These gentlemen are the Alpha Unit's trainees. You haven't seen them much since they have been helping out with construction. From left to right we have Kai Anders, tiger shifter. Cedric Ri'Emere, fae. Basil Barberry, witch, and the charming one is Lennox Chevalier, vampire."

Rheia nodded to the trainees.

Basil stepped forward his face serious. "We heard about your daughter, if you need us to do anything to help, just let us know. We got to know her when she helped out with our drills; I think we all fell a bit in love with the tiny angel."

Rheia blinked. "When did she help out with drills?"

Basil paled and turned to Lennox, their unofficial leader. Lennox smiled wide. "On that note, we are heading out. Goodnight, ladies."

The trainees didn't waste any time rushing out the door.

Rheia looked at Beth then Meryn. "They probably just meant that she got their water or something like that, right?"

Meryn and Beth nodded. "Absolutely," Beth assured her.

Together, they entered the dining room, and the men stood. Rheia sat next to Colton. The look he gave her told her that he missed having Penny between them at meal times, too. Taking a deep breath, she reached for his hand. His thumb slowly rubbed back and forth on the back of hers.

As Ryuu served their dinner, she turned to Colton. "When did Penny help out with drills?"

Colton choked on the wine he was sipping, as did Aiden. Colton turned to her, smiling weakly. "Do you remember when I said I'd tell you later?"

"What did you have her do?"

"Just ring bells, that's all, baby." Colton said, squeezing her hand.

"That's it?" Rheia asked. She knew there had to be more to the story since both men were sweating bullets.

"Yup, she used her ninja like skills to sneak past the different units and ring their tower bells. It helped the men look for an unseen enemy. She was amazing." Colton's face shone with pride.

"At least you didn't try to teach her how to shoot. I had to put my foot down with Radek over that one." Rheia picked up her fork and pushed her food around.

"I seriously need to call and ask him what in the hell he taught my daughter," Colton growled.

Rheia smiled. "It wasn't just Radek. Levi, Dax, Marco, and Athan would show her things as well. I never knew what I would walk in on next. I remember one day I thought Athan was teaching her about the different parts of the body and how they worked. The more I listened, I realized he was showing her kill zones that had major arteries. It'll be a miracle if she turns out half normal."

Colton was about to respond when they heard a loud banging on the door. The men jumped to their feet and hurried to the front door. Aiden swung it open, and Sascha rushed in cradling Penny. Behind him, Quinn and Oron ushered in an older couple.

"Penny!" Rheia exclaimed and pulled her daughter out of the large, white-haired shifter's arms.

"Sascha, report!" Aiden barked.

Sascha turned to Aiden. "After drills today, we relieved Beta and took over guard duty. Thirty minutes ago, we heard screams and breaking glass. When we entered the home, the ferals were being held at bay by a flickering wall of light. We dispatched those ferals and chased off the survivors. We called in Beta to track them and brought Penny and the Carmichaels here."

Aiden frowned. "Wall of light?"

Oron stepped forward and reached into his front shirt pocket. He carefully lifted out a tiny doll like body and, with sad eyes, handed it to Meryn. "Thank the Gods he had his necklace make him visible, otherwise I may never have found him."

"Felix! Oh, honey, what did you do?" Meryn cuddled the small sprite, tears streaming down her face. She looked around. "Ryuu! Ryuu!"

Ryuu rushed forward, "I am here, *denka*. Keep him close to your body to keep him warm. He used up a lot of magic keeping Penny and the Carmichaels safe." Ryuu picked up a tiny hand and a small blue current passed to the sprite. To everyone, it looked like his breathing became a lot easier.

Ryuu straightened and looked around the foyer. "Gentlemen, please escort our guests to the family room and wrap them in blankets. I'll be right back with warm drinks for everyone and some honey for our little warrior."

Colton and Keelan helped Mr. and Mrs. Carmichael to the family room and into chairs. Rheia sat down on the sofa and proceeded to inspect every inch of her daughter. When she went to check for a second time, Penny rolled her eyes and snuggled close. Colton sat down beside them and wrapped his arm around them both.

In the foyer, Aiden and Gavriel gave instructions to Sascha to continue their guard duty around the Alpha estate. When everyone was gathered in the family room, Ryuu began passing out cups of warm coffee and hot chocolate.

"We're probably the last people you want to help, aren't we?" Mrs. Carmichael asked, twisting her napkin in her hands.

Rheia looked up, surprised. "Of course, we'd help. You're Penny's grandparents."

Mrs. Carmichael looked from her to Colton. "But we took her from you."

Colton tightened his arm around them. "We just hadn't had a chance to work out a suitable arrangement, yet. You're family and we protect our own."

Mr. Carmichael patted his mate's knee. "Please, forgive Mina, we're both shaken up. My name is Gerard and this is my mate Wilomina. Thank you for everything you've done. We never believed that ferals would attack us in Lycaonia."

Aiden sat next to Meryn, who was still cooing softly to Felix and helping him with his honey. He looked at Gerard. "Can you tell us what happened?"

Gerard nodded, his hand trembling slightly as he covered his mouth. "We had just finished eating dinner. Mina made stuffed raviolis; they were always Elena's favorite. Anyway, we were cleaning up the kitchen while Penny colored at the table when the back door was suddenly kicked in. Mina grabbed Penny and I stood between them and the door, but we didn't see any intruders. Suddenly, sparks were flying. Every time one of those creatures hit the wall of light, they became visible for a moment. Mina was screaming her head off so it didn't take long for the unit warriors to hear and come to our aid. If we hadn't had that tiny little sprite with us, I hate to imagine what would have happened."

"They tried to take our grandbaby away from us, like they took Elena." Mina wept into her hands.

"Thank the Gods you sent Felix with Penny, Meryn," Colton whispered.

Meryn looked up with rimmed red eyes. "He's my little hero."

Ryuu stepped forward. "If I may? It has been an extremely long day for everyone and my *denka* is exhausted. Might I suggest everyone retire for the evening to get some rest?"

Aiden stood, nodding. "We'll leave the perimeter up indefinitely until we can figure out why they're attacking. Ryuu, can you get the word out to everyone, especially the trainees, not to approach the Alpha estate without clearing it with you? I'm afraid that means you'll have to raise and lower the perimeter as needed."

Ryuu placed a hand over his chest and bowed. "Of course; if it will keep my charges safe and able to sleep at night, I will gladly do so."

Keelan shook his head. "Aiden, we can't live like this. That spell is far from perfect."

Aiden nodded. "I know, but it's the best we have right now. Give the key to Ryuu; he'll act as gatekeeper."

Penny yawned and snuggled closer to Rheia's chest. For the first time since breakfast, Rheia felt like she could breathe again. She couldn't stop kissing the top of Penny's head, and she wasn't the only one. Colton hadn't stopped rubbing Penny's back since they sat down.

Mina looked at them, her eyes shining. "You're very good with her. She's a very considerate child. I knew she was trying not to hurt our feelings, but we knew she wasn't happy. Now we see why; she missed her parents." Mina's voice choked up.

Gerard rubbed her arm gently. "I think this is what Elena would have wanted, Mina."

Mina dabbed at her eyes and turned to Rheia. "You will let us visit, won't you?" she asked timorously.

Rheia's heart soared. Did this mean she and Colton could keep Penny? "You can visit any time you would like. In fact, once we get rid of these ferals, we'd love it if you'd watch her sometimes during the day or have her over for the weekend."

Mina smiled warmly. "Thank you. We wanted a chance to do right by our daughter, but seeing the two of you with her, I can't, in good conscience, keep you apart. It's obvious she loves you."

Rheia squeezed Penny tight. "And we love her very much."

Colton stood. "Come on; let's get our girl to bed."

Rheia nodded and Colton helped her stand with Penny still in her arms.

"Mr. and Mrs. Carmichael, if you will follow me? I will show you to one of our guest suites," Ryuu offered with a bow.

Everyone, including Darian and Keelan, had to kiss Penny goodnight. Penny, blinking sleepily, pointed to where Felix was snuggled close to Meryn. Rheia walked over and Penny kissed the tip of her finger and held it out to Felix. Felix kissed his finger and reached up slowly to touch fingertips with Penny. Satisfied that she had said goodnight to her friend, Penny relaxed against Rheia.

"That was too precious for words," Rheia heard Beth say as she and Colton walked into the foyer toward the stairs. She had only gone up three steps when Colton lifted Penny's drowsy body out of her arms. "Let me carry her up the stairs, honey."

Rheia looped her arm through his and they walked together to their room. Since Penny was already in her pajamas, they simply placed her in the center of their bed. Rheia stared down at her daughter and the reality that she'd almost lost her began to sink in.

Colton came up behind her and wrapped his arms around her waist. "I know."

She didn't have to explain why she was upset or defend her irrational fears because he *did* know. The tremors she felt behind her told her more than any words that he knew exactly how she felt.

"Let's get some sleep. I don't know about you, but I can't wait for this horrid day to end," Colton whispered. Rheia nodded and quietly they both changed into their pajamas. Before they climbed into bed, Colton took his time holding her against his body and sharing tender kisses. They both needed the simple touch of the other to chase the fear away.

Kissing her softly on the forehead, Colton stepped away and turned off the light. They got into bed on either side of Penny. From the moonlight coming through the window, they both stared down at their daughter. Penny frowned in her sleep and turned her head. Immediately, she and Colton reached out and took one of the girl's hands. Penny smiled and calmed down and they fell asleep connected to one another.

Rheia woke the next morning when she heard the door shut. When she looked up, Colton was walking in with a hot cup of coffee. She sat up and looked around.

"Penny?"

Colton placed the cup on the nightstand. "She's having breakfast with everyone downstairs; I thought you might need just a bit more rest."

Rheia scooted up and sat with her back against the headboard. "Any news?"

Colton sat on the edge of the bed. "No, we're still running patrols; there's been no sign of them."

Rheia sipped her coffee and then climbed past Colton to get out of bed. Instead of her normal scrubs, she pulled on a pair of jeans and a cowl neck fleece top, it was one of her favorites for keeping warm. To keep the hair out of her face she pulled her hair back in a ponytail. Since she wanted to get downstairs to Penny as soon as she could, she didn't even bother with makeup. She slipped on her sneakers and turned back to face Colton who was watching her with a contented smile on his face.

"What?"

He shook his head. "Nothing, you're just the most beautiful thing I've ever seen."

Rheia saw the adoration on his face and knew that he meant it. "Let's go see our girl. I'd like to get to know her grandparents more as well, since it looks like they'll be a part of our lives."

Colton stood and picked up her coffee cup. She took his hand, and they headed downstairs. Colton laughed as she practically dragged him forward; she was desperate to see her daughter, to hold her, and to know that she really was back.

"Good morning, Pumpkin Dumpling," Rheia said and scooped Penny up out of her chair. Penny wrapped her arms around her neck and kissed her cheek. She smelled like syrup. Rheia was so happy to see her that she didn't even mind the stickiness she felt on the back of her neck.

She sat her back down and Colton and Rheia took their seats on either side.

Ryuu set a fresh platter of pancakes shaped like small animals down on the table. When Ryuu caught her staring, he blushed and cleared his throat.

"I thought we would all appreciate the levity this morning." He kept moving around the table refreshing the platters. Ryuu had missed her daughter as well.

Rheia turned to Meryn. "How's Felix this morning?"

Meryn looked down at the soft fabric sling across her chest. "He's sleeping, but his color looks better today. He was so grey yesterday, I thought we'd lost him." Her hand cradled the small bundle carefully.

Colton looked at Meryn oddly. "How did you know to send Felix with Penny?"

Gavriel nodded. "I have been wondering that myself since yesterday."

Meryn shrugged, her head turning from one man to the other. "It just seemed like a good idea at the time."

"Fate works in mysterious ways," Mina said, sipping her orange juice. Both she and her mate were seated next to Keelan, looking much better after a good night's rest.

"Whatever the reason, I'm grateful for his help. Despite his size, he fought like a true warrior," Gerard said, commending Felix.

"If the two of you are up to it, I did have a few questions." Aiden said, putting his fork down.

Gerard nodded. "Of course, Commander, anything we can do to help."

"Did the ferals say anything to you before going after Penny?" Aiden asked.

Mina shook her head. "I don't think they were specifically after Penny, they were reaching for all of us, and no, they didn't say anything."

Gerard thought about it for a moment. "I have to agree, Commander. They tried to pull me out the door before I was able to break away to stand with Mina and Penny; I don't think they were after her specifically."

Colton cursed under his breath. "Couldn't they just tell us what they're after? It would make it a lot easier to kill them."

Darian laughed. "You're getting lazy, Colton. That's like hoping a criminal gives you a signed confession."

Colton looked at Rheia, then down at Penny. "I have good reasons for wanting to stay home a bit more. The sooner we can figure out their end game, the sooner we can all relax."

"Seeing you with Penny, it makes me wish we hadn't pushed Elena away. We missed so many years with them both." Mina smiled at Penny with tears in her eyes.

Rheia pulled Penny into her lap. "Can you tell us about her? Elena?"

Mina looked at Gerard, who nodded. Smiling, Mina turned to face her. "Elena was such a headstrong child, very much an old soul, like our Penny. She knew exactly what she wanted and went after it. That actually became the crux of our estrangement." She sighed then continued. "When she was old enough, we started pressuring her to visit with more chameleon families, in hopes she would find a chameleon mate. We're a dying breed of shifters and every new birth is desperately needed."

"But Elena didn't want to hear anything about it, she said she was in love and she wanted to be with her boyfriend, Reggie." Mina practically spat the name. "He was a wolf shifter that filled her head with ideas that we were trying to control her and she should move away with him, and that's what she did. One day, she packed up and left to live in the human world with Reggie. The only way we were able to keep track of her was by monitoring her on social media." She scrunched up her nose, "Watching one's child from afar is never preferable. When she finally mated with Brian, who ironically ended up being a chameleon, we were hopeful that she would return to Lycaonia to have their baby. Months and months went by without any updates on her Facebook or Twitter accounts. We assumed she was busy with the new baby and we were on the verge of reaching out to her when the Elder gave us the news that she had been killed last year."

Her voice faltered and Gerard pulled her close, continuing for her. "That's why we were so desperate to raise Penny. We failed to keep our daughter safe, but we have a second chance with our granddaughter."

Rheia shuddered and kissed Penny's head. "I can't even imagine losing a child."

Mina nodded. "Which is why when we saw you with Penny last night, we knew we couldn't separate you. I could never inflict that kind of pain on another mother."

"Sorry to butt in, but you said Elena was pregnant?" Meryn interrupted. Mina nodded.

Meryn turned to Aiden. "That sounds horribly familiar."

Aiden frowned. "But that happened last year."

Meryn paled. "Maybe I need to widen my search parameters more than I initially thought."

"Bullshit!" Darian exploded. "How could this have been happening right under our noses for so long and no one noticed."

Beth set her coffee cup down. "Because not all of them have been discovered. Of those that were, only a fraction were found by paranormals like the Vanguard. Even those we know about, the ones that were killed outside Lycaonia weren't tracked. They were treated like isolated incidents. It's only because of Meryn's reports that we knew to step back and look at the bigger picture."

Mina looked around the table. "You mean to say that our Elena wasn't the only one?"

Aiden shook his head. "You may have heard stories in the past few months about paranormal couples going missing from inside Lycaonia. It's bigger than that, couples have been going missing from all over."

"What is the council doing about this?" Gerard demanded.

"They've ordered different units, from each of the pillar cities to start their own investigations. They're feeding all of their findings through Meryn who gives us correlations and possible leads," Aiden explained.

"Why are they suddenly attacking like this?" Mina asked.

Gavriel shook his head. "If we knew, it is possible we could determine what they are after and stop them. But so far, the attacks have been random."

Groaning, Meryn reached down and pulled out her laptop from her backpack. "This is going to take for-freaking-ever. I'm going to have to not only widen the city search, but also go back a couple years, and I have to do all of this without caffeine? Fuck me."

"Remember Meryn, Adam and I both advised you to try and keep your stress down as well," Rheia reminded her.

Meryn nodded and smiled. "Sure, I'll get right on that. I'm confident the ferals will just pack up, go home, and play dominoes once we explain I can't be bothered with them because of stress. If we have any hope of figuring this shit out and putting a stop to them, so my baby won't have to worry about getting hacked and slashed in the front yard, then I'm going to have to put in a few extra hours."

Rheia stared at Meryn for a few seconds before turning to Colton. "Maybe getting pregnant right now isn't the best idea. I'm not sure I could survive without my caffeine."

Mina's eyes lit up as she looked from Meryn to Rheia. "Babies are such a blessing. If you need any help homeschooling let me know. I'd be happy to teach Penny, of course, unless you've made other arrangements."

Rheia looked at Meryn, who looked just as confused as she felt.

Meryn turned to Mina. "I'm sorry, what did you say about homeschooling?"

Mina turned from Rheia to Meryn and back. "Didn't you know? Paranormals homeschool their children until it's time for them to enter college or apprentice to a Master in a craft."

Meryn looked up at her mate, a disgusted look on her face. "No. Someone seems to have left that shit out. Seriously Aiden? Homeschool? I don't have time for that."

Aiden paled. "I didn't even think about it. It's such a natural thing in our world."

Rheia shook her head. "I'm going to be working at the clinic all day; I won't be able to homeschool either."

Beth frowned. "I also have a full plate. In addition to collecting and maintaining information for all of the unit warriors, the council has asked me to perform a sort of census for paranormals, to get a better idea of who is located where, outside the pillar cities. That could take me years."

Gerard chuckled. "It's a good thing you have Mina then." He turned to Aiden. "And I'm pretty sure your mother would be more than happy to help teach her grandchildren."

Aiden looked down at his mate. "See, baby, nothing to worry about. Now, let's see what we can do to get you to de-stress."

Meryn was about to respond when Aiden's phone rang. Meryn rolled her eyes. "There is no such thing as de-stress around here."

"McKenzie here. What?" Aiden shouted, standing quickly. Around the table the other Alpha Unit members stood. Aiden put the phone on speaker. "What do you mean the clinic was attacked? How's my brother?" Aiden demanded

"He's in bad shape. We need the other Doc to come patch him up. He's not healing fast enough, Aiden!" An anxious male voice shouted.

"Calm down, Ben. Can you bring him here?" Aiden nodded to Gavriel. The vampire kissed his mate and moved quickly toward the foyer, Darian and Keelan close behind him.

Rheia stood and placed Penny in her chair. She kissed her forehead and looked down at Colton. He nodded and stood beside her.

"We can't move him, Aiden. I think we're losing him," Ben said, choking up.

"We'll be there in a few minutes, baby brother. Hold on, don't you dare lose him!" Aiden ordered and ended the call. He looked up to find that Rheia and Colton waiting on him.

"Let's go."

Rheia turned to Mina and Gerard. "Can you please watch over her?"

Mina nodded. "Of course, honey, go save our doctor."

Rheia grabbed Colton's hand and together they ran toward the door.

CHAPTER THIRTEEN

of the Alpha Unit emptied out of their SUV right behind them. Quinn met them at the door and ran with them down the hall. They were almost to Adam's office when ferals began to pour from the rooms on either side of the hallway.

"It's a trap!" Darian yelled.

"Kill the woman! Find the slides!" A rough voice screamed from behind the pack of attacking ferals.

Rheia found herself sandwiched between Aiden and Colton, each firing his weapon into moving targets, almost without even looking in their direction. When their ammo ran out, Colton and Aiden roared loudly and let their claws free. In a perfectly coordinated dance practiced over centuries, Colton rushed forward and blindly flung the enemy back to Aiden who would gouge the feral across the neck and drop the body. They moved fluidly together in perfect synchronization until a sea of ferals lay dead at their feet. Colton lifted Rheia past the gore and they hurried on to Adam's office.

Ben looked up when they entered. "Where the hell have you been?" He stopped and looked at their blood-smeared clothing. "What happened?"

Rheia walked past him and knelt beside Adam on the floor. Someone had applied bandages to his midsection, but they were already soaked in blood. Slowly, she lifted the gauze and sucked in her breath, she could see his intestines protruding outside of a long, wide slash. She stood and ran from the room, Colton on her heels. She went to one of the empty examination rooms and began to pile the items that she needed placing them on a sterile tray.

When they arrived back in the office, she looked around. "Clear the room. I don't want any debris kicked up that could get into the wound. Ideally, we'd be in a sterile environment, but we don't dare move him." She looked over at Colton. "I'll need you to wash your hands and put on a pair of gloves; you'll need to hand me things as I call for them."

Colton immediately went to the sink to do as he was told. Rheia arranged the tools she needed on the tray and then joined him at the sink as Aiden emptied the room. When they turned back, Aiden stood by the door. He looked her in the eye. "I'm not leaving."

"If you're going to stay, don't move from that spot," Rheia ordered. Aiden nodded.

Slowly, she began the tedious process of putting Adam's insides back where they belonged. They lucked out in that he didn't have perforated bowels. After about an hour of flushing the wound and sewing multiple internal sutures, Adam's body began to heal itself. She watched in amazement as he turned the corner and the dissolvable stitches that she just put in began to melt before her eyes. In the end, all she had to do was hold the flesh together long enough for it to heal and seal itself.

To be on the safe side, she applied medical glue and taped his wound shut. Colton helped her lift him so they could wrap his midsection. Breathing a sigh of relief, she sat back and checked his pulse. His heart was beating strong.

"Can we move him?" Aiden asked, startling her. She had forgotten he was still in the room.

She nodded. "Yes, but be very careful with him."

Aiden opened the door. "Darian, Oron, you're on deck." Aiden moved out of the way, as the two huge fae stepped in and carefully lifted the large bear shifter.

They loaded him into the back of one of the SUVs and headed back to the Alpha estate. Meryn and Beth met them at the door and gasped at their clothes. Everyone was covered in blood, evidence of the carnage that had taken place at the clinic.

Rheia looked around. "Penny?"

Meryn pointed to the family room. "Mina and Gerard are keeping her occupied."

Colton exhaled. "Good. We're going to clean up. We'll be right back." Colton grabbed Rheia's hand and they headed up the stairs as Aiden and Meryn coordinated with the others to get Adam situated.

Once behind the closed doors of their bedroom, Rheia and Colton immediately headed to the bathroom and began to strip. They piled their soiled clothes into the separate tub and stepped in the shower together.

After working on Adam for so long, the hot water on her muscles felt heavenly. Colton's calloused hands gently massaged her neck and back.

Groaning, she closed her eyes. "We don't have time."

"Challenge accepted," he whispered in her ear.

Using a soapy hand, he teased and pulled at her nipples, sending current after current to her clit. When his hand traveled downward, she opened her legs wider to give him better access. At her back, she felt the hot, hard evidence of his arousal. His slick fingers slid on either side of her clit bringing her right to the edge.

"Colton, I'm there," she panted.

"Stand on the ledge," his deepened voice sent shivers through her body. Without even looking, she knew his eyes had shifted and his canines were out; she couldn't get enough of his wild side.

She stepped up on the small ledge that kept the water from flowing onto the bathroom floor. It gave her just enough height that when he bent her over slightly, he was able to slide deep inside her from behind.

"Hands on the wall," he ordered.

She did as he asked. He thrust into her and twisted her nipple. With his next thrust, his other hand teased her clit. The combination of pain and pleasure was driving her insane.

"They keep coming for you; I can't lose you," he growled and scraped the skin at her shoulder with his teeth.

"You'll never lose me because not even death could keep me away from you," she rested her head back against his chest as he plunged deep inside her.

Just as he brought her to the edge again, he bit down. She opened her mouth to scream, but nothing came out. Her body flew apart as he emptied jet after jet of hot cum into her. She struggled to catch her breath. Gently, he pulled from her body and began to wash them up in earnest.

Limp as a rag doll, she let Colton wash her hair and rinse her off. They got out, quickly dried off, and got dressed. Rheia put her hair back up in a ponytail and fished another pair of jeans out of her suitcase. She prayed Ryuu would be able to get the blood out of her fleece pullover; it was a favorite.

This time she opted for her college sweatshirt and another pair of sneakers. She watched Colton dress and took a moment to appreciate the beauty of his body.

"I lied, you know," she said, as he pulled on his shirt.

He looked over at her uncertainly. "Lied about what?"

"I actually prefer blonds," she admitted.

Grinning, he held his hand out to her. "I know."

They were walking down the stairs when the front door flew open and a lovely, blonde haired woman rushed in. She looked up and saw Colton. "Where is he? Where is Adam?" she asked frantically.

Colton let go of Rheia's hand and hurried down the stairs. He wrapped an arm around the woman and steered her toward the family room. "He's okay." Together they walked into the family room.

Rheia walked to the bottom of the stairs confused. Did Colton just forget about her? Who was that woman? Was she Adam's mate? Behind the blonde woman, Byron and another man stepped through the open door before closing it behind them.

"Rheia," Byron said simply and pulled her into a bear hug.

"Sir?" she asked. She knew that he was Aiden's father and an Elder, but had no idea how to address him.

"Sir?" Byron's frowned down at her. "Please, call me Byron. I heard that you saved my son's life; I can never repay you."

The grey haired man stepped beside Byron and bowed in a manner similar to Ryuu. "Forgive the late introductions, my name is Marius Steward. I am Lady Adelaide's squire. In case you missed her, Adelaide was the woman that sped past you a moment ago."

"*That* is Aiden's mother?" Rheia asked in disbelief.

Byron let out a booming laugh. "Yes, she looks too delicate to have mothered four hulking lads, doesn't she? Don't let that fool you; she's the strongest of us all."

Ryuu walked toward them from the kitchen. "As I explained on the phone, Lord Byron, please let me know when you need to leave and I will lift the perimeter." Ryuu hung the brass key and circle next to another brass shape on the wall next to the door.

She pointed to it. "What's the other one?"

Without missing a beat, Ryuu answered "Fireball."

Right, of course, what house isn't equipped with a fireball? What was I thinking?

Chuckling, Byron looped his arm through hers and, in a courtly manner, escorted her to the family room. Inside, the room was a circus. Every chair and sofa had someone sitting on it.

The entire Alpha Unit was there, cleaned up from the fight. They stood around telling Gerard what had happened. Adam was reclining, his eyes closed, on the chaise lounge. At his side, Adelaide fussed over him. Beth, Meryn, and Mina sat next to the men, peppering them with questions. Rheia looked around until she spotted Penny. The small girl sat in Jaxon's lap while he and Noah read her a story.

Colton looked up from Adelaide's side and he grimaced. He quickly crossed the room and kissed her on the cheek. "I am so sorry, my love, but Adelaide is almost like a second mother to me..." he started.

Rheia stood on tiptoe and kissed him. "It's okay, I understand. I got to meet Marius and see Byron again."

Colton shook Byron's hand and nodded at Marius. Byron turned to Aiden. "What happened out there, son?"

The room quieted and all eyes turned to Aiden. He turned to his father. "The ferals attacked Adam to set a trap. They made sure the injury was severe enough that he couldn't be moved, but wouldn't kill him right away, so that Rheia would have to go to the clinic. When we got there, the leader gave the order to attack and to find the slides." Aiden turned to Rheia. "Do you know what slides he was talking about? Because, whatever they are, they are willing to fight and die, down to the last man."

Rheia stared then remembered the small travel microscope case that lay forgotten at the bottom of her coat pocket. "Oh my gosh, yes. I have the slides I got from Adam the second day I was here; they're of the Mystery Man."

Colton shook his head. "Why would they attack now? Adam's had those slides for weeks; they could have taken them from the clinic at any time. The body, too, for that matter."

"What changed?" Meryn asked.

Rheia snorted. "The body went from being normal to a pile of goo."

"Then what?" Beth asked.

Rheia thought about it. "Then I collected a sample from the goo pile, we opened the windows to air out the room, then Aiden and Adam called the council while we came back here."

Beth turned to Byron. "Did anyone else outside the council know that we had the body?"

Byron shook his head then paled, realizing what that could possibly mean. "It's not possible. I refuse to believe that any council member would betray our people," he said, adamantly.

Meryn pursed her lips. "That may not be the case, Dad. Adam's office phone could have been tapped."

Darian crossed his arms. "It makes sense. All of this started after Aiden and Adam made that phone call."

Meryn pulled out a legal pad and began to make notes. "So, chronologically: Elena and Brian are killed; Penny goes to live with Rheia, and a year later, ferals attack Rheia's house. Why?"

Rheia was about to answer then looked over to where her daughter sat. "Pumpkin Dumpling, why don't you go color on Uncle Aiden's wall for a bit, okay?" She knew they were about to discuss some pretty horrific things that her four year old daughter did not need to hear.

Penny nodded and hopped off Jaxon's lap, grabbing her backpack and heading toward Aiden's office. When Rheia heard the door shut, she turned back to the rest of the room. "Marco believes the reason the ferals attacked was because of a news article written the week before. In it, the reporter links the murders of Penny's parents to more recent murders in the area and lists Penny as a survivor and possible witness. It also mentioned that Penny was adopted by a local surgeon."

"Bastard," Colton grumbled.

Rheia grinned at him. "I'm pretty sure my brothers paid him a visit."

Meryn took notes. "So after a year, the ferals get intel that Penny survived and what? Could ID them? That doesn't sound right. Even if she could identify them, so what?"

"We are missing something," Gavriel said, leaning against the wall.

Meryn twisted the pen in her hand. "Let's keep moving. Next, Penny and Rheia move here, the clinic is ransacked, and the gooey body is taken. After that, the ferals try to get to Rheia at the clinic but are subdued by Colton and Gamma. Ferals then attack the Carmichael home, but according to Gerard and Mina, everyone was a target, not just Penny. Finally, Adam is attacked at the clinic to set a trap to get to Rheia, because they believe she has these all important slides."

Beth reached up and took Gavriel's hand. "It's not over, is it? Even though you killed all the ferals at the clinic, it's not over yet?"

"This is pissing me off! I feel like I'm missing pieces to the puzzle." Meryn scribbled back and forth on her notes.

"I know how you feel. I told Radek the same thing earlier. It's like the pieces aren't fitting together right." Rheia crossed her arms, frowning.

Adelaide sipped her tea then set the cup down on the saucer. "I may not know about reports or surgery, but I have raised four boys." Everyone turned to look at her. "I remember once Adam and Aiden were assembling an intricate battle scene puzzle, but they couldn't make anything fit. They argued for hours; it was nerve wracking."

Aiden blushed. "That's a nice story, Mother; but I don't see how that relates to what is happening."

Adelaide looked at Aiden then over at Adam and sighed. "I really thought I taught you better than that. Do you remember why you had such a hard time putting the puzzle together?" she asked, raising an eyebrow.

Adam glared at Ben. "It was because Ben dumped his puzzle in with ours in a rush to go out and play."

Meryn gasped. "Adelaide, you're a genius."

Rheia chuckled. "Good one, Lady McKenzie."

The men all stared at each other with blank expressions.

Adelaide smiled at Rheia. "Please dear, call me Adelaide, I practically helped raise Colton, he's family."

Aiden leaned down next to Meryn. "What?" he whispered.

Meryn rolled her eyes. "We've all been assuming that everything is connected. That the ferals who went after Rheia and the ones who stole the body are connected, but what if they aren't? What if the puzzle pieces aren't fitting together because there are two separate puzzles?"

Aiden stood and smiled at the unit members. "Our women are amazing."

Gavriel and Colton nodded in agreement.

Rheia sat down on the arm of one of the chairs. "So back to the initial attack, why would they go after Penny?"

Mina waved her hand in the air. "Maybe for the same reason they went after my Elena, because Penny is half chameleon."

Meryn and Beth exchanged dubious looks. "Mina, I don't think that's the reason why."

Mina looked around. "Why else would she be attacked? Chameleon's are extremely rare. Some shifters hope their children mate with us so that their grandchildren and their bloodline gain our abilities."

Meryn held up her hands forming a 'T'. "Okay, timeout. What do you mean Penny is only half chameleon?"

Rheia stared at Mina. She was wondering the same thing; she had always assumed she was chameleon like her mother.

Mina blinked. "Didn't I tell you? Elena was pregnant when she left Lycaonia. Penny is the child she had with her wolf boyfriend."

"No wonder she was able to get past the units during the training drill," Colton said looking a bit shell-shocked.

Meryn's head whipped back to Mina. "When you say chameleons are rare, how rare are they?"

Mina sighed. "We're almost extinct. That's why we pushed Elena to try and find a mate among other chameleon families. How ironic that she did exactly what we wanted in the end. Since her mate ended up being a chameleon, their baby, had they lived would have been the first pure blooded chameleon shifter born in a decade."

Meryn let the legal pad drop and scrambled for her laptop. "No, no, no, no, oh no," Meryn muttered under her breath as her computer booted up.

Rheia stood. "What did you figure out?"

Meryn tapped away and then the color began to drain out of her face. She swayed a bit in her chair. Ryuu and Aiden were instantly at her side. "Meryn, what?" Aiden demanded.

Meryn shook her head as if trying to erase what she'd seen. "After breakfast, while you guys had your showdown at the clinic, I ran a wider search. All of the US, going back twenty years, you know, a huge sample, just in case." She swallowed hard. "I know why chameleons are so rare. They've slowly been hunted to extinction." She flipped her laptop around to show a map of the US. Red dots were scattered everywhere. "Over eighty-five percent of all reported paranormal murders in the past twenty years have been chameleons." Meryn began to shake so hard Rheia thought she was going to hurt herself. Suddenly, she stood. "Excuse me." Covering her mouth, she ran from the room. Rheia stood and darted out right behind her.

Sure enough, she headed straight for the bathroom. Rheia held her hair back as Meryn threw up her breakfast. She rubbed her back and wet a washcloth to lie across the back of her neck.

"I'm okay," Meryn whispered.

"Of course you are, you're doing beautifully," Rheia said removing the washcloth. "Feel like heading back?"

Meryn shook her head. "Not really, I bet Aiden's lost his shit. I really don't want to deal with him right now."

"I have my son under control Meryn, you can come out," Adelaide's amused voice said from the other side of the door.

Grinning at each other, Rheia helped Meryn to stand and they walked out.

Meryn turned to Adelaide. "How is he?"

"I made him sit on his hands in a chair. He'll be fine once he sees you up and around." Adelaide wrapped an arm around Meryn and led them back to the family room.

When they entered, Aiden started to stand but Byron cleared his throat. Meryn took pity on her mate and went directly to him. He pulled her into his lap and it looked like he wasn't letting go.

Rheia turned to Beth. "Have they figured it out yet?"

Beth shook her head. "Not unless they're keeping it to themselves."

Colton turned to her. "Please, oh wise women, show us the light."

"Goofball," Rheia said, and nudged him gently in the ribs.

Meryn leaned back against Aiden's chest and closed her eyes. "It means that ferals have been systematically collecting chameleons, for whatever reason, for the past twenty years. It means that they are larger and more organized than we ever realized."

Her words silenced the room.

Adelaide sipped her tea. "And that's just one puzzle. What about the other one?"

Rheia turned and looked at Adam who was trying to get comfortable on the sofa. "Adam had the body for weeks before I showed up. I removed the necklace and it went from solid state to liquid state in the matter of moments. But the ferals didn't know Adam had the body until he contacted the council to report the change."

"Did you notice anything when you looked at the slides?" Beth asked.

Rheia shook her head. "Nothing that Adam didn't explain. The first slide was from a normal paranormal, the second was from our Mystery Man before he disintegrated. The third was from our Mystery Man after he became goo, and the last slide was from a regular feral."

Meryn shrugged. "Does it matter? I mean, dead is dead, right?"

Rheia shook her head. "Not according to Adam. He said, that even after death paranormals decompose slowly, which is why he believed the Mystery Man was a normal paranormal because he was decomposing at the same rate as a paranormal. It only accelerated after the necklace was removed." Rheia stopped as a horrible thought began to take shape in her mind.

Rheia slapped her forehead. "I had it all wrong! But in my defense, it's partially Aiden's fault."

Aiden sputtered. "How... what's my fault?"

Rheia stood and began pacing back and forth. "At the clinic you told me that the necklace masked the smell of the ferals, making them undetectable. In my mind, I didn't question the necklace further, so we had no idea why the body began to break down, but it's as I just said, the decomposition only accelerated *after* the necklace was removed. That's why they wanted the slide samples; they knew we would figure it out." She faced the room and realized that not even Meryn was following along.

"Okay. Slide one, normal paranormal right? Slide two, Mystery Man before he went supernova. Adam and I assumed that the cellular decay that we saw was due to the body slowly decaying, because it was an *assumption* that he was a normal paranormal. Slide three, Mystery Man, the gooey state. All cells were in the process of breaking down simultaneously. Slide four, regular feral, all cells had some form of decay." She took a breath and continued.

"What if the decay we saw in slide two wasn't because he was decomposing slowly like a normal paranormal? What if the decay was there before he put on the necklace? What *if* he was already a feral and when he put the necklace on it stopped the cellular degradation? That necklace acts as more than just a Glade air freshener; it actually halts cellular decay, that's why there's no smell."

Beth gasped, bringing a hand to her throat. "So if a feral were to put the necklace on right after turning, there would be no way to detect what he was."

Gavriel looked between Aiden and Byron. "It would also explain why we suddenly have different types of ferals. In the past, they acted like mindless beasts, relying on brute strength to create terror and cause pain. But we are now seeing them starting to band together, laying traps, and acting with caution."

Rheia nodded. "It makes sense. If the cellular decay is stopped, they would retain higher brain functions."

Meryn stared down at her hands. "So to recap: we have an unknown and growing force of intelligent ferals that cannot be detected by scent who have been operating in secret for at least twenty years collecting chameleons to further make them invisible and have only recently grown big enough balls to start attacking unit warrior mates." She looked up and around the room.

"We are so fucked."

CHAPTER FOURTEEN

Mina turned to Meryn. "How did you arrive at the conclusion that they were collecting chameleons for invisibility?"

Meryn shrugged. "Kinda going out on a limb for that one, but it makes sense. We have invisible ferals attacking and they've killed hundreds of chameleons, I'm kinda just connecting the dots at this point."

Mina shook her head. "It doesn't work that way, to use our abilities you have to be born to it."

Keelan stepped away from the wall. "It is possible, if they are using a blood spell."

Mina gripped her mate's hand tight. "Nowhere is safe."

Her words galvanized the men into action. Byron and Aiden stood. Aiden set Meryn down in their chair and kissed her softly. "We need to call a council meeting and contact the other three pillar cities. We have some major decisions to make."

Ryuu left the room heading to the foyer to deactivate the perimeter.

Colton leaned down and kissed her forehead. "Gavriel and I will be going with Aiden; Darian and

Keelan will stay here. Gamma has also been assigned to patrol around the estate, you'll be safe."

As they prepared to leave, Ryuu walked in holding the brass perimeter charm. He looked at Aiden. "Someone took the perimeter down."

Frowning, Aiden looked around the room. "Who'd do that?"

Rheia felt ice slide down her spine. "Where's Penny?"

"I can't smell her down here!" Colton yelled. She could hear him calling for their daughter as he ran up the stairs. "Penny! Penny, where are you!"

Rheia ran from the room to Aiden's office.

"Rheia!" Colton called out.

"In Aiden's office!"

Colton, Meryn, and Aiden rushed in.

"She was supposed to be right here. She was supposed to be coloring!" Rheia turned to look at the colors and figures on the wall.

"Keelan and Ryuu, check the house, top to bottom! Gavriel call Sascha, check to see if they saw anything outside!" Aiden began barking orders as he ran from the room.

Rheia turned to Colton. "Where is she?"

Colton shook his head. "I don't know, but I will find her. I'll check around the house to see if I can pick up her scent."

Meryn pointed to the drawing. "Do you think she got scared drawing the attack scene from your house and hid?"

Rheia shook her head. "Why would she take the perimeter down?" She looked down at the drawing. "Besides, that's not our house, we don't have rounded windows." Rheia froze. Why hadn't she realized that earlier, this wasn't something Penny was drawing from her nightmares.

Rheia stared at Meryn and they both turned to look at the rounded window behind Aiden's desk, then down at the drawing. The terrifying figure that was staring back at them, Penny had seen looking into Aiden's office window.

"Colton!" Rheia screamed.

The sound of thundering feet heralded the men as they ran into the room. Colton burst through the doorway looking around for an unseen enemy.

"What?" he asked.

Rheia pointed down at the drawing. "Something has been stalking her outside Aiden's window."

Colton looked at the drawing and blanched. As one, the men left the room at a run, heading outside. Rheia and Meryn followed. As they turned the corner of the house, Rheia was just in time to see Colton throw his head back and howl; his body expanded before he burst from his clothing as a giant wolf. He rushed into the woods behind the house, Aiden and the rest of the Alpha Unit right behind him.

Rheia choked back a sob. "Does that mean... Is she?" She couldn't form the words.

Ryuu wrapped an arm around both Meryn and Rheia's shoulders. "He caught her scent; all we can do now is wait."

Rheia buried her face in her hands and prayed.

Colton tracked Penny's scent. When he came to a clearing, Colton heard the sound of a gravelly male voice.

"Come back here, you little bitch! You escaped me once; you won't do it again. You better listen to me; I'm your fucking father!" the angry voice snarled. The feral was wearing a necklace; they could neither scent nor see him.

Off to his right, he heard Aiden's voice as he approached the clearing. "Why do you need a child?" Aiden asked.

Laughter filled the air. "Look at you, fumbling around blind. You can't even see me; I'm invincible! Wearing this necklace hides me from the great Unit warriors. If you could only see how much the rules of your society hold you back, you would embrace freedom like I have."

Gavriel stepped into the clearing, his face a hardened mask as he scanned the surrounding area. "You want us to become like you? A monster that preys on children? Why are you after your own child?" Gavriel asked, in an effort to keep him talking.

"Because she is my blood. If I kill her and add her to my collection, she will tie me to what I took from her mother and her sniveling mate. It would make me even stronger. Not many have been able to collect a chameleon, they're so hard to find. How lucky it is for me that my bitch ex-girlfriend and brat are both chameleon, and I knew exactly where to find them. The fact that she was mated and pregnant was a gift from the Gods!" he shouted.

Colton heard the slightest sound to the right, the sound of feet running.

Penny!

Seconds later they heard a man shout right before he became visible.

"You little bitch! Get back here!" The man turned to the left, right as the unit warriors closed in on his location.

Colton didn't hesitate; he launched himself at the man who had stalked his daughter. He clamped onto the man's arm and shook. Pain exploded over his right haunch and he let go. He immediately jumped again, this time he was able to wrap his mouth around the murderer's neck. He bit down until he heard a crunching sound. He shook his head hard, back and forth for good measure, before he let it drop to the ground. He stepped back and let Aiden examine the body.

"Good work, Colton, next time, just let us shoot the bastard," Aiden grinned.

Colton growled. Aiden nodded. "I understand; if it had been my daughter, I probably would have mauled his ass, too. Now, we have to find Penny."

Colton opened his mouth, raised his head, and howled. Seconds later a tiny, squeakier howl lifted to the treetops. Colton looked around and watched as Penny stepped forward and literally melted into sight from the trunk of a tree. She *was* half wolf and half chameleon.

"No wonder she kicked our ass during drills," Sascha muttered.

Penny ran forward and threw her arms around his neck. Colton whimpered and licked her face. Sascha scooped her up and took the necklace from her hand. "Guess those bell drills paid off, huh, little lady?"

She nodded.

Aiden stepped close to Penny and ran a hand over her hair. "Sweetie, why did you go with him?

You did, didn't you? You took down the perimeter and went with him, why?"

Penny looked down at the ground then looked over at Colton. She pointed to him, then back toward the house.

Aiden cursed under his breath. "He told you if you left with him, he wouldn't hurt your new mommy and daddy, didn't he?"

Penny's eyes teared up, and she nodded.

"Oh baby, it's our job to protect you, not the other way around. You let Papa and Uncle Aiden deal with horrible men like that." Aiden rubbed her back.

Penny shook her head violently and pointed a thumb to her chest.

Gavriel stepped closer. "Did he tell you that it was your fault that your other mommy and daddy were killed?"

Penny covered her face with her hands and nodded.

Colton snapped and growled. He wanted to shift back, but didn't feel like flashing his daughter either.

Aiden pointed to him. "Your Papa is right. What happened to your mommy and daddy was not your fault. Do you hear your *Athair*? It was never your fault; it was because that creature was a sick fuck and was crazier than hell."

Keelan coughed into his hand. "Language."

Aiden flushed and turned to Penny. "Don't tell your mom I said that, okay?"

Penny smiled shyly then nodded.

Colton was about to step forward to nudge his daughter when his vision began to blur. He staggered to the left then collapsed on the ground.

"Colton? Buddy?" Aiden knelt down beside him. "Shit, looks like that fucker bit you." He turned to Sascha. "Take Penny back to the house; tell them to prep a vehicle to take Colton to the clinic. Tell Rheia that Colton needs her." Sascha nodded and took off toward the house, Penny held securely in his arms.

Colton closed his eyes and rested his head on the ground.

"Oh no you don't, you bastard. You are not leaving me alone to deal with Meryn for the rest of my life, not to mention your distraught mate and daughter. Fuck that! You better fight, brother," Aiden ordered, then gently lifted him up.

Asshole

Colton closed his eyes and darkness closed in.

In the darkness, he struggled to open his eyes. He looked up and saw his mate staring down at him. All he could see were her eyes, anxious and worried; a surgical mask covered the rest of her face. He blinked; he was so tired. He was just going to rest his eyes for just a moment.

The next time he opened his eyes, once again he saw his mate standing over him; this time he could see her entire face. She looked sad, tears trailed down her cheeks. He wanted to lift his hand, but couldn't move it. All around him was the smell of sickness and death. He couldn't fight the darkness, and it swept him away again.

Rheia paced back and forth in the large conference room Aiden had set up to discuss Colton's condition. After the first two days, Beth and Meryn returned to the Alpha estate to watch over Penny. Adelaide called Colton's parents and Rheia met them that first day. Both his mother and father hadn't moved since they arrived. Robert looked so much like Colton that Rheia had a hard time looking at him. She could see where Colton got his wavy blond hair, green eyes, and easy smile. However, it was from his mother, Alice, that he'd gotten his devilish sense of humor. She stopped pacing and turned to Adam.

"Why isn't he healing?" Rheia demanded. She'd been up for nearly seventy-two hours, ever since Aiden had carried her mate out of the woods and her own private hell had begun.

Adam shook his head. "I don't know. As a shifter, he should have healed this by now. But the wound, if anything, looks like it has gangrene."

Rheia took a deep breath. "It's rotting. Aiden said the feral bit Colton on the shoulder when they were fighting. The skin and muscle have begun to rot."

"Is he turning feral?" Aiden asked.

"My boy isn't a feral," Alice said, her voice crisp and even.

Aiden's tired eyes were sad. "I have to ask Aunt Alice, he would do no less for me."

Robert laid a comforting hand on Aiden's shoulder. "We know, son."

"Can you cut it out? Then allow the opening to heal like normal?" Darian asked.

Adam shook his head. "That was one of the first things we tried. We can never cut enough out. I'm afraid that whatever this is, it has spread to his blood. He's rotting slightly faster than his shifter healing abilities can cope with."

"Will he begin to rot on the inside, like one of those monsters?" Alice whispered.

"I'll put a bullet in his head first," Aiden growled.

The only reason Rheia wasn't furious was that she was grateful. Unlike a true feral, Colton was still a paranormal; he would feel the loss of every inch of skin that dissolved. A bullet would be more merciful. As it was, they were keeping him in a medically induced coma so that he wouldn't feel any pain.

"If he were able to heal faster, could he beat this thing?" Gavriel asked.

Adam and Rheia both nodded. "He damn near has it beat now, it just seems to be one step ahead," Rheia explained.

"I would like to donate tissue or blood, whatever is needed to help him." Gavriel offered. Alice gasped and Aiden stared.

Rheia looked around. "Okay people, newbie human in the room. What does that mean?"

Gavriel looked up, his eyes smiling. "Vampires heal faster than shifters. As an older vampire, I have ingested so many different types of blood that I am a universal donor. As old as I am, my blood will carry quite a bit of power with it. This offer is not made lightly. As his mate, if you agree to this, both of you will be tied to me forever."

Rheia couldn't wrap her mind around all of the power implications. "Will he live?" she asked.

Gavriel nodded. "I am almost certain of it. Had I known the situation was so dire, I would have offered sooner. As it was, I have had guard duty at the Alpha estate for the past two days and am only now getting caught up."

Rheia turned to Adam. "Do it. I don't care about all of the other stuff, if Colton will live, do it."

Adam stood, smiling for the first time in days. "Gavriel, if you would come with me, I just need a wee bit of your blood, maybe a bit of tissue. Shouldn't hurt a bit."

Gavriel sighed and glared at Adam. "It may hurt you." He clapped Aiden on the back as he walked by and left with Adam.

Aiden practically collapsed across the conference room table in relief. Rheia could see how deep his bond with Colton was, they were more like brothers than friends. Aiden sat back up and looked out at the room with bloodshot eyes, reaching into his pocket. "I'll just be in the waiting room, I need to update Meryn. Please come and get me the second his condition changes." Aiden started dialing and staggered from the room.

"He probably blames himself, poor boy. He's been protecting Colton since they were babies," Alice clucked. Rheia sat down next to her feeling like her eightieth cup of coffee was about to run out.

Alice leaned over and pulled Rheia into her arms. "Thank you. Thank you for doing whatever it takes to save my son. He's very lucky to have you."

Rheia hugged Alice back; she was probably the only other woman on the face of the planet who loved Colton as much as she did. "We're lucky to have him."

Alice pulled back and wiped at her eyes. "That's right, you have a daughter. I'm going to beat that son of mine senseless when he wakes up for not calling us the second he found.you. I still can't believe I'm a grandmother."

Robert sat down next to his mate. "We haven't had a chance to meet her, but we've heard some amazing stories from the leader of the Gamma Unit. He calls her the 'Ninja'."

Rheia smiled wearily. "I never did get the whole story about what happened. Colton promised to tell me later." She swallowed hard.

Alice patted her thigh. "And he will. My boy has this uncanny ability to make you want to pummel him and kiss his boo-boo at the same time. He's driving us mad with worry now, but I'll bet you anything, he'll wake up grinning." She sniffed and dabbed at her eyes with her handkerchief.

"All we can do now is wait. I'd give anything to see that grin again," Rheia admitted, laying her head on Alice's shoulder.

Alice took her hand. "Me too, my love, me too."

The first thing Colton became aware of was the fact that the inside of his mouth was dry. The second thing he became aware of was that the inside of his mouth tasted like ass. He peeled his eyes open and saw Rheia standing over him. He grinned up at her. "Hey, beautiful." His voice was so faint he could barely hear it.

Rheia burst into tears. Colton turned his head, looking around the room. Wasn't there anyone close by that could help his mate?

"It's okay, sweetheart," he whispered harshly.

She just continued to cry, great heaving sobs that were wildly out of control. Taking a deep breath, he mustered all his strength and tried to sit up. That got her attention.

"What in the hell are you doing? Lay back down!" Her tears slowed down and she was in command mode. Colton preferred her ordering him around to crying uncontrollably. "Water?" he croaked.

"Of course." Rheia picked up a large insulated mug with a bendy straw and held it for him. He managed to spill a good portion of it, but what he did swallow, felt heavenly. Every second he was awake, he felt his strength returning.

"Thanks, my love, I feel a lot better. What happened anyway? The last thing I remember is being in the woods calling Aiden an asshole."

Rheia stared. "*What happened?* What happened! What *happened* was you almost died!" She waved his cup around.

"I'm getting better."

She blinked at him. "Did you just quote *Monty Python*?"

He did, but the look on her face had him second-guessing admitting to it. "Maybe."

"Your mother was right; I want to smack the hell out of you and hold you close at the same time." Wearily, she sat down in the chair next to him and laid her head on his belly.

"You look like hell," he said, stroking her hair.

"It's your fault. You had to go be super dog, attack the feral, and get bitten."

"I'm not a dog. What does the feral bite have to do with anything?"

"The bite poisoned your blood and tissue causing you to rot."

Colton sucked in his breath. "I was rotting?"

"Yes, Gavriel had to donate blood and tissue to counteract the rapid decay to give your body a fighting chance. Oh, by the way, he said we're tied to him for eternity now," she yawned.

"If I had to pick a vampire to be tied to, he would be it," Colton admitted.

"You told me to tell you when you hurt me. Well this, you getting hurt and almost dying, hurt me. It almost destroyed me." Rheia turned and buried her face in his side.

"You know that this is part of my job. Do you want me to give up being in Alpha?"

Rheia sat up and shook her head. "No, but next time, let the men with projectile weapons kill the bad guy. Don't go after him with your fucking teeth!"

Colton grinned. "I hear and I obey."

Rheia gave him a sly smile. "You're in a good mood now, wait until your mother comes in. She's pissed at you, you know."

Colton racked his brain; her birthday wasn't until next year.

Rheia stared at him in astonishment. "You really have no idea why she's upset, do you?"

Colton shook his head.

"When were you planning on telling your parents you were mated and had a child?" Rheia asked.

Colton felt his stomach flip. "She's going to kill me."

"You'll live. Thank God, you'll live." She squeezed his hand.

Colton played with her fingers. "I saw you, in the darkness. At first, I thought I was just dreaming again, but it was really you. It was weird because it was just like my dream. At first, all I saw were your eyes, because you were wearing the mask and you were so anxious and worried. Then I saw your whole face and you were crying, and all I could smell was sickness and death."

"Before I met you, I had dreams with those images constantly; I thought they were telling me that you were sick and dying. I didn't realize it meant that I would almost die. If you hadn't been here, we would have lost Adam. Without you and Adam, I wouldn't have made it either. You saved me."

Rheia brought his hand to her lips and kissed him gently. "You're the one who saved me. Penny was the only light in my life until you. I'd closed my heart off to any potential love because I was afraid to lose it as I lost my parents. You bulldozed right past all of my hesitations and simply loved me. You helped both Penny and me to smile again and to laugh. You're the one who healed my soul."

Colton growled. "We're a good match, huh? Gods, I want you so bad right now."

Rheia looked down the line of his body to where his erection was tenting the blankets. "Unbelievable. You were dying not two hours ago and now you're up and at 'em."

Colton wiggled his hips and leered at her. "I have my priorities in order."

"Colton!" Colton heard his mother's voice coming down the hall. He stared down at his cock and tried to think of anything to make it go down.

Rheia was chortling beside him refusing to see the horror of the situation. He cursed his disobedient dick and in a last ditch effort, grabbed the pillow from behind his head and placed it in his lap. He fell back on the mattress, jarring his injured shoulder.

"Motherfucker!" he growled.

The door opened. "Colton Marius Albright, watch your language. You're not too old for me to wash your mouth out with soap. If you're well enough to be concerned about putting a pillow in your lap, I won't feel guilty if I have to use that medical grade antiseptic."

"Yes, Mother. You'll never believe what happened; I found my mate." Colton gave her his best little boy grin.

Alice put her hands on her hips. "Yes dear, I know. I want to talk with you at great length about your poor communication skills."

Rheia stood and motioned for Alice to take her seat.

Colton stared up at his mate. "Don't go. We're a perfect match, remember?"

Rheia turned to the door. "I'm going back to the estate to shower, check on Penny, and catch up on my sleep. You should be able to leave sometime tomorrow. Alice has volunteered to nurse you so I can finally get some rest. Have fun with your mother." She wiggled her fingers at him and shut the door behind her.

His mother looked at him and her eyes softened. "Are you in any pain?"

Colton wiggled a bit and slowly removed the pillow when he saw he was in the clear and put it back behind his head. "Not any more. It hurt like hell when I hit the mattress though."

Alice rolled her eyes. "Then you shouldn't have moved your pillow. Honestly, Colton, you act like I haven't seen you walking around with an erection before. You might have forgotten the two decades you were in puberty, but I haven't."

"Mother! Please, never, ever, mention me and the word erection in the same sentence again." Colton shuddered and looked around. "Where's Father?"

"He's sleeping now so he can relieve me later this evening. By tomorrow, we'll take you back to the estate. We're both dying to meet your daughter. Really Colton, how could you forget to call us?" She sounded so hurt that Colton reached out and took her hand.

"It wasn't safe, Mama," he said simply.

"Oh my sweet boy, don't you know there isn't anything I wouldn't do for you? It's my job as your mother to protect you, not the other way around," she chided him.

Colton blinked and thought back to why Penny had left the safety of the house. There wasn't much a child wouldn't do for their parents either.

He looked his mother in the eye. "I know."

Her breath caught and she smiled down at him. "I guess you do, now. Welcome to parenthood."

"I love you, Mama."

"I love you, too, Colton. If you almost die again, I'll kill you."

"Yes, ma'am."

CHAPTER FIFTEEN

Meryn, Beth, and Rheia laid blankets on the floor at the end of the hallway. Noah and Jaxon had the day off and were killing zombies on the X-Box downstairs while Penny and Felix played tag in the hallway. Ryuu had set up an afternoon tea on the floor for the women who were enjoying the lazy afternoon. Tomorrow would be pure chaos as the entire household prepared for the Midwinter's Ball, so she was thoroughly relishing this quiet time.

"Fuck!" one of the men shouted from down the hall.

"Anyone hurt?" Rheia called out.

"We're good," Colton responded.

Rheia went back to her tea, inhaling the gentle fragrance of bergamot and spice.

"This was a wonderful idea. It's so peaceful." Beth leaned against the wall.

"Watch out!" The sound of something large falling from a great height reverberated down the hall.

"Colton?" Rheia yelled.

"That was my bad!" Darian shouted.

Rheia turned to Meryn. "Did you know Colton's middle name is Marius?"

Meryn choked on her tea. "Seriously? How'd that happen?"

Rheia chuckled at the memory of Colton's mother telling her the story. "Colton's father is an international business guru. He can apparently turn dirt into profit. Anyway, he was away on travel a few weeks before Colton was due, despite Alice begging him to stay home. After being home alone for so long, Alice got tired of being bored, so she got in her carriage and went to visit Adelaide for tea. She was just getting ready to leave when her water broke. In the end, Marius delivered Colton and, much to Robert's chagrin, she gave him Marius as a middle name."

"It's why he feeds me. My father always hated visiting the McKenzie's; Marius spoiled me rotten. My mother unwittingly created quite a scandal naming me after House McKenzie's squire." Colton chuckled as he swaggered down the hallway. He held out his finger pouting. "I have a boo-boo."

Beth and Meryn said 'awwww' and Rheia rolled her eyes. Careful of their cups, Colton lay on the floor between the three women and soaked up their attention. Beth dropped small chocolates in his mouth and Meryn offered him her tea. Rheia kissed his finger and shook her head at his antics.

Aiden came around the corner covered in flecks of paint.

"Colton! Get your mangy ass away from my mate and get back to your station. We're almost done. I'd like to be able to air out the room before Meryn has to sleep in here tonight," Aiden roared.

Colton hopped up and gave the women a salute. "Coming, fearless leader. Keep your fur on because, according to Meryn, you are fugly without it."

"Colton!" Aiden barked.

Rheia shook her head as he walked away before turning to Meryn. "Is it true you hit Aiden over the head with the back of his toilet?"

Meryn nodded. Beth stared at her wide-eyed. "I KO'd his ass the first day I met him."

Rheia laughed. "Didn't you hurt him?"

Meryn shook her head and lowered her voice. "He liked it. Secretly he's a... a... mannequin... a machinist... Beth, what word am I trying to say?"

Beth was laughing too hard to answer.

"Meryn! Quit telling them I'm a masochist and come check out this paint color for the nursery," Aiden yelled from down the hall.

Rheia laughed along with Beth; Meryn was absolutely crazy, but that was part of her charm. Meryn got up and then whispered down at them. "Whoocha." She pulled her hand back and made a whipping motion.

"Meryn!" Aiden yelled again.

Meryn stood up straight pointing an imperial finger down the hallway. "That is Mistress to you, slave."

Colton's head popped around the corner with the biggest grin Rheia had ever seen on his face. "Hey babe, Aiden is turning purple, that can't be healthy."

Meryn walked past him. "He'll be fine. He's such a drama bear."

Colton held out his hand to Rheia. "Come see. We're done with Penny's room."

Rheia, Beth, and Penny hurried down the hallway. Since the trainees now had their own barracks, they had converted the guest suite adjacent to Colton's suite into Penny's new room. Walking through the door, Penny began bouncing up and down all over the room. The men had lost their minds. They had built her bed into a princess tower, complete with real ivy. Rows of bookshelves filled with fairy tales and stuffed animals lined one wall. They had made the entire length of one wall a chalkboard, with buckets and buckets of colored chalk. Everything was done in greens and teals instead of pinks and purples, but it still looked dainty and feminine. In one corner, Ryuu was putting the finishing touches on a small bistro style table with its own tea set.

He bowed. "Lady Penny, your tea is ready." He poured a small cup for her and an even tinier cup for Felix. Penny sat down and raised her teacup, sipping it prettily. Already, Rheia could see Beth's elegant influence on her daughter.

"Do you like it, Doodlebug?"

Penny nodded emphatically.

Colton walked up beside Rheia and wrapped an arm around her waist. "I may have gone a bit overboard with the toys and stuffed animals, but in my defense, they're not all from me." Colton jerked his thumb at what could only be described as Penny's own toy store. The entire corner from floor to ceiling was shelves of toys, dollhouses, puzzles, and dolls.

"Colton! Christmas is right around the corner, what are we going to get her now?" Rheia groaned.

Colton gave her a sidelong glance. "Don't worry; I already have it covered."

"What'd you do?"

"Nothing, well, nothing too big anyway."

"Speaking of presents, I still have one to give you," Rheia said taking his hand. "Beth can you watch her for a while?"

Beth nodded from where she stood at the long dresser. "I'm just going to organize her clothes a bit."

"Thanks."

Rheia led Colton from the room to their own suite. She went over to their dresser and pulled out a small pouch.

"What's that?" Colton asked, looking like a kid on Christmas morning.

"Something Adam gave me. Evidently, paranormals don't take blood tests to determine if they're pregnant. This be-spelled stone can detect the most minute form of life. I haven't checked yet." She held the pouch out to him.

Colton didn't move; he didn't even blink.

"Colton?" She walked over and waved her hand in front of his face.

He inhaled sharply. "Can we check?"

She handed him the pouch; he opened it before upending it, dumping the stone into her hand.

They both looked down.

Nothing. It remained a dull black stone.

Rheia sighed. "I was hoping I was. I know you want children so badly."

Colton smiled and plucked the stone from her hand. "That just means we get to try harder to perfect our methods."

She looked up at him through her lashes. "Do you think you can just knock me up as easy as that?"

Colton's eyes flickered to yellow. "Challenge accepted."

Rheia sucked in her breath. "Shit." She giggled and began to peel off her clothes, heading to the bed. She'd almost made it when a warm arm snaked around her middle and lifted her high off the ground.

She squealed as he dropped her onto the bed. He dropped the stone and pouch onto the nightstand.

"How do you want it, my love?" he asked kissing down her neck.

"Like our first time, hard and fast. I love it when you're barely in control."

"On your hands and knees," he ordered.

With anticipation thrumming through her, she got on her hands and knees. She looked over her shoulder and watched as he slowly stroked his cock. Every time he reached the head, he would flick his thumb into his slit and moan. Watching him stoked levels of arousal she didn't know she was capable of reaching. Lowering onto one elbow, she reached down her body and began to play with her clit.

"Shit baby, are you touching yourself?" he asked.

"You started without me, so I figured I'd better catch up."

"Ungrateful wench." He grabbed one of her ass cheeks in each hand and spread her wide. One hand moved then he was easing the head of his cock inside of her. She loved it when he took her at this angle; the head of his cock stroked her G- spot perfectly. She moved her hand away from her clit and held on to the comforter. She knew she didn't have long before he sent her over the edge; she could feel the pleasure mounting.

She could feel the strength in his hands where he gripped her and from the force of his thrusts. Something about that strength focused on pleasuring her made her head fall back.

Unlike before, she knew Colton didn't have to worry about not claiming her, so when he leaned forward and covered her body with his, she knew what was coming. She tilted her head to one side.

"Make me yours, Colton, don't hold back."

He roared and his hips began to piston at a ferocious pace. Every third or fourth thrust, he reached her cervix, just that bit of pain she needed. Screaming, she felt her orgasm flood her body with pleasure, like a dam bursting water over parched earth. Her body soaked up every wave of ecstasy.

He bit down on her shoulder and thrust twice more before filling her with his cum. She loved hearing him gasping for breath above her, knowing her body had driven him to the edge. When he pulled out, she moaned; her orgasm had clenched her muscles and he felt even bigger.

"Be right back, baby." Colton kissed her tailbone and walked to the bathroom.

As sexy as it was in the moment, cooling cum dripping down her leg felt gross. When Colton returned with a warm wet washcloth and began to wash her, she sighed happily. After he finished and returned the washcloth to the bathroom, he climbed back into bed with her and they snuggled up together.

"You said it gets better than this?" she asked.

"From what I hear. After a few years, I'll know every inch of your skin by heart."

"I can't wait." She stretched. "Did you want to eat lunch with the others?"

"Yeah, just let me rest my eyes for a few minutes." Seconds later, he was out like a light and snoring.

Rheia was definitely not tired, if anything, she felt energized. Slipping from under his arm, she went the bathroom and showered quickly. She pulled her clothes back on and looked over to where Colton lay with his mouth open, drool trickling down his chin. She smiled. She must be in love, because he looked ridiculous and yet she still wanted to jump him for more sex. She decided to give him a few more minutes rest before they went down for lunch.

Sighing, she picked up the pregnancy stone to slip it back in the pouch and nearly dropped it when it began to glow a deep amber color. She froze. She set the stone back down on the nightstand and stepped back. She picked it up again and the amber glow flared brightly.

She looked at Colton then at the stone, then down at her flat stomach.

"Merry Christmas, my love."

Smiling, she put the stone back in the pouch and tucked it into her pocket. She'd figure out a way to tell him later. Now she had to wake him up to eat.

"Meryn! You have to start getting ready!" Beth called out into the hallway. Even from the family room, everyone heard her clearly.

"I'm leveling up, be there in a minute!" Meryn shouted back, tapping away on her laptop.

"I still have to do your makeup and your hair!"

"No, you don't. I'll be ready before you."

"Perfection takes time! And really good make up!"

"Don't worry about it. I'll be fine."

"Argghh, she's hopeless! At least Rheia let me help her." Colton heard her say and then it was quiet.

The men were already dressed and ready to go and waiting in the family room. Rheia and Penny had come down first, looking enchanting. Colton thought his heart would burst. Beth had coordinated Rheia and Penny's dresses so that they complemented each other. Rheia's dress was a vision of fire, a red satin gown trimmed in white. Her hair was pulled back in a complex series of braids and her makeup was sheer and natural looking, except for the fire engine red lipstick. Colton had plans for that lipstick later. His princess was dressed in a layered white fluffy dress lined in red satin. She wore a half braid adorned with a simple red bow.

There were rumors floating around Lycaonia that Beth had threatened bodily harm on no less than three dress shopkeepers to get proper attire for his mate and daughter so last minute.

Beth had been upstairs since ten o'clock that morning. Gavriel had been forced to get ready in Darian's room since he was forbidden to go into his own suite. Meryn was laid out on the sofa in jeans, sweatshirt, grimy sneakers, with her laptop on her stomach. Rheia kept sneaking worried looks in her direction.

They heard heels on the stairs and the men straightened. Gavriel stood as Beth entered the room. She had chosen to complement her cool complexion and blonde hair with non-traditional Christmas colors. Instead, her dress embodied the essence of winter. The main body of the dress was skin tight and done in a very expensive looking teal silk and accented with deep blues and whites. She smiled demurely at Gavriel who was having trouble catching his breath. Then her eyes moved over to Meryn, her mouth dropped.

"Meryn!" she screeched. The men winced.

"Okay, okay." Meryn sat up and put her laptop aside. She grabbed a wadded up garment bag that had a muddy sneaker tread on it and headed toward the bathroom. Beth clutched at her chest and looked ready to have a panic attack.

Rheia stood and rubbed her back. "It's okay, everything will be just fine."

"Do you have any idea how long it takes to get ready for something like this?" Beth demanded.

Rheia and Penny nodded. They had just experienced 'getting ready' at Beth's hands.

"Okie dokie, let's boogie," Meryn said from the doorway.

Beth turned and Colton had to hide his smile. Meryn was decked out head to toe. Her hair was perfectly coifed and a single emerald teardrop necklace adorned her neck. Her dress was forest green and around the waist was a plaid that looked like it matched Aiden's tartan perfectly. She had on white gloves up to her elbows and more emeralds at her wrists. Even her makeup looked flawless.

Beth's mouth worked up and down. "How!" she finally exploded.

Meryn spun around, smiling. "Lady Fairfax gave me this. It's the Gown of Éire Danu. It really makes getting ready a breeze."

Beth swayed and Gavriel was at her side in an instant. "You're the owner of the Gown of Éire Danu?" She looked down at the floor, her fists clenched. "Meryn, I am going to kill you."

Meryn shrugged. "Do it later. I am dying to try the food at the ball. I was too nervous at the All Hallows' Eve Ball to try all the yummy food. Tonight, I am totally gorging."

Beth turned to Gavriel, a tragic expression on her face. He pulled her into his arms. "There, there, it is okay."

"Come on, peeps! I'm hungry." Meryn stomped her foot and headed toward the door. Aiden had to sprint to catch up with her.

"Darian, Noah, Jaxon, Keelan, Gavriel, and Beth, you're in the first carriage," Aiden explained once everyone was outside.

"Colton, Rheia, Penny, Meryn, and I will be in the second carriage. Have fun, everyone." Aiden turned and helped Meryn then Rheia into the carriage. Colton lifted Penny into the carriage and kissed her cheek. She smiled and kissed his nose. Grinning, he bowed to Aiden, allowing him to climb in next, before getting in last. He couldn't wait to see his girls' reaction to their first Midwinter Ball.

Colton watched as Sascha and most of the Gamma Unit monopolized his daughter. They were spoiling her rotten with small gifts and candies. Of course, that could be said for most of the units. They had all fallen in love with his tiny angel. Thank the Gods, Ryuu had volunteered to serve tonight, he was keeping track of all of Penny's gifts.

To his delight, Rheia hadn't stopped smiling.

"I want to try that white, fluffy thing again," she said pointing to the dessert table.

"You mean the coconut macaroons?"

"Those are not coconut macaroons, I've had those. These are like hugs from the Lord."

Colton laughed and steered her back to the desserts table. Rheia took one in each hand and ate one then the other. Colton picked up a few for himself; they were some of his favorite holiday treats as well.

Rheia looked around. "Where's Penny?"

Colton looked over the crowd. "Sascha still has her. I swear he's been with her all night. I think they bonded when he carried her in the woods." He popped another macaroon in his mouth.

"Maybe she's his mate?" Rheia suggested.

Colton inhaled to vehemently deny it and immediately began to choke. Rheia whacked him on the back a few times. When he could catch his breath, he straightened. "She is four. He better stay away from my princess, or I'll feed him his balls."

Rheia ignored him and laughed at his indignation. He glared at her. "I refuse to have that fluffy cat as a son-in-law."

He was still grumbling when, across the room, a waving hand caught his attention. He smiled. Rheia's present had arrived.

"Okay, enough with the macaroons, let's dance."

Smiling, Rheia took his hand. He led her to the dance floor and deliberately twirled her too hard, spinning her into the open arms of the man behind her.

"Oh my gosh, I'm so sorry," she said turning. When she looked up and saw who it was, she lost all sense of composure and began to bawl like a baby.

Colton was stunned. It wasn't the reaction he'd expected.

Radek Carson, Levi Sorrel, Dax Vi'Eaereson, Marco Rodriguez, and Athan Durant crowded around Rheia.

"What are you doing h... h... here?" she blubbered.

"Oh, Pumpkin Dumpling, you really didn't think you were going to spend the holidays without us, did you?" Radek asked, using his thumbs to dry her cheeks. She nodded.

Athan smiled at Colton. "Your mate invited us for a visit; he said that we would be the perfect Midwinter gift."

"You are; you all are." Rheia cried, trying to hug them all at the same time.

Out of the corner of his eye, Colton saw a blur of white and then Penny launched herself at Dax. Laughing, he threw her in the air and kissed her face. She beamed out at the room. The men sucked in their breath.

"Isn't she gorgeous?" Marco whispered sounding choked up.

Each man looked like he'd been hit between the eyes with a two-by-four. They passed Penny around until each man had a chance to cuddle her and get a smile of his own.

Colton reached into his pocket and handed Rheia a long, white, rectangular box. "Open it."

With trembling hands, she opened the box and gasped. Colton had dipped deep into his savings to get this made for her last minute, but her reaction was worth it. Rheia threw herself in his arms crying again.

"I love you so much." She buried her face in his shirt.

"You and Penny are my entire world, how could I do any less?"

She sniffled and looked up. "You love us that much, huh?"

Colton lowered his voice. "Indeed."

Rheia blinked. "Did you just quote *Stargate*?"

Colton smiled. "Maybe."

Penny reached out from Radek's arms wanting to see the necklace. Colton winked at Rheia, knowing she hadn't seen the inside yet.

"It's a locket, baby girl." He very gently pried it open and revealed miniature portraits of himself and Penny. He turned it. Inscribed on the back he had chosen: *My Healer.*

"Put it on me," Rheia ordered. "I'm never taking it off."

Colton opened the fastener and placed it around her neck. "Merry Christmas, my love."

"Sonofabitch!"

Everyone turned to see the silver globe over Keelan open, dumping pounds of purple glitter all over the witch.

Colton looked up to make sure he wasn't standing under anything.

"You get a free pass tonight, because of Penny, but you're fair game tomorrow," Sascha promised.

Colton gave him an exaggerated salute.

Radek raised an eyebrow.

Colton shrugged. "Just a friendly, ongoing, personal battle. They turn Keelan purple and taunt me about my mate giving them a physical, and we 'accidentally' electrocute them. You know, good clean fun."

Athan chuckled. "It almost makes me miss being in a unit. Almost."

Rheia turned to her brothers, "How long are you staying?"

Radek started to tousle her hair and noticed the braids. Grinning, he lowered his hand. "A couple days."

"I'm so glad you're here to watch me give Colton his present." She smiled up at him slyly and stood back from their semi-circle.

She reached down into the front of her dress and Colton wagged his eyebrows at her.

She laughed. "Not those."

She opened a small pouch and let the stone fall into her hand. Seconds later, it turned amber, lighting up brilliantly in the dim ballroom.

Excited whispers ignited all around them; paranormals knew what the light meant.

Colton tried to get air, but found that he couldn't. His entire focus was on the soft, warm light in his mate's palm. When he started to see dots, his knees nearly gave out A solid whack to the back had him sucking air into his starved lungs.

"Breathe, you idiot! And, congratulations," Sascha said, smiling wide. He picked up Colton's hand and shook it.

Aiden pushed his way through the growing crowd, Meryn in tow. He looked from Colton to Rheia to Colton again. "Brightest Blessings on your child!" he boomed, pulling Colton into a hug.

Meryn and Rheia were hugging and Meryn was jumping up in down with excitement.

Colton felt a tug on his jacket. Penny was looking up at him with a puzzled expression.

He picked her up and settled her on his hip. He walked over and pointed to the stone in Rheia's hand.

"Do you see that stone?" Penny nodded.

"It's a very special stone. It lets paranormals know right away if a mommy gets pregnant, that way every precaution can be taken to make sure that mommy and baby are healthy. Since the stone your mommy is holding his glowing, that means she's going to have a baby. You're going to be a big sister, Penny," he explained.

Immediately, Penny began to wiggle. Colton set her down and wrapped an arm around Rheia. They watched as Penny hugged Rheia's midsection and kissed her belly multiple times.

"Isn't she just the cutest little thing?" Aiden said proudly.

"You up to being *Athair* to my other child?" Colton asked.

Aiden clapped him on the back several times. "Of course! Also, Meryn and I both decided, we would like you to be *Athair* to our son as well."

Colton shook his best friend's hand.

"Daughter!" Meryn said stubbornly.

Aiden frowned and Colton laughed.

Aiden pulled Meryn into his arms as Colton did the same with Rheia. His whole world was now complete.

"I love you, Rheia Bradley. I love you, Penny Carmichael," he said kissing both of his angels.

"And I love you, Colton Albright." Rheia rested her head on his chest.

Penny looked from him to Rheia and back.

"Love you, Mommy and Papa."

Everyone around them quieted. Radek and the rest of Rheia's brothers crowded around. Behind them Sascha and the Gamma Unit pushed closer.

Rheia looked up at him then down at Penny. "What did you say, baby?" she asked, her voice shaking.

Penny pointed at her. "Love you, Mommy." She then pointed at Colton. "Love you, Papa."

Colton whooped loudly and pulled Penny into his arms. He threw her in the air, laughing, unable to keep the joy from spilling over.

"I love you, too, Penny! You're our perfect Christmas miracle." He and Rheia snuggled her close.

He had his mate and daughter and another child on the way.

Life didn't get better than this.

EPILOGUE

Darian slipped away from the festivities. He smiled widely at the strangers who passed him in the hallway, nodding his head and tipping his hat at the ladies. He got into the carriage and whistled as it wove slowly through the quiet streets of Lycaonia. Everyone in the city was at the Midwinter Ball.

The carriage dropped him off at the Alpha estate and he let himself in. He walked up the long staircase and headed to his personal suite. Once the door closed, he loosened his tie and walked over to dresser.

He stared into the mirror, his reflection visible by the light of the moon. He relaxed his face and let the smile slide away. He'd been dreaming of his mate almost nightly, but in his heart, he knew it was too late. He watched as his lavender eyes flickered to black.

He was almost lost.

Thank you for reading!
I hoped you enjoyed My Healer.
For a full listing of all my books please check out my website **http://alaneaalder.com**

I love to hear from readers so please feel free to follow me on Facebook , Twitter, Goodreads, AmazonCentral or Pinterest.

If you liked this book please let others know. Most people will trust a friend's opinion more than any ad. Also make sure to leave a review. I love to read what y'all have to say and find out what your favorite parts were. I always read your reviews.

Don't forget to sign up for my newsletters so you will receive regular updates concerning release information and promotions.

OTHER BOOKS BY ALANEA ALDER

Kindred of Arkadia Series

This series is about a shifter only town coming together as pack, pride, and sloth to defend the ones they love. Each book tells the story of a new couple or triad coming together and the hardships they face not only in their own Fated mating, but also in keeping their town safe against an unknown threat that looms just out of sight.

Book 1- Fate Knows Best
Book 2- Fated to Be Family
Book 3- Fated For Forever
Book 4- Fated Forgiveness
Book 5- Fated Healing
Book 6- Fated Surrender
Book 7- Gifts of Fate
Book 8- Fated Redemption

Bewitched and Bewildered Series

She's been Bewitched and he's Bewildered...

When the topic of grandchildren comes up during a weekly sewing circle, the matriarchs of the founding families seek out the witch Elder to scry to see if their sons' have mates. They are shocked to discover that many of their sons' mates are out in the world and are human!

Fearing that their future daughters-in-law will end up dead before being claimed and providing them with grandchildren to spoil, they convince their own mates that something must be done. After gathering all of the warriors together in a fake award ceremony, the witch Elder casts a spell to pull the warrior's mates to them, whether they want it or not.

Each book will revolve around a unit warrior member finding his destined mate, and the challenges and dangers they face in trying to uncover the reason why ferals are working together for the first time in their history to kill off members of the paranormal community.

Book 1- My Commander
Book 2- My Protector
Book 3- My Healer
Book 4- My Savior
Book 5- My Brother's Keeper

Made in the USA
Middletown, DE
29 May 2022

66393805R00161